THE

DAY FOR

THE

DEAD

EVEN THE DEAD GIVE UP THEIR SECRETS

By

Sim Parsons

Cover design by Rebecca Parsons

ISBN - 13:9781675220863

DEDICATION

To my dad for all his support
and the sudokus

TIKAL

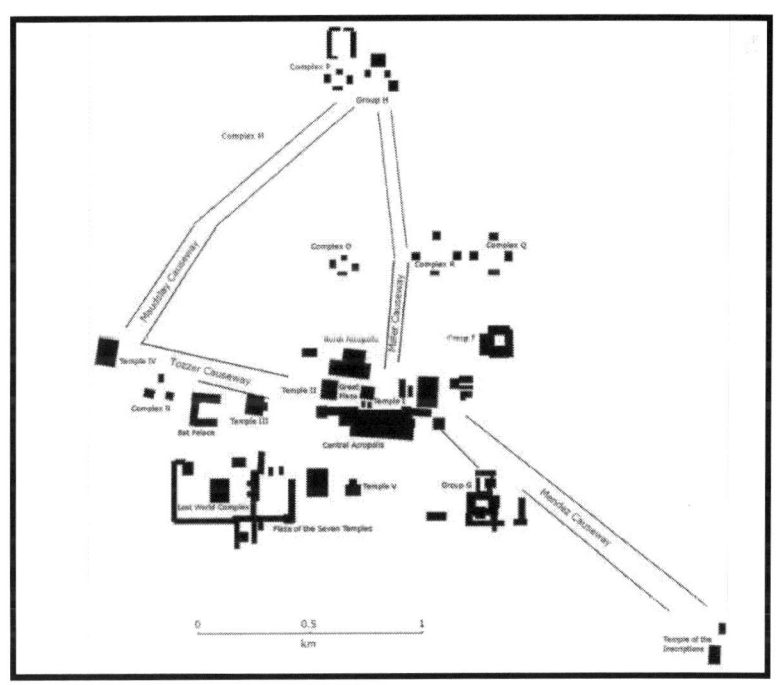

ONE

The attic felt airless and forgotten. A vacillating pendulum of light brushed the darkness. The low-wattage bulb was still swinging from her blind attempts to locate a switch. Stooped low under the eves, she pushed a packing case to one side and peered into the gloom. Stacked boxes and bags crammed the roof space.

A rustle from the corner induced a shudder. Images of disease-infested rats, scuttling nearby, filled her with revulsion. Childhood projects on the Black Death and an unrestrained imagination had left an indelible mark.

With each diminishing oscillation, the darkness closed in. Something stirred to her left, forcing an instinctive response from her cramped limbs. Twisting awkwardly, she caught a stack of shoeboxes and sent them tumbling into the shadows. Photographs and letters cascaded from their place of rest, disturbing dust and sending spiders scuttling for cover. In frustration, she closed her eyes and steadied her breath, the fear of rats now driven from the front of her mind by more mundane and practical considerations.

Although most items seemed to have tumbled nearby, a few colourless photographs had fluttered to the far reaches of the insipid pool of light and there was no way of guessing how many lay unseen, just beyond her straining vision.

Recovering one of the fallen boxes, she found the flimsy sides crumpled in her hands. There was something foolhardy in trying to preserve precious, photographic moments in so fragile a container. The other boxes appeared no sturdier. The darkness, like some physical presence, was intent on concealing the dead man's past.

Cautiously she worked her way back towards the trapdoor and the landing below, leaving the scattered photographs and faded envelopes in their new, random arrangement. Her left foot found the edge of the ladder and she eased her way back down. Her jeans and t-shirt were matted with dust and her hair silted with cobwebs. The thought of a hot shower away from this dingy façade of a house, a change of clothes and a glass or two of something alcoholic was hugely tempting. It was Friday afternoon and far too late to start sifting through all those boxes; the job could wait until after the weekend.

Brushing herself down, she descended the threadbare stairs to a shabby kitchen. Anything of any value had already been removed and the bare shelves and empty cupboards were a stark contrast to the jumble above. A local firm had cleared the place and a skip near the front door, piled high with broken furniture, revealed how little worth the dead man's possessions had been. Only the attic still lay undisturbed.

She stared around the carcass of a kitchen noticing the lighter patches on the walls, scars of discarded pictures. Twin, grime-streaked windows peered out from above the sink. Like cataract-glazed eyes, they offered a blurred view of a straggling garden, shrouded by a shapeless laurel hedge. It was a strange, solitary house, isolated from the rest of town and yet in some ways fitting as the last residence of a reclusive man.

The next owner would probably bulldoze the place and start afresh. She reminded herself again why she was there and stepped across to where her coat was hanging. Draped from a hook on a scuffed backdoor, it added the only splash of colour to an otherwise drab room. She reached into one of the generous pockets and extracted a small torch.

What she was being paid for was to investigate the dead or more precisely those interred without kith or kin. Lonely individuals laid to rest with no one to mourn or even mark their departure had become a staple of her work.

Paupers' funerals, not the most sensational journalism in the world, now and then struck a rich seam. More often than not their photos and letters were sad testaments to a life not shared or one drawn out beyond relationships. Sometimes so sparse were the pickings, the deceased might as well have been a shadow for all the impact they had on the world. But occasionally, and only occasionally, a hidden history was worth the digging.

Her newspaper had an on-going understanding with a local firm specializing in house clearances. In return for free advertising, S & K. Household Clearances let *the Gazette* know where and when properties were being cleared and gave them a brief window to dig up stories of local interest.

Her initial qualms at being loaded with such a morbid job and her colleagues' gravedigger jokes had run their course. Ferreting through the personal effects of the dead had initially seemed wilfully intrusive but no one cared, and anyway who else was going to tell their story?

Over the past few months, she had unearthed a range of "hidden gems", as her editor was in the habit of reminding her, usually before assigning her yet another public health funeral. A wealthy widow, whose intestate demise and drab lifestyle had hidden her riches from local gossip, was soon the talk of the town as the paper attempted to track down potential beneficiaries. A forgotten war-hero interred with his memories was also worthy front-page news, although the salacious exploits of a rediscovered, 60s porn star and the belated exposure of a former paedophile, living alone under a new identity, sold far more copies.

Several of her recent articles had even been syndicated to the national press and the whisper amongst the staff at *the Gazette* was that "Juno's going places!"

She now enjoyed the process of gathering together evidence of a person's existence and re-forging an identity. As someone who had always travelled light through life, accruing little as she went, the range and number of papers and mementoes tucked into the recesses of dead peoples' homes were often baffling but always informative. Certificates of past achievements, records of former acquisitions, faded love letters, photos relegated to collect dust, financial statements from another era and even records of previous generations: strange, forgotten indexes.

So much of the past was irretrievably interred with the bodies. Last year there had been almost 4,000 so-called 'paupers' funerals' throughout the UK and the number was on the increase. It was a source of work that was not likely to dry up, at least not in the foreseeable future.

Patching together a life combined her journalistic desire to root out a good story and a sense, garnered from her interest in history, that the past informed the present. She had always believed that the dead had tales to tell but only recently realised their commercial appeal to the living. It was her job to provide the conduit for such narratives.

Her degree in History had partially qualified her for such a role, delving into archives of original-source material, but it was *the Gazette* that had honed the skill. At university her research had woven strands of the past into a consistent tapestry, however unappealing or unremarkable it appeared to the world in general. The newspaper had inverted this search and taught her to look at the impact of the big picture first. Only then should she unpick the individual threads if they were of interest to the public.

The public, or more specifically their readers, were of paramount importance, or so her editor would have her believe. Although public interest was a high-minded sales pitch, schadenfreude and other peoples' dirty washing sold far more papers.

Returning to the attic, it was obvious any hope of sorting through its contents today was a forlorn one. There were just too many boxes to search in the limited time she had set aside. She had been led to believe that the job would be no more than a cursory browse. S & K. Household Clearances had obviously not ventured up into the loft and had based their advice on the paucity of objects in the rest of the house. The reclusive tenant had apparently not bothered to unpack many of his possessions. Maybe he had not intended to stay or the house had not provided sufficient space.

The torch beam shamed the low-wattage bulb, spiking the furthest depths of the attic and the shamble of boxes. The size of her task was daunting but its very scale promised rewards. An uneventful life did not usually warrant a horde of memorabilia. Her eyes tracked the narrow beam, methodically calculating the work ahead: over thirty containers of varying shapes and sizes all labelled with dates! At least that should assist with a coherent reconstruction of the dead man's life.

She placed the torch on the floor near her feet and began to scoop up the fallen photos and letters. Black and white prints, coloured shots and envelopes with foreign stamps were all heaped together. She did not register individual items, only that a broad range of exotic locations and ethnic faces stared out at her from the growing collection. The deceased had obviously travelled extensively and that might provide the angle she was looking for. She could already imagine the headline - "WORLD TRAVELLER ENDS JOURNEY ALONE".

Within a few minutes she had finished and was ready to leave, but as she retrieved the torch it illuminated a gap between two of the larger boxes. The sheen of yet another stray photograph caught her attention. Awkwardly, it had drifted just beyond easy reach.

On her knees, she managed to wriggle an arm into the tight space. Her imagination was working overtime envisioning monstrous arachnids, fanged and venomous, mistaking her wriggling, white fingers for tasty treats. Her index finger brushed the edge of the picture, and with commendable self-control, she eased it towards her.

As it emerged from the gap, dusty but undamaged, she was startled by a noise from below. Somewhere downstairs something had moved. Anxious that someone else might be in the house, she hurried to the top of the ladder calling out as she went.

Reaching the landing, she shouted out again but there was no answer. Hesitantly, she stepped across to the stairwell aware of the floorboards creaking beneath her feet and the brooding silence below. Her heart was working overtime. Subconsciously, she grasped the good-luck charm that hung around her neck, a tear-shaped moonstone set in silver. She did not believe that she was a particularly nervous person, but all alone, burrowing through a dead man's possessions and disturbed by unexplainable noises was enough to put anyone on edge.

At the foot of the stairs, the kitchen was as empty as when she had first entered the house so was the adjacent living room. She felt a chill run down her spine and quickly hooked her coat off the back door, stuffing the few items she was carrying into its pockets. Her voice sounded strained as she called out for the third time, "Is anybody there?"

Enough was enough and without a second thought for the open loft or the bare bulb left glowing inside, she swept up her car keys from the windowsill.

As she turned away from the door she sensed rather than saw something move beyond the streaked windows. In the dusk-dimmed garden, something had stirred. There was someone out there. A sense of urgency to quit the dead man's house welled up inside her.

TWO

It was much later that evening when she objectively tried to assess what had spooked her. She was no novice when it came to searching deserted properties still redolent of their former occupants. The signs and the smells of the recently deceased clung to all the homes she had visited.

Solitary searches in cramped, unventilated attics and odd, untraceable noises had become an accepted part of her job, but something about the experience today had got to her.

She had been too scared to properly register what had caught her eye in the garden. All she recalled was a shadow passing across the window and she had bolted like some terrified child. It had surely been nothing more than the last vestiges of sunlight catching some windswept bush or tree and yet in that briefest of glimpses, the shadow had moved with more purpose than any wind-stirred vegetation. And it had been moving towards the door.

Her fumbling attempts to unlock the car had seemed to take an eternity whilst behind she had sensed a presence moving through the house. Finally, the key turned and she had thrown herself into the driver's seat. Her little red Fiesta, so hesitant on bitter winter mornings, had not let her down and immediately burst into life. Jamming her foot on the accelerator, she fishtailed out of the drive and onto the deserted country road.

At the first bend, she briefly spared a glance in the rear-view mirror. Near where she had parked, someone was standing in the road staring after her. Then they were gone, hidden by the corner and the hedgerows.

It was irrational, but the sense of somebody close behind did not ease despite the distance quickly placed between her and the house. Frequent glimpses over her shoulder could not repress the sense of an unseen presence crouching behind her seat or stop the hairs bristling on the nape of her neck. She switched on the radio, found a pulsating track and turned the volume right up, to drown out the pervading anxiety.

Arriving home in a blare of music and a squeal of breaks, a slight headache was just starting to throb behind her eyes. The calm of her irregularly shaped, one-bedroom apartment with its familiar sights and smells, plus the effects of a hot shower and a very large gin gradually restored some sense of normality. Her earlier panic now seemed slightly ridiculous. She had a vivid imagination but had learnt to keep it in check as a matter of self-preservation.

Her parents had died in a car crash before she was old enough to have any memories of them and a distant relative of her mother's had brought her up. The relationship had always been a tempestuous one, to say the least. At an early age, it had been made quite clear to her that Aunt Agnes, as she insisted on being called, had neither the time nor inclination to take on a child. Over time the tension increased and the arguments escalated, while the periods between the altercations grew ever briefer.

She had taken refuge in an alternative world of make-believe and from an early age had learnt to be self-dependent, populating an imaginary world with friends and fantasies. Many of her childhood hours were spent, "Away with the fairies," as more than one school report had testified. What they did not realise was that it was more than what psychologists termed, "A developmental stage in engaging with a wider world." It was a carapace to keep reality at arm's length.

When she finally escaped to university all contact with her aunt had been severed. The 'over-active imagination' had lasted, but the real world had gradually hemmed it in.

So why had she allowed her imagination free reign on this job? Actually, she had not given it permission for flights of fancy, more like it had made a break for freedom from her psychological, secure unit. She must have visited a score of vacated properties in the last two years searching for "hidden gems", but none had got under her skin like this one. At times the job had educed feelings of sorrow, pity, distaste and even amusement, but the sense of unravelling a story and straightening out a person's history had always placated her emotional unease.

Did it have anything to do with the envelope lying unopened on the table? After six years with not a word from her aunt, out of the blue, a letter had arrived. She recognised the writing immediately, having forged more than one excuse to her school in that dull, expressionless style. Like the woman herself, it was an unembellished hand of short, sharp strokes, lacking in any flourish, patience or creativity. The letter had arrived at the office and played on her mind ever since.

It was a part of her life she had tried to leave behind, an unfortunate cul-de-sac that led nowhere. She had made it clear when she left that any attempt to renew contact or drag her back into that joyless world was unwelcome. So why on earth would her aunt be trying to re-establish contact now? She pushed both letter and thoughts out of sight and mind and returned to the job in hand.

Never before had she run away from an assignment. Well, at least no one at work was going to hear about this incident. She was stronger than that and neither childish fears nor unsolicited letters from her former guardian would get in her way. She still had Monday, before the rest of the house was cleared - time enough to sort through the attic.

She refilled her glass and slipped an instant meal-for-two into the microwave. They offered better value than those for one, although the uneaten portion often lay forgotten and festering at the back of her fridge.

Her mobile, recharging on the work surface nearby, trilled into life with the opening bars of Kelly Clarkson's 'Stronger', a theme tune that had stayed with her since university days.

She guessed who it would be before she even registered the caller identity. Her editor Anthony (never Tony) had a habit of contacting her at irregular times, always concerning work. His hours either represented the most assiduous work ethic or absence of any social life. Over the last few years, she had come to realise that it was the latter. His job was his life and he seemed to feel it necessary to impose similar working conditions on all his staff.

The call lasted longer than usual. She briefly detailed her visit to the house without any of the histrionics and her plan to return to sort through the miscellaneous boxes.

The extended conversation was largely in respect of the details his sub-editor had tracked down concerning the deceased, a Leonard Fosse. She had seen a picture of him with neat chestnut-coloured hair framing a strong, clean-shaven face, a Roman nose and wide-set green eyes. In the photo, staring sceptically at the camera, he appeared tall and skinny, dressed in a casual, dark travelling suit and a white shirt. It seemed Mr Fosse had only been in his late 30s and had started to rent the house some ten months previously but had remained a stranger to locals.

His regular postman had registered that the house appeared deserted much of the time and assumed the owner worked away from home. The post he had delivered was largely made up of circulars with hardly any personal correspondence. Nobody else seemed to have had or remembered having had any dealings with him. Mr Fosse's first memorable impression on the town's inhabitants seemed to have been his death. He had collapsed two weeks ago, outside the newsagents, and was dead before the ambulance arrived, surprisingly, given his age, the victim of a massive heart attack.

Research had shown that Fosse had been a professional freelance photographer mainly in the Americas. His published work over the last decade recorded the personal effects of a rapidly changing political landscape: ragged urchins of a Brazilian favela stood beneath a rigid

Christ the Redeemer, Canadian Inuit fishermen dwarfed by a multinational oil tanker, poverty-stricken, Southern States' share-croppers reflected in the chrome of a gleaming limousine.

They had managed to download various examples of his work, the most recent, from sixteen months ago, captured rows of Mexican-looking peasants harvesting opium poppies overseen by a lounging, armed guard.

Surprisingly for such a seemingly distinguished career, they were struggling to find many personal details. His profession explained the foreign faces and striking locations of the photos stashed up in the attic and promised to make for a rewarding return visit.

"Strange, he does not seem to have had a life of any note outside work," Anthony continued, without giving any sense of being aware of the irony in his statement. "Let's hope some of his stuff will be more revealing. Hopefully, we can put together a double-page spread of some of his photographs you find in the attic alongside a biography and maybe tie them into global events.

"If the photos are as good as the ones online, and not yet published, we might spark some interest from the big boys. It'll make a nice change from our usual lament for the latest victims of austerity."

The eagerness in his tone was evident as he outlined his intentions. She smiled to herself at his enthusiasm, undimmed by years of covering the mundane and the unremarkable that made up the bulk of their copy. The call concluded with her promising to contact him by Monday lunchtime to let him know if she had unearthed anything worthwhile.

All concerns for her earlier, disturbing experience were forgotten as she removed the steaming pasta dish from the microwave and inattentively ate whilst trawling the Internet for background details to the secretive Mr Fosse. Why had a successful photographer, who had not published anything for over a year, hidden away from the world in a miserable house in the middle of nowhere?

THREE

The weekend passed in a whirl. Two of her university friends, Rosie and John, were throwing a house-warming party. They had been 'an item' ever since Fresher Week at the start of their respective courses.

As with most undergraduate relationships, they had their highs and lows but had clung together after graduating, probably for mutual security rather than anything more romantic. Now their contrasting careers had brought them into geographical proximity, they were clambering up the housing ladder together, as a couple.

She threw a few things into a small case and early Saturday morning sped up the motorway to her friends' new apartment, a trendy redevelopment of a Victorian warehouse just outside the city centre.

From the moment the familiar female voice over the intercom ushered her up, she was swamped with noise, friendly faces, news and reminiscences. Over a dozen of Rosie and John's friends, mostly from college days, had made all or part of the weekend.

She did not know what was more exhausting, catching up with each other's lives and reliving college days or trying to sleep on an uneven, inflatable mattress squashed between two other make-shift beds. It was a weekend of laughter and promises, but she was not sad when Sunday evening rolled around.

Although it was great to catch up, she was troubled on the return journey with ambivalent feelings. Tales of work and careers had dominated much of the conversation, but the underlying theme that ran through the entire weekend was partners: actual or potential. Everyone seemed to be entering into, engaged in, or leaving a relationship, with all the expectations and baggage that entailed. Amongst her contemporaries "We" was starting to replace "I".

As usual, the subject of relationships had left her cold. Well, not so much cold as shut out. It reminded her of school days when everyone was talking about the latest Reality TV show that she had not been allowed to watch. It was a world of common references shared by all her peers that had little or no bearing on her life.

University had not been a time for serious romance, more a series of drunken, fumbling liaisons. None of the men or women she had been with had lasted. Something was always missing. Once the physical desire was quenched there was still an unsatisfied need, something lying beyond articulation. Not one fling had ever developed into anything she could call a proper relationship.

Since then she had fallen on chaste times. Long working hours, older, married work colleagues and an unremarkable social life had taken its toll. Even the few holidays she had managed to finance, travelling to various foreign locations of historic interest, had been largely solitary affairs. A brief thing last summer in Tuscany with an American backpacker, Brad, had quickly died out when they returned to their respective lives, and the passion had faded as inevitably as the tan. She suspected that the sex, like the cheap Chianti they had shared, was better left in Italy.

She pushed the thoughts from her mind as she squeezed the small car into a parking space opposite her apartment. Case in one hand, she let herself in, wearily climbed the stairs and contemplated the compact open-plan apartment. It felt safe and comfortable, but she knew instinctively that her life story would unfold somewhere else other than here.

The Gazette was a solid starting point for a career, but she was ready to move on. When it was time to go, no misplaced sense of loyalty or work-based comradeship would hinder her decision. Even Anthony had hinted that she had probably outgrown her role on a small-town paper.

She undressed, dropping her clothes carelessly over a chair and slipped under the duvet, drowsily mulling over where alternate career and life choices might have taken her and who she might have been if circumstances had been different.

FOUR

Dragged from the depths by her alarm, she struggled to surface. She was definitely not a morning person. Several mugs of strong coffee were her daily defibrillator.

With thoughts of the dust and dirt that lay ahead, she opted for a pair of faded jeans and a grey Boston Red Sox sweatshirt, one of the few mementoes she still had of Brad. She grabbed a roll of black plastic garbage bags to transport any items of interest and her warm coat and was on her way as the second dose of caffeine fired up her nervous system.

The weekend had been so busy that she had hardly afforded a thought for Friday's incident and those she had spared were more along the lines of what she would need for a half-way decent article. Before leaving the flat, she once again registered the unopened letter thrust beneath the fruit bowl where she had left it.

Approaching the turn off to her destination, her rattling Fiesta gratefully slowed. She was surprised not to be able to spot the house above the hedgerow. Maybe she had not driven far enough although she was certain on her last visit it had been visible from this turn. As the stretch of hedge dwindled away, she realised why. The unremarkable two-storey house was now no more than a burnt-out husk. A fire truck and several other vehicles were parked on the road. Firefighters were still dealing with the smouldering shell. Smoke trailed up from the charred rubble and merged with the lacklustre sky. It was hardly recognisable as the building she had poked around, just a few days before.

The nauseating stench of the charred floor and wall coverings shrouded her car and seeped through the ventilation system as she drove past and pulled up nearby. The roof and second floor had collapsed in on the ground floor leaving only a smouldering, skeletal frame.

Despite an overwhelming sense that she had just lost a potential centre-page spread and that Anthony was not going to be best pleased, there was another story here. She contacted the paper to see if their photographer was available and then took a few back-up shots on her mobile.

An hour later she had given an edited version of her previous visit to the police and *the Gazette* photographer had been and gone. Perched on a stile across the road from the ruin she watched the firemen pack away their equipment.

Anthony had accepted her suggestion for a replacement, day-in-the-life article focusing on one of the members of the fireteam and now she just had to choose a likely candidate. She had her eyes on the most photogenic member of the crew, not one of the regular troop but a smart, uniformed officer, probably in his early thirties and by the look of him someone who must have spent a fair amount of time in the gym.

Leaving aside any personal interest, he would make an ideal subject for the new article. Fair-haired, clean-cut, rugged features and a winning smile, he was definitely worth closer inspection. She had watched him taking notes, apparently assessing the damage and occasionally addressing members of the regular fire crew. Hopefully, the photographer from the paper and caught him in action. A photo of a good-looking guy in uniform never hurt sales. Her interest in him though was not entirely one-sided. Several times she had caught him glancing in her direction.

Her reveries were disturbed by a winter chill as the wind

strengthened, gusting dead leaves around her ankles. She slid her hands into her coat pockets for extra warmth. Her left hand struck the miniature LED torch and her right touched some forgotten card or paper. The fire crew started to reboard the fire truck and the objects were forgotten as she slipped down off the stile.

She crossed the road in time to waylay her intended subject. He did not seem surprised at her approach and had obviously been aware of her presence. She handed him her business card, an action that still gave her a little thrill, and explained her "professional" interest in him. He met her gaze with unwavering, gunmetal blue eyes and introduced himself as Tom Webster, before politely excusing himself with a deep Mid-Atlantic accent. He had urgent business back at the station that needed immediate attention but could meet her there later, after three. She accepted, shook his hand and watched him climb into a black, Series 5 BMW before pulling away.

The tactile memory of his handshake stayed with her after the car had disappeared: long fingers, surprisingly soft skin and a gentleness that belied his obvious physical strength.

Finally alone, she took one last look at the charred ruins and then turned towards her car. Had she been economical with the truth? She reviewed the account she had provided the police sergeant. The description of her previous visit to Fosse's house and her reason for returning had not included the light left on in the attic or her panicked departure. Had she not considered it important enough to mention? Surely neither had any relevance.

Her hands reached back into her coat pockets searching for the car keys and once again her fingers encountered the item in her right pocket. She drew it out and realised it was the last photograph recovered from between the boxes in the attic. Disturbed by the unexplained noise and in a hurry to be gone, she must have absent-mindedly pocketed it.

The dusty print revealed a stepped pyramid in a jungle clearing. She applied a crumpled tissue to the picture, wiping away some of the accumulated dirt and pocket fluff that obscured the image. Gradually it developed some clarity.

It was an interesting photograph and had Leonard Fosse's usual stylistic qualities, a group of individuals framed by a contrasting landscape. A monument buried in a primaeval forest dwarfed the subjects. The small picture was still too grubby for a detailed examination so she carefully re-pocketed it and headed home to change out of her smoke impregnated clothes.

Showered and back in smart workwear, she returned to the office. After catching up on her in-tray, she turned her attention to the photo. A cotton bud and some rubbing alcohol were the first requirements. Surely Fosse's premature death and a single picture rescued from his fire-decimated house still warranted an article? The man had a reputation as a photographer and that meant his work should be of interest to their readers.

As yet, she had not told Anthony about the photo - no point getting his hopes up if the picture was unsalvageable. The first job was to see whether it could be cleaned up and then whether it lived up to first impressions.

An alcohol-impregnated, cotton bud slowly restored lustre to the image. Colours began to emerge in narrow strips. Dense jungle, spreading to the horizon, developed a rich green tint. A hewn-stone structure at the heart of the picture thrust above the encroaching vegetation as if attempting to escape its grasp, while forest tendrils snaked over the lower steps in an attempt to hold it down. Capping this stepped pyramid was a solid, square building constructed from massive slabs and crowned with an impressive stone headdress. A perpendicular flight of steps ascended to a squat central entrance, black and forbidding.

The sky was largely clear except for the top right corner where storm clouds were gathering. Shafts of splintered sunlight cut through the ominous cumulonimbus to cast elongated shadows from right to left. The photo had been taken from a considerable height to achieve an aerial perspective. The overall effect was a sense of some primal force looking down on civilization's attempts to resist nature and the elements.

She turned her attention to the figures, frozen in time. They were not artfully posed but irregularly distributed, caught unaware in an instantaneous, human tableau. She found a magnifying glass in her desk and leant over the print.

Two of the individuals in the shot were wearing military-style, khaki clothing. One such character crouched halfway up the sheer steps, intently staring through a set of binoculars. The other person in the lower left-hand side of the picture seemed to be leaning over an earthbound shape. She blinked hard and readjusted the glass slightly to refocus the image. The shape came into sharper relief. The crumpled form was another individual whose face would have been visible apart from a stain on the photograph. It was impossible to discern what the person leaning over them was doing.

The last two characters towards the centre of the picture had also been caught mid-action. They seemed to be arguing. A man with his back to the camera had his arm raised, gesticulating or threatening. One foot was off the ground as if caught mid-stride. The character he confronted, a young woman, was leaning away from him, hands raised in apparent supplication.

She blinked, rubbed her eyes and shifted the glass fractionally to pull the girl's features into focus. The magnifying glass slipped from her hand, bounced off the edge of the table and landed on the carpeted floor. She made no attempt to pick it up. Fortunately, there was no one around to register her shock.

After a few moments, she exhaled. In that instant, as the girl had drifted into sharper focus, she had been confronted by her own face. The girl in the photograph was her.

FIVE

Something about your own picture was instantly recognisable, not just the looks but also the stance, demeanour and some internal quality evident in the features all combined to capture the unique identity.

She slowly bent and retrieved the undamaged magnifying glass and moved around the table so that her shadow no longer fell across the photo. This time her attention immediately honed in on the cowering girl, the only female in the picture.

It undeniably looked just like her, shoulder-length anthracite black hair and a slightly elongated face with regular, rather petite features. The body was tall and slender and the short-sleeved t-shirt clung to her, accentuating her small breasts and hinting at the intense humidity. The matching walking shorts, loaded with pockets, revealed long tanned legs and thigh muscles stretched taut from the alarmed posture. Olive green socks and well-scuffed walking boots completed the outdoor attire.

She steadied her hand and gazed at her double. The image was slightly thinner than her and the skin more tanned. The defensive pose also made her appear more angular than she believed herself to be, but it was the pose that ultimately forced self-recognition. Caught in that instinctive, defensive reaction, the figure not only had her looks but also mirrored her automatic physical response to aggression and fear.

Sitting down heavily, she wracked her brains. It made no sense. What was a professional photographer doing with a picture of her and more to the point when and where on earth was it taken? She had no recollection of having ever visited such a location and none of the other people was familiar. She did not even recognise the clothes she was wearing. The frozen, mute figures were acting out some personal narrative that made no sense but cried out to be heard.

Yet again she was letting her imagination get the best of her. It was coming up to 2.30 and almost time for her meeting at the fire station. Later, when she had more time, she would run it through the office software to improve the image quality. Once she had done that she would obviously notice the differences. Her doppelgänger would look no more similar than one of those celebrity lookalikes.

Before leaving, she briefly met with Anthony in his shelf-lined office stacked with files and lit only by artificial light. Dressed in a tired, grey suit and a patterned, green tie, Anthony was as usual immersed in work. He paused long enough to discuss her intentions for the fire officer article, set a tighter deadline now the Leonard Fosse story had literally gone up in smoke and brought to her attention several other local events needing her attention.

She kept thoughts of the salvaged photo and its potential for a new article to herself. Better to say nothing until she knew exactly what she had.

Tom was already waiting for her in the shadows, outside the station side-door, nonchalantly leaning against the wall. No one else was around and he had changed into dark jeans, a tan brushed leather jacket and a collarless white shirt. He looked just as eye-catching out of uniform and rekindled her enthusiasm for the interview.

He was even taller than she remembered and the blond hair was now swept back in a James Dean, pompadour style. His sculpted features were tanned and suggested a physical, outdoor existence. She could imagine him on a Harley-Davidson, appearing over a rise of some American interstate, cutting a trail through a wild, iconic landscape. He smiled at her with the same broad, closed mouth smile she had noticed earlier. Close up his eyes were clear and more steel grey than blue.

He accepted her offer to buy him a tea at the small café across the road and they were soon settled at a corner table with a view of the street outside.

Sitting across the table from her, his gaze made her feel slightly apprehensive. It had a penetrative quality that was difficult to read. He listened attentively to her idea for a feature with only an occasional question and suddenly she realised she was doing most of the talking. She had forgotten the first rule of interviewing - always remember who was the subject.

In an attempt to bring the conversation back round to him, she removed her jotter pad and asked if he minded her taking a few notes as aide-mémoires. She explained that most journalists now used digital recorders, but she preferred to edit material as she went along. He nodded and waited for her to start. His silence was off-putting as if she was the one under scrutiny.

"Can we start with why you wanted to join the fire service?" she asked, finally meeting and holding his stare.

"It's really not that interesting," Tom replied in a soft, self-deprecating tone. "I just knew that whatever I did, it had to be of some practical use."

"A worthy sentiment," she interjected.

"I hope so. My father was a police officer and my mother a nurse. I grew up in a world where practical skills were highly valued and usually employed to assist others. I always believed I should make a difference."

She found the determination in his tone appealing; it had a sense of purpose and energy. "I noticed an American inflection?"

"My mother was originally from Boston. She left her home for London and my father but never left her accent. I guess some of it must have rubbed off on me."

She gradually gained an insight into the person sitting opposite her. There was nothing exceptional in his story: his physical fitness was a requisite of the fire service's entry requirements, his success a determination to put misspent school days behind him. As a regional fire officer, he now investigated the causes of fires for legal and insurance purposes.

The nature of his work meant he was never in one place for long and kept irregular hours. She could have fabricated such a history without ever leaving the office, but it was when she pushed him on details of the fires he had investigated that his accounts took on more originality and impact. It was as if his personal history was not of great interest to him whereas the causes of conflagrations and attempts to hide them were a real passion. She had never realised just how technical fire service work could be. He loved the job but was rarely able to take time away.

"I am now in the enviable position of having accrued two months leave which has to be taken soon. The force has a policy of, use it or lose it," he said and then casually added, "Any suggestions?"

"What a great opportunity. Let me give it some thought," she replied, imagining how he might look on a beach, stripped down to swimwear. "I thought I was doing well with two weeks owing. Have you travelled much in the past?"

"Only family holidays. Spain a few times when I was younger." He paused before switching the subject of the conversation back to her. He wanted to know how she had first become involved in journalism.

As usual, when asked about her past, she ignored her childhood and started with university and how History had been her only real choice. The path into journalism followed when she realised it employed many of the same skills. "I read somewhere that a historian is often only a journalist facing backwards."

He smiled at the saying but then brought her back to family and childhood. The earlier unease passed and she found she was talking about the death of her parents and her painful upbringing, things she had only fully shared with her closest of friends.

He seemed to have the ability to elicit information without seeming to pry. He would have made a good journalist. Maybe it was a technique he required for cross-examining witnesses to fires. It was strange how people were often willing to share private and intimate information with total strangers; a lucky break for journalists, but it also explained the demand for councillors, psychiatrists and therapists as well as the popularity of confessional TV shows.

During a natural pause in the conversation, she glanced at her phone and realised they had been talking for over an hour. Although she had all the information required for the article, she was reluctant to let Tom leave. He was easy to talk to and as Rosie would say, "A real piece of eye candy," and he showed a genuine interest in her. It had been a long time since she had felt so quickly at ease with an attractive man.

The conversation turned to what she had found at Leonard Fosse's drab hideaway. Tom seemed fascinated by *the Gazette's* habit of rescuing photos and documents from the houses of the deceased with the hope of resurrecting their stories.

She had just started to describe the clutter of boxes in the loft and the photos she had dislodged when his phone rang. He apologised and said he had to take it. He listened to the brief call without responding and only acknowledged the message with an "ok" sign off and then excused himself, "I'm sorry, but I lost track of time. I'm going to have to go."

Her disappointment at his abrupt departure was obviously written across her face because he added, "I'm needed back at the station, there's something I still have to do, but perhaps you'd like to join me later for a proper drink?"

"That would be great. There's a new place, 'Jazz Notes', just opened in South Street. My editor has asked me to give it the once over. D'you fancy trying there?"

"Sounds promising. Shall I pick you up?"

"No that's alright. I've also got some unfinished work. I'll meet you there at eight?"

He seemed happy with the arrangement and they left the café together. Tom watched her climb into her Fiesta and drive off before walking away from the fire station and heading down an adjacent side street.

Back at *the Gazette* offices with the intention of writing up her interview under the working title, 'A Burning Desire!' she scanned her notes and continued to think about Tom whilst mentally ticking off staff as they left. As usual, Anthony was the last to go. His mood had improved since earlier and slipping on his well-worn duffle coat, advised her not to work too late and departed with a wave. The main door closed behind him and she was finally alone. She waited until his car, also grey and worn, pulled out of the office car park before retrieving the envelope containing the photograph.

Image enhancement was not a new skill for her. The first stage was a high definition scan to digitalise the hard copy, which she saved as a TIFF file. Once uploaded to Photoshop she increased the pixel dimensions and used filters to remove some of the background noise and discolouration. Gradually the image on the screen dissolved and reformed as each process ran its course. Two or three of the stages had to be reversed when the resulting layer was less clear than the previous version. Eventually, she decided that it was about as sharp and bright as she and the program were able to accomplish.

Aware that it was already seven-thirty she saved the image to her documents and then emailed it to herself. She had been staring so intensely at the quality of the copy that she had not really engaged with what was in the picture – a case of not seeing the trees for the woods, a reversal of the normal adage. She would look properly when she got home, but she did not intend to give Tom an excuse to leave before she arrived.

26

SIX

The venue was an anti-climax the evening was not. Tom was already there when she arrived, perched on a raised metallic stool at the bar. He caught her reflection in a wall of smoked glass mirrors and swivelled to acknowledge her.

As soon as he had ordered them both a drink, they retreated to a table away from the myriad of speakers that were drowning the place in soupy, soft jazz, more muzak than music. Stark pinpricks of light illuminated their progress across the floor. Once settled in a quieter corner, the conversation picked up from where it had left off.

"Did you manage to sort out the problem at the fire station?" she asked.

"Done and dusted. Just needed a signature. Anyhow you've had your chance to interview me, I think it's only fair I find out a bit more about you."

"I've already told you all about how I ended up at the paper and what I do there. What else would you like to know?"

"You're the journalist. What do you normally want to get out of your interviewees?"

"Usually a few facts, something quotable and it doesn't hurt to have something contentious."

"Well for fact's sake you can start with the obvious. What's Ju short for and are there any boyfriends on the scene?"

She laughed and relaxed into the evening. "It's Juno, but I got tired at school of being teased with 'D'you know?' so I've stuck with Ju ever since. And no boyfriends currently."

"So far so good, what about the memorable quote?"

"I quite like 'journalism being the first rough draught of history', but I can't take the credit for that one."

"How about something contentious. Any secret aspirations?"

"Such as?"

"You know, Pulitzer Prize, Miss World, Forbes listing, global dictator?"

"I'll settle for being the first Pulitzer Prize-winning, billionaire beauty queen. Global domination has never been high on my bucket list."

"An underachiever eh?" Their laughter was shared, sincere and unlocked any reserve she still harboured for this man she had met only a few hours ago.

At some point, she offered to get them another drink and to her amazement realised she was already tipsy. Swaying slightly as she clambered down from her high-rise stool, she was reminded that she had not yet eaten. The alcohol had gone straight to her head.

The place had filled up and unsteadily she zigzagged her way through the youthful crowd towards the bar. She could not believe a single drink could have such an impact - what a lightweight.

Behind the bar, a large girl shoehorned into an ill-fitting, immodest dress looked appalled at her enquiry about a menu. The idea that they might serve food or even crisps was obviously anathema to her.

Returning to Tom with two over-priced drinks, the measures of wine mere droplets in the fishbowl-sized glasses, she checked to see if he had eaten. He had but seemed happy to join her for a takeaway.

"What were you doing earlier that was so imperative you had to forego dinner?" he asked.

She set her glass back down on the table wondering if she should tell him. As she had noticed earlier, there was something about him, his stillness and self-assurance that encouraged confidences.

"You know I told you that last Friday I was at that place that burnt down, looking for a story. For some reason, something spooked me and I left in a bit of a hurry. What I didn't realise was that in the rush, I pocketed one of Fosse's photographs. It looks to be some kind of jungle temple that still might make for an eye-catching article."

At the mention of the photo, something in Tom changed. Something about his posture and his gaze made her hesitate. For an instant, his interest in her was just a little too intense, no longer a relaxed first date, more like a cat drawn to a flutter of wings. Her eyes dropped to the wine glass and by the time she looked up the impression had passed. It was nothing but the dim light, alcohol and lack of food playing tricks on her mind.

Over time she had grown accustomed to diverse responses to her imaginative speculations, from outright hilarity and disbelief to enthusiastic confirmations, although the majority tended towards the dismissive end of the spectrum. Tom's response to the discovery of her doppelgänger was different. Apart from when she first mentioned the photo, he remained impassive and inscrutable and she found it impossible to predict his final response.

"I am surprised you made it here at all," he said.

She looked at him questioningly.

"I don't think I could have left such a mystery unresolved. It would be constantly gnawing at my curiosity, which reminds me, you still haven't eaten."

Her stomach rumbled as if in agreement.

"How about I treat us to a pizza of your choice and you give me a chance to have a look at this mysterious photo?"

She nodded and accepted his offer, pleased not just at the thought of imminent sustenance but in being able to share her bewilderment at the mystifying picture.

Despite having to queue for their pizza, they were back at her apartment sooner than expected. She felt a sense of relief that she had left the place in a reasonable condition: no unfashionable knickers or bras left on show, no piles of unwashed plates stacked in the sink and no Tracey Emin style bed. She uncorked a bottle of Australian Chardonnay and poured them both a decent sized glass.

"You mentioned an unexpected letter arriving from your aunt. Is that it under the fruit bowl?" Tom asked.

"That's it," she replied.

"How did she get your address? I thought you said she had no idea of where you were living."

"Somehow, she found I worked for *the Gazette* and sent it there. It's been sitting on the table since last Thursday, a reminder of a time I'd rather forget. What would you do?" she asked, returning from the kitchen with a couple of plates and some cutlery.

"Bin it or read it, but don't leave it dangling."

"Can you open it? I think it might spoil the evening if I did."

Tom carefully opened the letter and scanned the content. "She's succinct, I'll give her that. It just says that it is important you get in touch. She is not well and has some things she needs to discuss with you face-to-face."

"She never had anything worth telling me when I was growing up, so I can't see any reason to discuss things now."

"Maybe she's worried about her health and sorting out some kind of will. From the look of the address, it wouldn't take you more than a few hours to visit and see what she wants"

"The only thing she ever gave me was this necklace and that was my mother's. I don't want anything from her." And with that, she took the letter off Tom and shoved it back in the envelope.

They ate while she powered up her computer and downloaded her emails to find the one from *the Gazette*. The sour taste from her aunt's message was forgotten as she opened the picture on her screen. She was pleased with her efforts. The small, stained image was now bigger, sharper and brighter. Tom's subdued, foreign-sounding imprecation suggested that he had already spotted her doppelgänger.

"You don't think I am being fanciful, do you? That's me or my spitting image, isn't it?"

He nodded slowly in response without taking his eyes from the screen. "Can you blow it up any further?" he asked.

The image was increased in size to a point where it started to show signs of pixelation. What was now clear was that the girl she thought of as her mirror image was scared, very scared. Her awkward stance, defensively angled away from the intimidating man, indicated the nature of her response, but in more detail, the face was truly fearful: taut features, mouth agape, eyes wide and strained.

"She appears shocked," Tom observed in a hushed tone. "What do you think was happening?"

"I don't know, but to me, she looks more than just shocked. I'd say she looks bloody terrified."

"Do you recognise anyone?" he asked, looking up from the screen for the first time and observing her response.

"No, none of them. If it wasn't for my image, there's nothing here that I recognise, not the clothes, nor the people, nor the place!" Her tone sounded strained even to her own ears. Tom reached out a hand and reassuringly laid it gently on her arm. "I wondered if it was some kind of trick. You know image manipulation. But what the hell would a total stranger be doing messing about with my picture?"

"Why don't we start with some of the other elements? That might get us somewhere. We should be able to find out where it was taken. I can't believe that such an imposing monument isn't well known and the clothes might provide more information." His thoughtful approach and reassuring touch calmed her and together they began a more purposeful analysis.

Each Individual's attire and activity was scrutinised in turn and assessed for clues. The shock of realising how frightened her lookalike appeared, paled when she re-centred the picture on the two characters to the left-hand side of the frame.

The stain obscuring the face of the slumped body had not been removed with the filters and enhancements but was now clearly visible as blood. The features were masked because the face was a gory mess. The hair was shoulder length and could have belonged to a man or a woman. Slumped and limp, the body was largely concealed by the individual bent over them.

"Obviously this person is badly hurt," she said, pointing at the prostrate figure. "So why the hell aren't the others doing anything about it? Why is the person with the camera taking pictures and not helping? I'd have thought they'd all be concerned with sorting out some kind of first aid."

The shock of recognising herself diminished as the picture compounded the initial mystery with ever more disturbing questions. The figure leant over the invalid could be aiding or assaulting the injured person, it was impossible to tell. His tattooed arms were either supporting or smothering the limp form. The character perched halfway up the temple, with the binoculars pressed to his face, appeared oblivious or unconcerned with the events below.

She looked away from the screen and Tom caught her worried look. She wondered whether he was thinking the same as her. "What the fuck do you think's going on here?" she said, her voice trembling slightly.

"I don't know, but I would be surprised if this was an accident," he replied in a tone that suggested he had already decided that the injury was intentional.

"What do you mean?"

"I've seen enough accidental and premeditated injuries to know how people respond to both." His assured tone left no room for debate.

"Maybe the photo's staged," she said, in an attempt to refute the implications.

"Maybe!" he replied unconvincingly. She allowed the subject to drop and offered to make them coffee, more as a diversionary tactic than a need for caffeine. The suggestion was gratefully received and while she busied herself with the percolator, he searched the Internet for images of jungle temples.

By the time she returned, he had remarkably brought up an image on the screen that was almost a carbon copy of the pyramid in her photo.

"At least I think we've found the setting for your photograph. It's Tikal, an ancient Maya complex." He looked at her for a response. "Have you ever been to Central America?"

"No, no I haven't, nowhere near. Go back to the picture," she directed.

Sure enough, as he split the screen between the two pictures they were almost identical except for one or two minor differences. The colour of the Internet image was of a lighter grey and some of the stonework looked in better condition as if recently repaired. The picture Tom had found was also taken from a lower perspective. The details below the website placed the temple in northern Guatemala.

"I have an idea," she said. "In the image you found, the steps around the base have been repaired, which makes me think the website picture is more recent than Fosse's photo where the same steps are crumbling. It also looks as if some work has been done on the left-hand side of the temple. If we were to trace a range of pictures of this temple taken at different times we might be able to see when the repairs were carried out.

"If this photograph is Fosse's, I can probably find a date range when he might have been in Central America. One of his last published photographs, just over a year ago, was from Mexico. Prior to that many of his photos were published and should provide evidence of his location at specific dates. The two date ranges might help us home in on a time. With place and time established, I'd have two key elements in trying to make sense of this."

"I can see why you're a journalist," Tom replied with a smile. "Look, we're both tired and have been staring at this image for far too long. My vision's starting to pixelate. What if I do some research over the next few days? If you email me the picture I can have a trawl of the web and try to pin it to a specific time, as you suggested. Hopefully, that might throw a bit more light on your alter ego."

She suddenly realised just how tired she was and accepted his offer with thanks. He scribbled down his email, drained his cup and stood to leave. She passed him his jacket from the arm of the sofa and turned away just as he leant forward to kiss her. She turned back, vainly attempting to recapture the moment, but it had passed and he was already heading down the stairs and out the door with a final, "Goodnight."

If she had not been so tired or if so many things had not been going on in her mind, she might have kicked herself at her poor timing.

Later, encased in her duvet, her sleep-smothered thoughts lingered on Tom. She could see why he was good at his job. His calm, analytical approach to the photo and the speed he had identified Tikal as the location were impressive.

She recalled the sense of his presence next to her at the table, his smell and the touch of his hand on her bare arm. Her imagination slipped through the night to his bedroom, or what she fancied it would look like, but before her fantasies warranted an adult viewing certificate, sleep overpowered her.

SEVEN

The following week dragged along like some weary child. The frequency with which she glanced at the various timepieces that apportioned her daily routines was totally out of character.

Sure enough, Tom was as good as his word and had been in touch even though another job had dragged him away at short notice. He had been unable to date the picture with any precision. The research into Tikal placed the photo somewhere between eleven months and ten years ago. Repairs to the temple were irregular and interspersed with long periods of inactivity.

He had managed to unearth a newspaper report from ten years ago commenting on the fact that further funds had been found by UNESCO who had originally listed it as a World Heritage Site in 1979. The attached photograph presented the temple in a poorer condition than her print, but then there was no evidence that the picture for the article had not been resurrected from the archives.

The last repairs he had traced were completed only eleven months previously. One of his emails suggested that he might be able to extract more information from the original print. His department had access to some high-tech machines that might be able to do even more with the photograph.

The email also included a Wikipedia-style historic overview of the site, which supposedly dated back to fourth century B.C. and had been at the centre of one of the greatest Maya kingdoms. The central stepped temple reminded her of pictures she had seen of the massive pyramids at Teotihuacan just outside Mexico City. She was amazed at the scale of the place. So far archaeologists had discovered 3,000 structures and calculated up to one hundred thousand people might have lived there.

There were competing theories as to why it had undergone such a rapid decline in the ninth century: deforestation and drought were hard to believe surrounded as it was by dense jungle, while disease, earthquakes and volcanic eruptions all sounded like some disaster-movie. Alien invasion was one of her favourites but did not seem to have much going in its favour. So completely had the ruins disappeared into the jungle that Cortes, brushing past Tikal in 1525, was oblivious of its existence.

Her own research added to the details Tom had discovered and spurred on her curiosity. She returned to the photograph regularly, but it refused to surrender any more of its secrets. The characters' dramatic tableau remained unintelligible and her other-self persisted, petrified in time, unable to answer questions.

For some irrational reason, she was reluctant to lend the original photograph to Tom, keeping it safely locked in her desk at work. She had not seen him since the evening at the bar and might have thought that he had tired of her and her fanciful quest if it had not been for the occasional text and email. The ungodly hours they arrived reminded her of the time-consuming nature and unusual hours of his work.

Nothing more had come of the house fire and her activities there. The police had called once to check a few of the details and to let her know that it appeared to be a case of faulty wiring. A sergeant, with an irritatingly patronizing tone, had informed her that she was fortunate not to have electrocuted herself.

This new information put her mind more at ease. That surely explained the noise that had scared her: a trip switch cutting out, a fuse blowing, wires overheating - all potential culprits. As for the shape in the garden, nothing more than wind, shadows and a supercharged imagination. And the person she thought she spotted in the rear-view mirror was more than likely just a local, checking on her over-dramatic departure.

The front-page article on the fire had attracted little interest or feedback from the public. She suspected most of their readers had never known of the existence of the house in the first place.

Her article on Tom was not what she originally intended. Disappointingly *the Gazette* photographer had not managed to capture Tom clearly. Every shot had him turning away, bending down, or partially concealed by a member of the fire crew, almost as if he was camera shy. Even the snaps on her mobile had failed to catch anything halfway decent. Instead, they had gone with an action shot of the firemen dousing the last embers of the skeletal staircase.

Although the story had moved away from personal interest to civic responsibility and was more generalised, it suited Tom's wishes. He had been reluctant to be painted as 'a man of action', claiming it might irritate those in the heat of battle, the actual firefighters. He had sown the seeds of a more generic approach during their interview. To emphasise the physical demands of the job, she had headlined it "Feel the Burn!"

Despite not being what Anthony had originally expected, he was pleased with the final piece. Therefore, she responded to a request to join him in his office with neither undue concern nor expectation.

"Come in, Ju. Have a seat," he said, half-hidden behind his cluttered desk. "I'll cut to the chase," he continued, looking up from a letter he was holding and smiling. She shifted a stack of papers off the only available chair. "I've received a letter from an old acquaintance at *the Guardian*. It would seem they are looking to fill a vacancy on their staff and have been impressed by some of your work. My friend wants to know if you'd be interested in applying?"

She sat speechless, stunned by the news, initially imagining it to be some sort of practical joke. Obviously, she had considered the possibility of moving up to a national paper but only hypothetically.

"How did they hear about me?" she asked, trying to take on the full ramifications that such a move would entail.

"Well apart from the few stories we managed to sell on, I might have dropped your name into the conversation from time-to-time. You've been here over two years now and certainly proved yourself. It will be a real shame to lose you, but you cannot stay here forever. There's more to the news than the forgotten dead, vandalism and road works."

"That's not fair!" she proclaimed. "What of the piece I did on local drug suppliers targeting schools or the one on the failings in…" Anthony cut her off midway through her list.

"That is exactly why you should be leaping at this opportunity. You've cut your journalistic teeth here, but they will go blunt if you spend most of your time chewing the cud of regional news. A national will provide the opportunity to get those journalistic incisors working properly. You have real potential, so make the most of it."

Deep down she knew he was right. A daily, national paper might provide her with a world of opportunities. News would finally mean global events not just the local and the parochial.

"Thank you, Anthony. I know you're right; it's just come as a bit of a shock. How soon do they need a response?"

"If you want my advice, I'd organise a meeting as soon as possible, just in case they change their mind. The paper isn't looking for you to start until the beginning of next month so you have a few weeks to sort yourself out. Take the leave owing you and find yourself a base in London. Lord knows when you will next have time to yourself." He smiled at her look of apprehension. "If it doesn't work out, there is always a desk for you back here."

The conversation continued for a while, ironing out some of her concerns. It was decided she should work to the end of the day to clear her assignments whilst he contacted his acquaintance at *the Guardian*. She thanked him profusely and agreed to follow his advice.

Returning to her desk, her head was full of questions, and the afternoon passed in a haze of daydreams. What would this new career step mean and how might her life change? Work colleagues quickly latched on to the fact she might be leaving and an impromptu celebration or belated second-anniversary party was organised for the following evening. She suddenly thought of Tom. If he was back by then, maybe he could be persuaded to accompany her. She sent him an innocuous text tempting him to "a small gathering" without specifying the reason for the celebration. She wanted to tell him her news in person.

Not expecting any reply until much later, she was surprised to receive a positive response within minutes. The suggestion that he pick her up from her place the following evening was gratefully acknowledged.

Before the end of the afternoon, Anthony's contact, Ruth, who turned out to be a Resources Manager at *the Guardian*, had phoned her directly to arrange a visit. It was organised in two days' time, to discuss the potential job and "remuneration package". She appreciated the personal call although Ruth's brusque manner and harsh, cockney edged inflection were not immediately endearing unlike the soft, regional accent and slower delivery to which she had become accustomed.

Later, back at her flat and with time on her hands, she felt in a bit of a limbo not knowing literally whether she was coming or going. A small box with her few personal items, retrieved from her office desk, sat untouched on the carpet. Instead, she turned her attention to the web to calculate the exorbitant costs of London living. What would she need to earn to make the new job a viable proposition? A damn sight more than she was being paid now, that was for sure. She weighed up all the pros and cons until her mind ached with chasing considerations round in dizzying circles.

Whatever her eventual decision, she had two weeks of unplanned holiday to relish, an opportunity she had not had since university days.

If the meeting at *the Guardian* went well she should take Anthony's advice. Searching for a new flat to rent would be the sensible thing to do but not how she wanted to spend her impromptu holiday. Checking her bank account, she found it was healthier than imagined - an indication of how hard she had been working and her uneventful social life.

She toyed with the idea of another trip to Italy. She did not think she could ever tire of that country. She remembered a Verdi quote she had come across while researching one of her articles; "You may have the universe if I may have Italy." Everything about the place enchanted her, but mainly it was the expressive nature of Italians. They seemed so much more in touch with their emotions than the British. She recalled an unfulfilled New Year's resolution, inspired by a Christmas spent in Sienna, to learn Italian. The trouble was that as a visitor to another land you only scratched the surface. How could a fleeting visit ever lead to a true understanding of a place or its people?

Rising from the kitchen bar, her attention was drawn again to an A3 copy of the mysterious photograph lying enigmatically on the living room table. Research notes on Tikal, the Maya and Guatemala now surrounded it. A new idea sparked, kindled and began to burn. Was the idea of a holiday in Central America ridiculous? Could such a trip be organised at such short notice? She had the money and the time, plus the research into the Maya had truly inspired her. If the mystery of the photo was not enough wasn't the unexplained disappearance of an ancient kingdom, sufficient grounds for visiting Tikal?

A module of her degree on the European Renaissance had thrown out grappling irons of interest well beyond Europe. Explorers such as Columbus, Vasco da Gama and Magellan opened up the New World and connected the previously fractured worldview. She saw their exploits as the seeds of the troubled times she lived in, but it was Cortes and Pizarro who had really fired her curiosity. Their blazing trails of discovery and destruction through Central and Southern America, fired by their lust for fame, power and wealth, had turned them into the stuff of legends. History had intermittently re-evaluated them as either heroes or villains. It could be the trip of a lifetime. Why not, what was stopping her?

The rest of the evening was spent in a whirl of excitement planning the expedition. She found her cheapest transport, at just over £500, was an eighteen-hour KLM flight to Guatemala City, changing planes at both

Amsterdam and Panama City, followed by a seven-hour bus journey. Flores, the nearest town to Tikal, was some three hundred miles northeast of Guatemala City. It might be easier to catch an internal flight.

Last-minute vaccinations for Typhoid and Hepatitis A could both be booked in London and she could easily pick up sprays to stave off any mosquitos. No visa was required for a stay of up to ninety days and travellers' tales of the crime levels in Guatemala City or the humidity and heat at Tikal at this time of the year were not enough to dint her rising enthusiasm. Even the thought of an annual rainfall that could drown a person standing on a stool was an insufficient deterrent. Once she had the bit between her teeth, as Anthony used to comment, she was not easily swayed from her course.

Her enthusiasm and excitement continued to build as she read up on the vast forests around Tikal, part of a two million hectare biosphere reserve extending up into Belize and Mexico. Tikal National Park was one of the few World Heritage sites that had achieved its status both for archaeological importance and extraordinary biodiversity. Amongst the 2,000 different plants so far recorded, there were over 200 types of trees. As for wildlife, it was alive with 300 species of bird, 5 types of cat including jaguars and 7 sorts of monkeys. The website she was using even had a soundtrack of the howler monkeys' deafening dawn chorus, louder than either a thunderclap or a jet engine and a damn sight more unnerving.

Over the next few hours, she booked her international flight with KLM and the one-hour connecting flight with Avianca to Flores, the main base for trips to Tikal. This not only avoided the protracted bus journey but also meant that she no longer needed to navigate Guatemala City. A metropolis whose unhealthy reputation for crime and prostitution earnt it a top ten place in the list of the world's most deadly cities.

She also found a reasonably priced, traditional hotel, *Casa Maya Donna*, in Flores that advertised daily excursions to the ruins of Tikal and Yaxha and even overnight trips to Palenque in Mexico. All three looked to be fascinating archaeological sites although Tikal was her priority.

With a few small additions, her wardrobe would suffice but there were other things she needed: mosquito spray, suntan lotion, guidebook, toiletries, suitable footwear and a water bottle. The list grew until it formed two columns.

Sometime after midnight, she turned in, but sleep proved hard to come by and she watched the clock hands turn two before she drifted off.

EIGHT

The following day flew by. She booked an appointment for jabs at a travel clinic in central London, printed out flight tickets, managed to purchase most of the items from her list and hardly stopped until late afternoon when she found herself back at the apartment with her equipment, clothes, documentation and backpack scattered across the floor of the living room.

This was still the state of her apartment when Tom arrived at six-thirty. He was dressed in a cream, three-piece suit and a grey tie and looked good enough to eat. She was proud to have this man accompany her and knew they would be the source of much conjecture.

She was glad she had also made an effort, opting for her strapless, black, velvet cocktail dress, lace underwear, black net stockings and heels. Her lipstick was appropriately fire engine red as was her nail varnish. Her hair was worn up and the effect was completed with a brief spray of Italian perfume to her neck and cleavage. She could not recall the last time she had glammed up, and who knew what the evening would bring!

During an earlier call to Tom she had let on about the reason for the celebration and they had arranged to eat before joining up with her colleagues at a bar across town.

Entering her flat now his response was all she could have desired. He ignored the disorder, responding instead to her appearance with a low whistle. Only after he had stopped admiring her did he take in the chaos that covered the floor.

"What on earth is going on? Are you doing a runner? Not paid your rent for a while?" he said, carefully stepping back into an uncluttered corner of the room and assessing the items on show.

She swiftly piled everything together to create space and hide the sensible, non-sexy, travel underwear before informing him of her spur of the moment decision to travel to Guatemala.

He seemed truly pleased with her news. "That's great I'm just sorry I didn't manage to find out anything more specific about the photo. I'll be really interested in what you discover." He paused, "I've a suggestion. Your meeting at *the Guardian* is tomorrow morning and it just so happens I'm not working. How about I drive you there? It will save you the hassle and I quite fancy a day in London. I take it that's where the newspaper's based?"

The unexpected offer was leapt at. Her sense of direction was not good and navigating the capital had always proved a headache. "That would be great, Tom. Yes, London it is, near King's Cross. Are you sure you can afford the time?"

"Of course!" He smiled at her again. "Come on Ju, let's go and get something to eat and you can let me in on your travel plans," he replied, whilst ushering her towards the stairs.

They ate at a small, authentic Italian restaurant that her colleagues had recommended. She outlined her trip and her remote hope that the people who worked at Tikal might be able to throw some light on the picture.

"Maybe the local guides have records of accidents or injuries to visitors at the ruins," she mused.

Tom took a real interest in all her plans, right down to flight details and hotel arrangements. The conversation moved on to the forthcoming informal interview and the possibility of a move to London. She would have liked to have stayed longer at the restaurant and shared an intimate evening with Tom alone, but there was no way she could miss a celebration organised in her honour. They moved on to the party venue, regrettably foregoing dessert and coffee.

The evening with her work associates passed pleasantly enough. As the drinks flowed, gossip spread and comments about her and her secret escort started to circulate. She guessed most of the women envied her, assuming she had already bedded him. Tom seemed oblivious to the flirtatious comments and the increasingly lascivious looks that came his way as the evening wore on.

Most of the men, not surprisingly, were more interested in her. Male colleagues she worked with every day of the week suddenly treated her as if she was a different person, the effect of a bit of slap and a short black dress was remarkable.

The curtains closed on the party with farewells, embraces and best wishes for the future. As she and Tom were about to take their leave, Anthony apologetically called the drink-befuddled gathering to order. His grey work-wear suit had been exchanged for an equally uninspiring pair of beige trousers, brown sweater and chocolate brown loafers. The following alcohol inflated tribute to her verged on the panegyric, concluding with the presentation of a bottle of champagne and an apology, "I'm sorry it's not very imaginative, but you didn't give us much time."

The hug afterwards and mumbled private expressions of regret at losing her were more touching than she had expected and more valued than the public accolade. With a slightly unsteady voice, she thanked him again for all his support and the assembled company for how welcome they had made her feel at the paper and then with Tom beside her, they left the party.

Weaving their way back towards her flat, their hands met and his fingers gently closed around hers. His touch, soft and tentative, recalled their first meeting. Again she was struck by the incongruity of so powerful a body with so gentle a touch. It felt protective but not as sensual as she had expected, more comforting than arousing.

At her door, she turned towards him and this time did not move as he leant in to kiss her. She raised her head to meet his lips. His kiss was firm and moist but briefer than she would have desired. He drew back slowly, turning down her offer to come in for a coffee, and gave her a strange, indecipherable look before taking his leave with a promise to pick her up first thing.

Watching his BMW disappear round the corner, she wondered what had gone wrong. Why had he left so abruptly? Did he not fancy her? That was definitely not the impression he had given during the evening.

Letting herself in, she went directly to the full-length mirror in the bathroom. Despite the alcohol and faltering walk home, she still looked "desirable". Most of the men at the party would not have turned up their noses, but obviously Tom was not one of them. She should not have drunk so much, it had got her aroused and she wanted him. Anyway, whatever the reason, it was too late now, plus it was shortsighted to consider starting a relationship on the eve of moving away. It was not the time to get involved.

This did not stop her thinking about him though as she stripped and slipped naked into bed. The way she had felt when he had taken her hand, his lips on hers, it should have felt so right and yet something had been lacking. It was that sensual thrill; that electrical charge that came with the first touches in any passionate encounter that had been missing. "Oh well, his loss," she thought remembering the manner one of her friends at university, a self-styled, self-deluded Casanova, excused his failures.

She stretched luxuriously enjoying the feel of the cotton duvet on her bare body and her fingers reached between her thighs to draw out the pleasure he had deprived her of.

That night her dreams were troubled: howling cries, shadows solidifying and dissolving, forests sentient to her fear. She ran, her heart pumping, her breath straining, thorns raking her flesh, creepers grasping at her limbs. Breaking from the trees she found herself in a clearing infront of a set of perpendicular steps that vanished into the storm clouds above. Behind her she could hear a voice, Tom's voice, calling, pleading. The words were indistinct yet the meaning was clear. He needed her. He was in trouble. She must help him, but something held her there. Another presence, at the top of the steps, was stronger than his. They too were in trouble, however, their pain was felt rather than heard or seen. She tried to turn, but heart-rending inertia gripped her. The cries from behind intensified whilst the presence above grew stronger, enveloping her in a tidal wave of despair.

She woke with a start: shivering at the already fading illusions. The curtains were not fully drawn and a slither of moonlight fell across the floor to rest on the table and the photograph of Tikal.

NINE

The morning seeped in, dull and chill, not boding well for the day ahead. Breakfast was a non-starter, either because of nerves or last night's excesses, and a fruit juice and coffee were all she could manage. She dressed formerly in a slate grey, woollen, skirt suit that accentuated her height. Heels added to the effect and compensated for her youth in terms of confidence. She was careful and precise with her make-up and sparing with the perfume. It was important to create the right impression.

She wanted the job based solely on her ability as a journalist but was not so naïve as to believe that first impressions were not of paramount importance. Recent research had shown that most interviewers took only 385 seconds to make up their minds about a candidate.

Her handbag held a file of some of her more important articles at *the Gazette* along with details of the clinic booked for her travel jabs.

On autopilot, she cleaned her teeth and was just examining her reflection in the bathroom mirror for the third or fourth time when the buzzer went. It was a relief to hear Tom's voice at the other end of the intercom. Instructing him to wait there, she quickly grabbed what she needed and descended to the street. He greeted her with a peck on the cheek and ushered her around the corner to where his car was parked.

The early hour and absence of traffic meant they were soon out of town and on the motorway heading east towards London. Tom had learned that the National Film Theatre had a John Ford retrospective, which he planned to take in while she was being interviewed. There was an exhibition of stills from some of his films including those shot in Monument Valley, an iconic setting for numerous westerns.

Most of the journey passed in an easy silence, which she used to scan some notes she had printed about *the Guardian*: its history, structure, political bias, as well as various sales data. When they pulled over at a service station for a break, she used it as an opportunity to buy that day's publication. She believed in being fully prepared. Back in the car, she read the main articles thoroughly and the editorial, attempting to draw a clear sense of house style and any inherent values. Apart from occasional questions, Tom seemed happy to let her read in peace.

As they approached Reading, they joined the daily London influx of traffic and their journey slowed, the last twenty miles taking longer than the first ninety. They were still in good time for the appointment and the skies had cleared by the time they arrived outside the newspaper offices, a slick, modern, black metal and glass structure emblazoned with the paper's emblem. There was nowhere to park so Tom briefly pulled up in front and they arranged to meet later outside the National Film Theatre. He smiled reassuringly, squeezed her arm and wished her luck before she climbed out. He drove off to the blare of horns from temporarily delayed traffic. She drew in a deep breath, straightened her skirt and nervously approached the entrance.

The informal interview, inoculations and reunion with Tom all went like clockwork. She had decided to take the job before she even met Ruth. Once through the tinted glass doors, the sense of bustling energy and purpose was tangible. She felt inspired and animated from her very first step inside.

Ruth was a deceptively small woman dressed in an expensive, ash-grey, power suit. Her asexual haircut and firm handshake reinforced her assertive tone. The diminutive resources manager oozed self-confidence and energy as she whisked her around the high-tech offices and introduced her to the team she would be working with.

Her potential role and annual salary along with fringe benefits were spelt out as they toured. She was not asked for examples of her work and assumed they had already been inspected online and by the time they were halfway round she was ready to sign along the dotted line.

Ruth seemed pleased to welcome her on board and promised that there would be someone designated to show her the ropes when she officially joined them. She returned to Ruth's office to sign a contract and collect some paperwork and was then led back to the bright, modern atrium she had first entered. Ruth concluded their meeting by handing her a business card and informing her that if she had any issues she should not hesitate to contact her, whatever the hour. A brusque handshake and she was standing back out on the pavement in front of the building, where she had stood only an hour previously.

Deciding to walk to the clinic rather than catch a taxi allowed her space and time to assess her hasty decision. The roads were lined with vehicles and the pavements dense with bustling humanity - so many lives brushing past one another and yet seemingly oblivious to each other's presence. Even after only a few years working for *the Gazette* she was recognised around town, acknowledged and greeted, her sense of self-identity shaped by social interactions. Who was she in this heaving mass of people, surrounded by life, yet more alone than ever?

By lunchtime, she had received the necessary jabs, picked up some anti-malarial tablets and worked her way to the South Bank to meet up with Tom. They decided to grab something to eat at the National Theatre café just along the embankment. Tom had seen an advert for a lunchtime jazz quartet in the theatre foyer and the car was parked in the theatre's underground car park.

Over lunch, he listened to her animated description of her future place of work and skimmed the printed job description, which looked to be very fluid. She eventually remembered to ask him about the John Ford exhibition. He described some of the stills on display that had taken him right back to childhood westerns. A number were etched into his memory whilst others had inspired him to track down some of Ford's lesser-known films.

They finished lunch and decided to get out of London before rush hour engulfed them and by two they were back at the car. As they drove up the exit ramp and turned right towards Waterloo Bridge she noticed a large poster on the BFI advertising the Ford retrospective. Very briefly, she caught sight of some of the dramatic shots Tom had referred to. Her eyes reached the bottom of the poster just as they turned away from concrete and glass structure. Her final glimpse was of the opening date of the exhibition on the 24th, still two days away. How on earth had Tom managed to pre-empt the official opening?

She was on the point of asking him, when a speeding car cut them up. It seemed to have appeared from nowhere, travelling well above the speed limit and only Tom's lightning reactions avoided a major collision. The other driver did not stop and in a squeal of tyres was immediately lost from sight in the tangle of traffic. Tom swore under his breath, *"Pisado!"*

"Bloody hell that was close," she said, exhaling deeply. "What did you call him?" she asked, surprised not just at his speed of reactions but also his foreign-sounding expletive.

"Oh, *pisado*. It's one of the few words I picked up from holidays in Spain. It means something like being a jerk"

"Well, that's a new one on me. Do you always swear in Spanish?"

"I was sent to a Catholic school so English invective was taboo, but foreign insults usually slipped below the radar and to my ear often sound so much more expressive. I mean doesn't '*kurwa mać*' sound better than 'for fuck's sake'?"

"That doesn't sound Spanish."

"No, that one's Polish. One of the advantages of going to a multi-racial school." The conversation about the onomatopoeic qualities of language, especially when used for insults or protestations of love, continued through London and back on to the motorway.

They arrived outside her apartment as the light started to fade. She invited Tom in, but yet again he declined. Unfortunately, he was needed elsewhere. He made his apologies, said his farewells and was gone before she had even retrieved the door key from her bag.

She was disappointed that he was not free that evening for a farewell drink or as previously intimated, to take her to the airport the following day. A job had come up that required his immediate attention although he would not know the specific details until he checked in later. She thought some of Anthony's demands at *the Gazette* had stretched acceptable working hours, but Tom seemed to be at the beck and call of Fire Service 24/7. He promised to try and phone and to contact her as soon as she returned.

Before he had let her know of his change of plans, she had decided that if the opportunity arose she was ready to ask him to stay, even if it only turned out to be a one-night stand. She wanted to be held, feel the touch of his skin on hers, enjoy the physicality and exhilaration of sex with him and share her bed. The news of his immediate departure, brief kiss and receding view of his black beamer felt like a real anti-climax to the day.

Re-entering the small flat, her disappointment soon lifted. Anticipation bubbled up again as she took in her travel gear strewn across the floor. Who knew what would happen when she returned and moved to London. Tom's job could take him anywhere at any time, so why not London?

The evening was spent packing her rucksack and checking paperwork. She carefully rolled up the copy of the photo that seemed to have initiated her change in fortunes, slipped it into a cardboard tube and laid it alongside a leather folder with her passport, travel insurance and e-tickets. The original, retrieved from work the day before, she slid between two oversized books on a shelf.

Realising how tight time would be on her return, she also tidied the flat and phoned Anthony to inform him of her decision to take the

London job. He sounded strangely subdued at her news. Bizarrely, she did not tell him that she was going to Guatemala, just that she had booked a holiday, and he did not seem inclined to ask for details. Tom was still the only person who knew of her full plans or of the existence of the photograph.

Her train of thought was disturbed by the unexpected buzz of the intercom. Who on earth would call at such a late hour?

TEN

Squeezed into the window seat by a bickering, overweight couple, the flight to Panama threatened to be an interminably long one. There were more direct flights that would take only half the time, but they were prohibitively expensive.

The first leg to Schiphol passed in a blur. It had been a rush to catch the early morning flight, followed by a tedious wait-over, before transferring to the next plane with the nagging doubt that her backpack might not be coming with her. Once settled on the trans-Atlantic flight, she had a chance to reflect on last night's unexpected events. She eased her earphones into place, clicked on her playlist and tried to ignore her neighbours' sniping at each other.

It had been Tom at the door. He had called in a few favours and the job that had been so urgent could hang fire, so to speak, for twenty-four hours. He was freshly showered, dressed in a loose-fitting, blue, linen jacket, collarless white shirt and flourished a bottle of champagne.

"I couldn't let you leave without saying goodbye properly, could I? I was going to bring some flowers, but it's probably not worth it as you are not going to be here."

She replayed her memories of the evening. Yet again they had gone over her plans for Guatemala. Tom plied her with champagne and they returned to discussing the image on her computer screen. She pointed out a few new clues she had identified. Fainter, dark streaks trailed from the prostrate body along the step to the bottom left corner. She speculated that it could be blood, in which case the injury had happened somewhere out of shot and the body had been carried or dragged there. She re-centred the image and drew his attention to the lower right corner of the photo where she had noticed another dark patch. With the cursor, she traced around the magnified shape. The outline formed an elongated human shadow.

"I think there were other witnesses to this incident and the more people that were there, the greater the chance of me finding out who this woman was…is."

She moved the image towards the fiercely gesturing figure in front of her doppelgänger. At the base of his skull, just below the blond hairline, she had spotted some kind of mark. Initially, she had thought it was yet another blemish on the original photograph, but closer observation had shown that it was more solid and looked as if it could be a birthmark or a scar.

On the point of mentioning this feature to Tom, she realised that he had moved behind her and was leaning over her with his hands resting gently on her shoulders. She could smell his aftershave, a woody, spicy fragrance. It was hard to concentrate with him so close. She could feel his breath on her hair as he leaned over her to pick up her empty glass. He refilled both their glasses and carried them to the sofa, a silent invitation for her to join him.

"With the risk of sounding tedious, allow me to toast your journalistic flair and a successful quest." He raised his glass. "Ju, I believe if there is a story worth discovering, you will unearth it. If your double is out there, you will find her."

"Do you really think so?"

"I'm betting on it."

Joining him on the sofa, neither did anything to resist the sagging piece of furniture slumping beneath their weight. She snuggled into his side and his arm curled round to cradle her shoulders.

It was late when Tom finally made a move to leave and although the snuggling had moved onto gentle kissing and caressing it had gone no further. They were both still fully dressed. The champagne was gone and so was the best part of another bottle that needed to be used up. Before Tom was halfway off the sofa, she had suggested that if he did not feel up to driving he could bed down on the couch. He accepted and she disappeared to the bathroom where she opted for an over-sized t-shirt. Her normal habit of sleeping naked was just a bit too risqué. If she ended up like that, well, that would be a different matter.

This seduction, if that's what it was, had to be the most gentle and tentative she had yet encountered. She would never style herself a dominatrix, although she was not reluctant to take the lead or set the parameters when it came to sexual relations, but there was something about this man that made her hesitant about pushing the pace. If, for the time being, Tom was only prepared to accept this level of intimacy then she would not force the issue and spoil not only what they had but also what they might have in the future.

When she returned to the sitting room, Tom was already cramped up on the small settee under the fluffy blanket provided. He looked ridiculous, bracketed and crushed by the dog-eared arms of the sofa and curled into the hollow in the middle, like a man in a child's hammock.

"Look, this is stupid. You are not going to get any sleep on that thing. My bed's big enough for both of us," she said, giggling at his contortions.

"Are you sure? I really don't mind. I've slept on smaller. Mind you I was about ten years old at the time."

"I'm sure," she replied, watching him awkwardly unfold himself.

The sight of his naked torso with sharply defined abdominal muscles and powerful shoulders sent a thrill through her body. She had thought his face and hands had been tanned from regular outside work, but his whole body was of a similar light brown colour, largely hairless and stretched tight over a muscled sub-frame.

While he picked up the blanket that had slipped to the floor, her eyes quickly scanned the rest of him. His strong legs were covered in a light down of blond hairs. In his bent posture, his thigh muscles strained at the black cotton of his boxers. He turned away from her to retrieve the cushion that had also tumbled to the floor and embarrassingly she was still gazing at his arse as he stood up and turned towards her. Mind you, it was an arse definitely worth staring at.

It felt strange sharing her bed with another person. She had occasionally shared the bed with female friends who had stayed the night but never with a man. She turned away from him to switch off the bedside light and whispered, "Goodnight."

He leant over to kiss her on the cheek and for an instant, she felt his body against hers: the bare skin of his thighs against the curve of her legs, his defined chest pressed into her back and his pelvis cushioning her bottom. She could feel him turning hard as his body briefly pressed in on her. She felt wet with desire and turned to him at the very moment he rolled away.

What on earth was she to think? How could he get her so aroused and not want more? All the signals had been there. She thought she had made it obvious that she wanted him. It would have been so easy to have let the earlier contact go further, to have reached in under each other's clothes, to have slowly worked buttons, zips and hooks free and have let their hands explore each other's body.

She had felt his physical desire, impressively intrusive through her casual nightwear. Semi-naked, sharing a bed and both aroused - what more did it need? She lay back, struggling with her thoughts and desires and what made it worse was his breathing, soon low and regular. It took her far longer to let the passion seep away.

When she woke he was already up and dressed and while she got herself together and packed the last few items, he made them breakfast.

The conversation during the journey to the airport was stilted and the parting kiss, though lingering, lacked intensity.

During the flight she went over the events, time and again, first castigating herself for not being more sexually forceful and then rationalising the missed opportunity as a blessing. Her life was at a crossroads and where he was heading she had no idea. She was a survivor and could cope on her own. After all this time, did she really need emotional baggage just as new horizons were opening up?

She was not sure whether it was her animated facial expressions, troubled by conflicting thoughts, or some associated sound escaping her lips, but she opened her eyes to find the oversized, argumentative couple now silent and gawking at her in a bemused manner. This effectively curtailed any further daydreams. The rest of the tedious flight was only punctuated by uninspiring meals and unremarkable films.

By the time they arrived at Tocumen airport in Panama, a functional, bland hub, she felt tired, dirty and irritable. The couple in the seats nearest the window had resumed their mutual accusations. Her luggage had been booked all the way through to La Aurora airport in Guatemala, so at least she didn't have to worry about whether it had caught up with her yet. She found a Subway on the first floor of the concourse and despite the hour, grabbed a breakfast role and large coffee. The airline's offering had not been something to relish.

Her connecting flight was on time and the two-hour journey passed uneventfully. Although tired, a sense of anticipation at arriving at her destination country kept her alert and observant during the reunion with her backpack. Check-in, for the final sixty-minute dogleg of her journey, was a straightforward process.

La Aurora was another functional, indistinctive complex, although the people had started to look different. She had noticed slight changes at Panama, but there she had remained on the international flights' side of the terminal. Now she had to pass beyond passport control and weighed down with her bag, had to orientate herself in swarms of local travellers with their noisy entourages.

The usual suits, sportswear and casual clothes merged with brightly coloured, traditional weave shawls and jackets. Woollen caps and straw hats over wizened faces, bundles of immense size wrapped in blankets and pungent smells, stirred her senses. It was so un-antiseptic, alive with colours, odours and emotions as raucous families welcomed home one of their number, lovers passionately reunited and friends flamboyantly greeted each other in an attempt to outdo other reunions nearby.

In her tired state, it should have been overbearing, but the energy and emotions on display were a real tonic. That was until the sign flashed up on the departures board.

ELEVEN

The internal flight to Mundo Maya airport in Santa Elena had been cancelled, not delayed just cancelled. The disinterested woman at the Avianca desk could provide very little information. Some technical hitch meant the plane had to go through a range of safety checks. Flights would be restored "as soon as possible" was as precise a prediction as anyone was prepared to make. There was still some availability on the following evening's scheduled flight, but there was no guarantee that might not also be cancelled. The woman at the counter could not even provide an immediate refund for the ticket, just the paperwork.

The thought of spending her vacation in La Aurora International Airport was nothing short of purgatory. To have come this far only to be faced with a barrage of "maybes" and "ifs" was intolerable.

At the general information desk, she asked about alternative means of transport to Flores, still some 480 km away. The man serving seemed distracted and the noisy queue behind was steadily growing. He thought a taxi to Flores would cost about 2,000 Quetzal, over 200 pounds, while the bus from Guatemala City was a tenth of that price. He told her which bus companies ran services to Santa Elena, a district of Flores, and then passed over a handful of transport brochures before moving on to the next customer.

It was late, she was tired and decisions had to be made - not a good combination at the best of times. In a space away from the crowds she sat down, her backpack protectively close beside her. The brochures were difficult to follow even though they were allegedly in English. For the sake of saving a few hours, it was not worth the extra £200 to hire a taxi directly from the airport to her destination and anyway she would feel safer on a public bus than a long journey with some unknown cab driver as her only company.

Maybe the sensible thing was to book into a hotel for the night and catch a bus first thing tomorrow, or should she risk the night bus and not waste another day travelling? None of the bus companies seemed to operate routes via the airport, which meant either decision would necessitate heading into the city first. It was not something she had planned or desired. Guatemala City's top ten listing for danger was not a statistic that appealed.

"Can I help?" asked an old man, sitting opposite.

He had been watching her trying to make sense of the various options. She had noticed him briefly when she sat down but paid little attention. Being addressed directly, she was able to look at him properly. He was smartly dressed, grey-haired and had wrinkles to spare. The lined texture of his face and hands contrasted to his crease-free suit. His smile was warm and his enquiry unthreatening.

"I see you are trying to sort out our local transport system," he said. She thanked him and explained her predicament and with that, he rose awkwardly from his chair and with the help of a walking stick moved to sit down beside her.

After formally introducing himself he explained that he was waiting for his granddaughter's flight. His English was good and it turned out he had been an English language teacher and enjoyed any opportunity to refresh his skills. She explained her situation again and he searched through the brochures until he found the Linea Dorado bus details.

"That's probably your safest option if you are set on travelling tonight. Their buses are safe and reliable and you have the choice of an 8 pm or a 10 pm departure. The seats recline and I think they serve up a snack during the journey so it's quite comfortable and should get you in early tomorrow morning. It's many years since I last took that route, but I remember it being reasonable."

"Where do they go from?" she asked, still uncertain as to her best option.

"They have a depot in Zone 1," he said, withdrawing a pen from his jacket and circling the address on the company's flyer.

"Zone 1?"

"Oh yes, sorry I forget that the city's system of zones is not universally employed. Guatemala City is divided into over twenty zones each one with its own distinctive character. Certain zones should be avoided, especially at night."

"Is Zone 1 alright?"

"Yes and no. It's the oldest part of the city with the cathedral, national theatre, Plaza Mayor and many budget hotels and therefore attracts most of our tourists. It's safe enough during the day as long as you stick with the crowds. It would be hard to do otherwise - it's very busy. Night is a different matter. The tourists attract the poor of which we have many. Hold-ups at knifepoint are unfortunately becoming more common, actual violence is still rare. There are always police officers patrolling nearby and I think it would destroy tourism if visitors started to lose any more than their purses and wallets. You'll be fine if you get a taxi directly to the bus station. The yellow cabs from the official rank outside are a good choice. Just don't go wandering."

"I read about Guatemala's high crime rates. Which zone's should be avoided?"

"None of those above 16 are safe. *Mara Salvatrucha* runs many areas of the city."

"Mara who?"

"*Mara Salvatrucha* or *MS-13* is a criminal gang. They and Barrio 18 have carved up most of the city and are behind the different cliques that are allowed to operate. Drugs, extortion, robbery, prostitution and murder are all controlled by them."

"Are you sure it's safe enough to catch the bus?"

"You'll be fine. The problems come if you stray into the wrong area. So Zone 3 right alongside Zone 1 is definitely not for tourists. It's not so much gangs as garbage in zone 3, Basurero. It has the largest rubbish dump in Central America, awash with raw sewage. Sadly, it also houses some of our poorest people as well as the dead."

"The dead?"

"Our city graveyard is located there, right alongside all the rubbish. The life expectancy of our poor is not great. Maybe there is some sense in having their final resting place so near their homes," he said, with a rueful smile.

"Are the zone's clearly marked? I mean could a person accidentally end up wandering into a no-go area?"

"You'd know Basurero. You would probably smell it before you saw it. Poverty is all around you: in the buildings, the clothes and the faces. Many of the locals can only survive by foraging on the dump. The stench is sickening. Vultures circle overhead and there are wrecked cars and graffiti everywhere, but don't worry the taxi does not have to go through that area to get to Zone 1."

"Have you any idea of how long the journey to the bus station is?"

"At this time of the night, it's not much more than a twenty-minute drive. He'll take you directly north up the Avenida La Reforma past our national stadium. I think the one-way system then takes you up 11 Avenida. It's a busy, well-lit main road all the way."

The Arrivals Board flashed a change of status to his granddaughter's flight and he unsteadily rose to his feet. "Just remember to get a taxi from the stand outside and show him this address," he said, pointing at the bottom of the leaflet she held. "It shouldn't be any more than 60 quetzals and you'll be there in twenty minutes. Use a yellow or green cab and get him to drop you off directly opposite the bus station ticket office where you can buy your ticket and wait safely for the bus."

"Do taxis take credit cards?"

"If you have not got any local money I suggest you use the machine here at the airport rather than try to use your credit cards. I hope you enjoy your stay. Guatemala is a troubled country, but its treasures will stay with you forever."

She thanked him profusely and watched him leave in the direction of the Arrivals before she finally made a decision.

The cash machine issued a wad of quetzals that she sorted so that only a few of the lower denomination notes were visible in her purse. Then with a sense of apprehension, she left the safety of the air-conditioned concourse.

Outside it was dark but nowhere near as hot and humid as she had expected. People were milling around, arriving and departing, dropping off and picking up, and there was an organised taxi rank with a small queue not far from the main exit doors. It was at this point, wary of her surroundings, when she thought she recognised a man who had been hanging around earlier.

He had been waiting near the information desk when she had been sorting out her travel arrangements. There was nothing out of the ordinary about him: medium height, buzz cut, dark hair, jeans and a white t-shirt. A shadow marked the front of his t-shirt, not a patch suggesting thick body hair but a specific shape that rose to just below the neckline. What made him stand out from the crowd was his lack of travel accessories. Everyone else seemed to be loaded down: suitcases, bags, documents and children all around. He had nothing but a phone.

At one point, when she had turned from the desk to look at the clock suspended above the concourse, the stranger had been bending over, apparently adjusting a lace in his trainers. In the process, his t-shirt hung loosely and revealed the top of a tattoo that must have stretched right across his chest, explaining the distinctive shadow she had noticed earlier. The visible part of the tattoo seemed to be the top section of some gothic-style letters forming three angular peaks, a double ridge followed by a single one, like a capital MA.

She had thought no more about it, her only real concern at that time had been how the hell she was going to get to her destination. She had only spared him the briefest of glances. Amongst the crowd, he was just another person waiting for something or someone. Yet here he was again, some twenty minutes later, leaving the terminal at the same time as her: still on his own, still with a phone pressed to his ear. She spotted him while looking around for the taxi rank. Although he had left the airport immediately after her, he turned in the opposite direction and was now waiting beside the curb, thirty metres from where she stood in line for a yellow cab.

Arriving at the front of the queue she forgot about the stranger. A cab pulled in sharply to the blare of horns from other taxis waiting across the street. It appeared to have cut in on the line of waiting cabs. Maybe the driver had identified her as a foreigner and therefore a sucker for a hyped fare or a generous tip. 60 quetzals was what the old man had thought and 60 quetzals was what she intended to pay.

Once inside the car she felt relieved, although the driver did not speak much English he seemed harmless enough. Small and chubby, his broad smile revealed several missing teeth. He acknowledged the address and associated map on the bus company brochure and chatted away effusively in Spanish as the meter started up and the car rolled away from the curb.

She spared one last look back towards the stranger who was now climbing into an oversized, American-styled car that had pulled up alongside him.

They were soon on the main road heading away from the airport. The meter seemed to be behaving itself and the basic compass app on her phone agreed they were heading north. She briefly glanced out of the rear window just to check the stranger's car was not following. Headlights drawing closer, falling back, overtaking and turning off formed an ever changing, dazzling collage. It reminded her of a documentary she had seen about lions hunting zebras and being confused by the constant interchange of patterns. They found it near impossible to focus on a specific target. She knew how they felt. She turned back to face the front, eyes stinging from staring into headlights and focused on the road ahead.

TWELVE

They had been driving for about fifteen minutes with no apparent cause for concern when they approached a roundabout dominated by a multi-coloured, concrete statue sitting in a circular pool. On the other side of the roundabout, she could make out floodlights from the stadium, so far so good.

The driver, still chatting away, unexpectedly turned left at the island and off the road they had been following since leaving the airport. Hadn't the old teacher said they would go directly north past the stadium? She leaned forward and tapped the driver on the shoulder interrupting his flow of words.

"*Transportes Linea Dorado?*" she asked, remembering the local name for the bus station.

"*Camino cerrado por delante,*" he replied, without showing any obvious concern.

"I don't understand," she said, her anxiety level rising.

"*Camino cerrado por delante,*" he repeated. "*El accidente.*" He continued talking although very few words made sense. She knew "*camino*" was road and "*accidente*" was probably accident. Was he telling her that the road was closed because of some accident? Why the hell had she not thought to download a voice translate app?

They were still driving along a fairly busy, multi-lane road with traffic heading in both directions, no need for panic. She opened up the compass app again. They were travelling west and at some point must turn right. Why hadn't she bothered to download Google Maps before she left? At least then she could have checked exactly where they were in relation to the bus station. Trying to download it now was proving ridiculously slow. They had already crossed several intersections, surely if it was an accident that had caused this diversion they should have turned right and be heading back north by now.

"I want Transportes Linea Dorado, please. Zone 1," she repeated, leaning forward so she could see his face reflected in the mirror. She could hear the rising tension in her voice and realised she was clasping her moonstone necklace in her right hand.

"*Si, si, Linea Dorado.*" His face in the rear-view mirror betrayed nothing. The stream of Spanish words kept flowing and the car continued at the same steady pace.

Was she being ridiculous? The kind man at the airport had said the yellow cabs were safe. They were still on a major thoroughfare and the buildings outside were well-maintained, commercial properties, not the poverty-stricken zones he had warned her about.

But suddenly things changed and she knew she was in trouble. The driver turned left not right as expected and the road immediately narrowed. She glanced once more at the compass app. They were heading south. Even an accident could not justify heading in the opposite direction to the one she wanted. Another turn and the well-maintained, low-rise buildings gave way to walls covered in graffiti. Traffic died away and the few people on the pavements looked desperately poor. It was then that they passed a sign announcing "*Centro de Salud, Zona 3*".

With difficulty, she fought the rising panic and considered her best option. She had no idea of the number for emergency services and even if she did, what could she tell them? She was in a battered, yellow taxi whose driver was ignoring her directions. Christ, she was being kidnapped. Nightmare scenarios ran through her head. Apocryphal stories of unlucky travellers, enflamed by her imagination, twisted the sickening knot in her stomach ever tighter.

She had to stay calm, think. What had she learnt while researching Guatemala? Kidnappings often meant taking a person to a cashpoint and extorting the maximum possible. Violence and rape were not common crimes against tourists compared to theft. She reached down into her backpack and pulled out her key ring and closed it in her fist with the largest of the keys protruding from between the clenched fingers.

The driver was squat and overweight, no great specimen of manhood. If it was just money he wanted she would hand it over immediately. There was no point in risking violence for something that could be claimed on insurance, but if he made a move on her she would fight for all she was worth. She was not going to allow herself to be his victim.

She had never physically hurt anyone before, could she do it now? If he stopped and tried to drag her out of the car she had to aim for his face. Self-defence classes at university had suggested targeting the eyes. Even if he was not hurt badly, the shock had to give her enough time to escape. She was no slouch and he was in no shape to chase her, but what if he pulled a knife or a gun? As the taxi slowed she quickly transferred her passport and money to her jacket pockets and pushed her silver charm inside her top. Wait till she was out of the vehicle and free to move then make a break for it.

There was no time to think further. The taxi was rolling to a stop. Apart from battered cars and piles of rubbish, the road was deserted. She knew the direction they had come from. It was not far back to the busy roads where she could throw herself on the mercy of other drivers.

The keyring was cutting into her palm with the pressure of her grip. The car finally stopped and the driver opened his door and stepped out onto the road. She turned her fist down to hide the protruding key and slid to the far side of the cab. The minute he opened a door and made a grab for her she would kick out. Maybe that was what he was expecting.

Although petrified, she knew her best chance was to take him off guard. Most women in a similar situation would probably scream, kick and claw immediately unless threatened with extreme violence. If she appeared to be compliant through fear it might give her the element of surprise, an instant where she could lash out, hurt him sufficiently to give her an opportunity to run.

Did he just want her money or did he want more? Her whole body was shaking with fear. She slid further across the seat and grasped the door handle behind her with her spare hand. Whatever she did it had to slow him long enough for her to reach the main thoroughfare, otherwise, he would be back behind the wheel and run her down, long before her screams for help could be answered.

At that instant, poised between flight and fight, a set of headlights suddenly illuminated the nightmare scene, interrupting the driver mid-gesture. With one hand on the door handle, she could see that his other hand held a knife. His repulsive tongue flickered snake-like through parted lips as if savouring the fare and spittle dribbled from the corners of his mouth. All child-like qualities had vanished. His expression was now sickening, full of loathsome intentions. This was no robbery. The tableaux held; his leering smile transfixed in the beams.

Slowly he straightened and turned his attention away from her until he faced the other car's lights. As he moved away from the door, she swivelled to stare at the other vehicle parked ten metres behind. The headlights blinded her to any details apart from the two figures climbing out from the front seats. They walked round into the beams and waited. Menacingly silhouetted, it was obvious at least one of the men was armed. His right arm hung loosely down by his side and was extended by the outline of a gun.

Her driver stopped halfway between the vehicles and the two men slowly approached him from either side. Surely if they were going to shoot him, it would have happened by now. One of the silhouetted figures raised his right hand, index and small finger extended the others closed like a pair of horns, obviously a sign or symbol. They reached her driver without any violence occurring. Some sort of exchange was going on. Was the time to make a break for it now? The road ahead was a dead-end and the other way would mean getting past all three of them. They glanced in her direction as if guessing her intentions.

One of the pursuers moved out of the headlights with a phone to his ear and she recognised the man from the airport, the one without any baggage. He must have followed her all the way. What did he want? Was she just another soft target to be picked up on arrival? He was talking to someone on the phone. Although she could not hear the words it was apparent that the call was important, both his body language and the heightened attention the other two paid to his call was evident.

Finally, he snapped the phone shut and turned to the others. Something was said. There was no debate, no discussion, just immediate compliance to whatever instruction had been issued. The two men turned back to their car and her driver returned to his.

As he approached she gripped the key ring even tighter, but he seemed to have lost interest in her. Without a word, he slid back into the driver's seat, did a U-turn and drove back the way they had come. She dared not take her eyes off him but realised from the light behind that the other car was tailing them.

They were soon back amongst traffic. This time the driver was silent, only occasionally glancing at her in the mirror. Had they decided to take her somewhere else? If they had intended to rob, rape or kill her surely the deserted street was as good as any other vile place. Maybe they were taking her to a cashpoint, but she had already withdrawn her daily limit. If she gave up all the currency she had picked up at the airport could she make them understand? Maybe they would keep her prisoner until after midnight and force her to use the card a second time.

The thought that she might be held for ransom flickered across her mind but was quickly dismissed. Families had to have money for that kind of crime. Yes, she was a tourist and therefore probably wealthy compared to many Guatemalans, but no one knew who she was and she had nothing about her that might hint at money.

They were driving along a dual carriageway with plenty of other cars heading in both directions. When they came to a crossing and had to stop at lights she would throw herself out of the car. Even if they only slowed, she decided that would be the time to make a break for it. Surely someone would stop and help. She grasped her rucksack with one hand and the door handle with the other. However fleeting the opportunity, she was determined to take it.

The lights seemed to be set against her. Not one turned red as they sped along, neither did traffic slow them down sufficiently to make jumping out of the moving vehicle a possibility. She tried to catch sight of a sign or street name and with a shock realised that they were back outside the national stadium, heading north again on the same road as before. The driver had still not said a word.

Less than five minutes later they were outside the Linea Dorado bus depot. The driver stopped but made no move to get out. Her limbs, so long rigid with fear, unlocked and she made a bolt for it, throwing herself and her bag out of the car and hurtling across the road. She did not look back until she was inside the doors of the bus terminal. She expected at least one of the men to be right on her tail, but no one followed and by the time she looked back, both cars had disappeared.

The people waiting in the terminal were all staring at her. The way she had burst in, panting and fearful, must have alarmed everyone. An armed guard was scrutinising her, his hand just relaxing from the handle of his gun still resting in its holster. She saw a sign for the toilets and was soon hidden in a cubicle. Gradually her breath returned, adrenalin stopped pumping and her legs felt like jelly.

What had happened? She had been on the point of being robbed? Raped? Murdered? And then? Nothing. The driver had not even demanded his fare. Why had the other car followed her from the airport and who was the man with the phone? He seemed to know the taxi driver. What could have been said during that call, obviously something important? Had they been calling for guidance or instructions? Was that how gangs operated?

She felt her fate had rested on that one phone call. Someone did not want her hurt. The two men following had not only stopped whatever atrocity was about to be committed but also provided an escort all the way to the station. Was it as the old teacher had said? Too much violence was bad for tourism and future pickings. Was she not considered rich enough to bother robbing? It made no sense. Someone had given instructions for her to be left unharmed. Not only unharmed but to be delivered safely to her destination. Why?

When she finally felt up to moving she washed her face and re-entered the waiting room. Although she had missed the eight o'clock bus, the ten o'clock still had availability. She bought a single ticket and took a seat where she could keep a watch on the street outside. The presence of other people and an armed security guard put her more at ease, but until she was safely on the bus she was fearful that her salivating kidnapper might change his mind.

Not until they had boarded and left the city outskirts behind did she finally relax. She took one last glance back. Away from the city lights, the conical shapes of several volcanoes were now visible in the moonlight. Smoke drifted from one of the craters. What a truly dangerous place to live, both natural and social threats seemed endemic. Whatever it took, her return journey would avoid going anywhere near Guatemala City.

She tilted her chair back and closed her eyes and tried to sort out the events of the last few hours, but sleep soon overhauled her. She was oblivious to the long journey, stops they made, even the refreshments brought round on a trolley.

THIRTEEN

When she finally woke with the first rays of daylight, the bus was pulling in to Santa Elena bus station. She felt as if she had undergone the most extreme physical work out. There was not a muscle in her body that did not complain. She hobbled off the bus and into the waiting room, chose a seat facing the door and sorted through her papers to find the number she was supposed to call. The hotel offered a free pick-up service from both the local airport and the bus station.

By the time anyone arrived the noise and bustle around her had died down and only a handful of travellers were still waiting. A man entered from the street. After her recent experience, she was reluctant to approach him although his white shirt, red tie and slicked-back, dark hair fitted the description of the person who was supposed to pick her up. He had a sign tucked under his arm and as he turned to look round the waiting area she caught sight of her name on it. She approached him and introduced herself and was greeted with a broad, intensely white smile.

The journey in a dilapidated jeep lasted just over five minutes. She could have walked it if she had known where she was heading, but in her current state, she was glad of the lift. In strongly accented English, the driver introduced himself as Felipe, the owner of the hotel *Casa Maya Donna*. He chatted enthusiastically throughout the brief ride pointing out landmarks and points of local interest. They drove out of the nondescript town of Santa Elena, across a causeway spanning part of a lake and onto the remarkable island of Flores.

The hotel was a traditional, two-storey, Spanish colonial-style building set around a courtyard dominated by a central water feature, a tiered fountain. An overhanging, tiled roof created shaded loggias on three sides. The stuccoed walls were of a muted, ochre colour and there was a harmonious symmetry to the whole place.

Whilst Felipe sorted out paperwork, she stood in the double doorframe of the main hotel building looking out onto the attractive, sunlit courtyard. Various couples and small groups sat round tables chatting quietly over breakfast.

She returned to the counter to sign her name and to ask if there was a trip to Tikal the following day. Felipe could not have been more helpful. He added her name to the list to visit Tikal in the morning and then carried her backpack up to her room. He briefly pointed out the few features of the room and then left her with a breakfast menu. Standing on her balcony, staring out at the peaceful scene, it felt a million miles from the horrors of Guatemala City.

By the time she had showered and changed out of her travel clothes, she was ready for breakfast. Finally, her muscles seemed to have unclenched and her frayed nerves felt soothed if not quite sedated. She took breakfast on her balcony, revelling in the sunshine and silence. The courtyard had emptied and she sat for a while deep in thought. It was mid-morning before she summoned up the energy to leave her room to explore the historic town.

Flores was the other side of the coin to Guatemala City. Meandering along cobbled streets, she realised she was just one of many tourists taking in the sights. Only a mile or so in circumference the small island was little more than a dot in Lake Petén Itzá and was secured to Santa Elena by a narrow, tree-lined causeway.

Despite its diminutive size, the island prided itself as one of the last places to succumb to Spanish dominance, indeed the last independent Maya state. Cortés had not had the time to conquer it in 1541 and it had remained free from Spanish control for the next 150 years. It had been destroyed in 1697, rebuilt and inhabited ever since which also made it one of the oldest continuously inhabited settlements in the whole of the Americas. It was now a major tourist destination and she could see why. The picturesque, colour-washed buildings, complete with red-tiled roofs, arches and balconies, included cafes, hotels and restaurants aplenty.

Wandering without any real intentions or direction, she stopped off in shops and cafes whenever it took her fancy. Several items were acquired in a blue-washed bookstore including a map of the area and a small guide to the flora and fauna of the region.

Further on she stopped at a chemist and replaced the shampoo and moisturiser that had been confiscated at the airport security check. She was in the process of paying when a small pair of scissors and a nail file set caught her eye. She liked to save cuttings from newspapers and magazines when she travelled and even though she knew the manicure items would probably be confiscated going back through the airport, they were cheap and not something she would particularly resent losing.

Although 15 hours and some 300 miles distant from yesterday's terrifying experiences she still found herself regularly scanning the streets for potential threats. Away from the refuge of her hotel, her body was operating some kind of automatic defence mode she was unable to suppress. In cafes she found herself sitting at the corner table with her back to the wall. A backfiring motorbike forced an instinctive cry of alarm. A boy running past her caused an involuntary flinch and a flurry of nearby pigeons led to a spilt drink.

Her nerves were shredded, not just frayed. She thought she was tough enough to cope with most things, but then yesterday had not been "most things" and her frenzied imagination had been doing contortions ever since.

Violent, sickening images of what the taxi driver had intended to do with her and what would have happened if the phone call had been different, kept playing out in her mind. Would all three of them have taken her there and then? How long would the violation and the pain have endured? Would they have let her live afterwards or would someone have found her defiled body dumped with the city's refuse or floating in the sewage?

She had justified the purchase of a pair of scissors and nail file for routine activities, but deep down she knew it was fear. The nauseating memory of the leering taxi driver, knife in hand, clung leech-like to her thoughts. Her palm was bruised and still hurt from the force she had gripped her key ring. It might have worked as a weapon, but something honed and concealable would prove much better.

She had learnt to deal with other shit in her life and this was no different. In the end, nothing had come of her fifteen-minute abduction. She mentally chided her treacherous thoughts and drove them back into the recesses of her mind along with all her other wild imaginings.

By the time she finally returned to *Casa Maya Donna* she felt less jumpy. A refreshing cold shower and a chilled Gallo beer, sitting contentedly on her balcony, further distanced yesterday's ordeal. A few more drinks and the house special, Chicken Pepian with a spicy pumpkin and sesame sauce, and she was ready to turn in. The aches had subsided, so maybe the shock had finally passed. Someone dropped a glass and she did not leap out of her chair. She could cope. She would not allow herself to be anyone's victim.

Despite exhaustion and a sense that she had come to terms with her terrifying experience in Guatemala City, the night proved to be a restless one.

Back in her room, she untied the mosquito net and slipped underneath, ensuring it enveloped her whole bed. Initially, sleep came quickly but was then troubled by a cascade of intense dreams tumbling in on top of each other like some surreal film trailer.

Alternating images of jungles, temples and volcanoes formed backdrops for brightly clad peasants fleeing from shorn, tattooed gang members. Planes, buses and taxis sped between locations until spinning and bewildered she found herself cowering in some claustrophobic, dark place.

A storm dispersed this narrative only to dissolve to the sultry stillness of a jungle clearing. There she was again, fully absorbed with a camera whilst behind her, a yellow snake uncoiled from an overhanging branch. Its alternating double and single, black ridge markings were like an external spine running the full length of its sinuous body. Its jaws slowly separated to reveal knife-like fangs.

Oblivious to the menace, she went on fiddling with the camera while the snake coiled round and down the trunk until it reached the ground. Fraction by fraction, it slithered towards her, a flickering tongue testing the air for her presence. In her shadow it paused, ready and tensed, head engorged with venom. She tensed, awaiting the imminent explosion, violent penetration and venomous ejaculation.

The scene cut again, sweeping her to the gloomy interior of a wooden hut. Hunched figures, immobile in the shadows, stared at her squatting in the corner. A small metallic object glimmered in her hand. Fire expunged this scene and there was Tom, naked and drenched in sweat, battling through choking smoke, a machete his only weapon to slash at the flames.

Waking abruptly from these disturbing nightmares it was impossible to unravel the collage of feverish impressions, but she was left with a clear impression of the final one that wrenched her awake.

Locked in a small, oppressive space, the only light filtered through the horizontal gaps in the walls. There was someone else with her, unidentifiable, slumped in the shadows. She turned to the wall and realised she was scratching at the boards with a small, sharp implement, a nail file. Gradually the scratches formed letters, slowly and fitfully, each one a struggle. The child-like scrawl began to take on meaning; "HE" transformed to "HEll" and then took on a curl to cry out "HElP".

The words vanished in a flash of blinding white light and an accompanying scream that pitched her from her sleep.

For a few seconds, she was dazed, wondering where she was and what had happened. Had she screamed or had it been part of her dream? She waited to see if anyone had heard anything and would come to investigate. Only the throaty call of frogs disturbed the night. No one had heard anything or if they had were not going to get involved.

Her heart pounded so loud she could hear it in her ears. She dragged herself into the bathroom as if she had been drugged and sponged a cold, wet flannel over her face and neck.

Back in her bedroom, she slumped into the chair by the window. Her heart rate eased and the patchwork of intense dreams seeped away leaving only blurred recollections. The nightmares had been so vivid they had to mean something, but she could not hold on to them. Like wisps of hot breath on a cold morning, they diffused and dispersed.

The phone's screen showed it was 2 a.m. Her thoughts turned to Tom and why he had not responded to the brief text she had sent earlier letting him know she had arrived – safely! Returning to her dishevelled bed, she lay on top of the bedding and allowed her eyes to flicker shut.

FOURTEEN

The remainder of the night passed without further dreams, but come morning she felt as if she had been wrung out in a tumble drier. Her mind felt dull and listless. What with the grogginess and the intense nightmares, she wondered whether the last-minute vaccinations or the anti-malaria tablets were having an adverse effect.

Unable to get warm water from the shower, she was content to allow the cold immersion to tingle some life back into her. By the time she was suitably dressed and ready for breakfast, several Paracetamol were already kicking in.

A local driver who spoke little to no English took them to the ruins. On their way out of Flores other groups joined the party. With a full coach, they headed across the causeway with Lago Petén Itzá sparkling on both sides. It was a truly beautiful setting and a tonic for the disturbed night.

They drove through the less lovely conurbation of Santa Elena before turning north. Passing close by the tip of the lake, the water looked as smooth as glass. Jade green near the shore it dissolved into an aquamarine blue further out that mirrored the motionless wisps of cloud. The pitted road passed semi-hidden haciendas, ramshackle shacks and rough clearings interspersed with growing clusters of trees. She recognised cedars, the odd mahogany and the tall, stately silk cotton tree, the national tree of Guatemala, but many were unknown to her.

After about forty minutes the sun disappeared as the forest swallowed up the road. She could sense the rising anticipation amongst the other passengers as the soaring canopy enveloped their bus.

She struck up a conversation with an elderly, English couple sitting next to her. They were newly retired and had arrived in Flores a few days earlier and spent the time acclimatising and seeing the town. They seemed more interested in the gastronomic delights and atrocities of the restaurants where they had eaten rather than the flora and fauna around them or the ruined city ahead.

The others on the bus were a mixture of nationalities. There was an American family with two teenage children, a young Dutch couple on a backpacking expedition and a sizeable Chinese group with their own tour guide in tow. A multitude of cameras, guidebooks, drinking bottles and sun hats were also on view.

They turned left onto a minor road, not much wider than a single track and after another mile pulled into a parking area. The air conditioning had been on inside the bus and as they stepped out the heat smothered them.

The group assembled alongside the vehicle and a small, wizened guide approached, introducing himself as Hernandez. His English was remarkably unaccented and the tour commenced with an outline of his plan to start with the museum followed by a tour of the site. Lunch would be at the nearby Hotel Posada de la Selva and after they would be free to wander until four when they needed to be back at the bus.

Although still early, the humidity was palpable and within a few minutes, her clothes were beginning to stick to her. Before they even reached the museum, various drinking bottles appeared from backpacks and bags.

Although Hernandez was enthusiastic and informative in describing the various museum artefacts: a glowering mask, a ceramic figure, skeletal remains adorned with jade jewellery, her concentration was elsewhere and part of the way through the tour she slipped away. Much of the information on the Maya she already knew from detailed research into the picture. Now she just wanted to locate the site of Fosse's photograph.

Stealing away from the back of the group, she left without anyone apparently noticing. The heat outside seemed to have intensified in just the last twenty minutes. Turning right, she took the trail through the trees following signs for 'The Great Plaza'. Intent on finding the place she had travelled five and a half thousand miles to see, she passed partial excavations, groups posing for photos, a guide talking in Spanish, all with barely a glance. She wanted to gaze at the temple in the photo with fresh eyes before it had been contextualised. Her work at *the Gazette* had taught her to approach both the living, and even more importantly the dead, without preconceptions and if at all possible remain objective.

Only as she reached the Grand Plaza did she allow herself to take in her surroundings, a rectangular grassed area some sixty metres in length, dominated at either end by two stepped pyramids that soared above the tree line. Elongated steps flanked one side of the plaza along with a number of carved menhirs. Beyond, stood another interconnected series of impressive buildings, while opposite, the jungle encroached. The size of the buildings was evident by the insignificant scale of the tourists milling over and around them.

Standing in the centre of the plaza, she felt a charge surge through her. It was immediately recognisable, but she knew instinctively that it was more than just the recollection of a carefully studied photograph. It felt more like déjà vu. She was certain that at some point in time, she had stood on that very same spot and had been similarly awed by the towering ruins and encroaching forest beyond.

Removing her daypack, she extracted the cardboard tube with the photo. So little had changed. Apart from the shadows and the number of people, the temple looked almost identical. Some of the stonework had been repaired and appeared less grey, but otherwise, the photo could have been taken that morning.

She looked down at the print again and then turned and walked purposely towards the temple at the west end. Although there was a rope around the base and warning signs forbidding people to climb on it, she had noticed a couple ignoring the sign and scrambling to the top, unchallenged by any of the guides. She bent under the rope and started up the precipitous steps.

The pyramid was in three sections, but the stairway formed an unbroken causeway to the mausoleum at the top. Although determined, her breath became strained and her body soaked in perspiration before she had climbed more than halfway. The last section really tested her stamina.

Turning at the top, she gazed the length of the plaza. No one seemed to be paying her any attention. She sat down, regained her breath, took a swig from her water bottle and opened her guidebook.

The temple had been a loving gesture by a king to his wife to preserve their existences together in the afterlife. Although known as The Temple of Masks only two badly eroded, distorted masks now remained at the top of the steps to oversee the shrine. Her guidebook gruesomely noted that a depiction of a naked warrior, painted blue and bound to a stake during a ritual dance, had been discovered here. Blood flowed from his genitals and a white symbol painted over his heart warned tattooed archers of the forbidden spot, the point to avoid if the suffering was to endure. The disparity between the structure's loving intention and its brutal embellishment was grotesque.

She stared out over the plaza at the king's mortuary temple, the Temple of the Great Jaguar, at the east end of the Plaza. Its name was derived from carvings of a king sitting upon a jaguar throne. Probably six metres higher than the queen's burial structure, and composed of nine sections, it represented stages to the underworld. So much of Maya culture seemed obsessed with the afterlife. She dried her hands on a scarf in her bag and once again uncurled the photo.

The man in the photograph with the binoculars would have been sitting about two-thirds of the way up the king's mortuary temple, looking towards the partially reconstructed Temple of the High Priest, to her right.

Her doppelgänger and assailant would have been below her, between the two gravestone-style slabs guarding the crumbling steps.

The site plan placed the person leaning over the prostrate body at the base of five steps leading to the North Acropolis. The shadow on the right of the photo was in front of Maler's Palace.

She marked all their positions on the plan in the guide, but there was something wrong with the angle of the photograph. It had been taken from above her. Even standing on the highest step, she was well below the camera angle. She turned and looked at the shrine and roof comb towering another fifteen metres above her. Whoever had taken that picture had to have been on or above the tomb, and there was no obvious way to climb up.

FIFTEEN

Suddenly from the base of the steps, someone was shouting at her and signalling agitatedly for her to descend. Her initial incomprehension soon cleared as she realised he was a Tikal official, baseball-capped, beige uniformed with telltale license dangling from his neck.

Warily she clambered back down, finding the sheer descent far trickier than the ascent. The irate guide waited, fuming at the base of the steps. "Can't you read the signs? You are forbidden to climb this monument. Not only does it cause damage but it's also extremely dangerous," he snapped as she arrived safely back on terra firma.

She was profusely apologetic as the young guide went on to detail some of the accidents that had befallen previous, unwary visitors. She continued to apologise and gradually the young man calmed down.

"Are you on your own?" he inquired in a more civilised tone.

She explained that she was part of a group but had wanted to experience the site at her own pace. He nodded and then surprisingly offered his services as a private guide, "You will miss so much if you have no one to show you around."

"I'm not sure I can afford a guide and anyway I've already read a lot about the site." She ran off a series of excuses, but he would have none of it.

"Look, I won't charge you anything. If you want to give something afterwards, that's up to you. I have an hour before my next official tour and have to hang around so I might as well practice on you. If you already know everything I have to say, I will pay you. How about it?"

"How can I resist such a sales pitch?" she smiled, finally giving in. At the back of her mind was the thought that she had no idea what to do with the photo now, and having come all this way might as well enjoy a personalised tour.

Her guide introduced himself as Michael. He was probably only in his late teens or early twenties and slightly built, with an earnest face and eyes the colour of caramel. He had identified her as an American or European from her pale skin and was anxious to try out his linguistic skills ahead of his first large, English speaking tour group.

"My father was a big fan of American films and named me after Michael Douglas. I think he always hoped I'd be a film star rather than follow in his footsteps." Only then did she realise his English had a slight American twang.

"How long have you been a guide?" she asked, warming to the young man.

"Oh, not long. Actually, this afternoon is my first time in charge of a really big group."

She listened to him with growing interest as he led her towards the North Acropolis. He described how until the '60s the Maya had been mistakenly considered a peaceful, philosophic and astronomical society. They had a very advanced understanding of astronomy and a complex series of calendars to go with it, but it was only when their hieroglyphs began to be deciphered that historians' rose-tinted spectacles started to demist.

These so-called glyphs, a mixture of words and sounds, described battles, sacrificial offerings and torture. The kings, rather than being high priests of astronomy, had apparently been vainglorious despots lauding it over vast feudal fiefdoms often at war with neighbouring kingdoms.

According to Michael, the general consensus was that "The Maya used sacrificial blood as the mortar for their ritual lives, to sustain their deities." Their frequent wars resulted in large numbers of prisoners becoming the life-blood and labour of the victors.

The nature of your fate seemed to depend on your place in society. High-ranking prisoners of war were sacrificed, whilst lower status prisoners were used for slave labour.

For ordinary sacrifices, the victim was bound to an altar and their still-beating heart extracted with a flint knife. For important captives, such as rival kings, decapitation was the method of choice but not before being variously beaten, scalped, burnt or disembowelled. Finally, their headless bodies were cast down the steps from the top of a temple or dragged down into the caves below the city to be offered to the twelve gods of Earth who resided in the Underworld, otherwise known as the place of fear. Michael's grisly history lesson had obviously been designed with less squeamish visitors in mind.

They paused in front of a series of megaliths close to where the injured body had been in the photo. Michael explained that these were stelae, memorials to the kings of Tikal, and the glyphs carved into them, the source of most of what was known about the Maya.

He continued to explain how much was still left to be discovered including a period of thirty years entirely missing from their detailed calendar.

"They believe Tikal was conquered during that time by Caracol, a city in Belize, " Michael explained, "but the biggest mystery is what happened to the vast Maya civilization at the end. The last date on any stelae at Tikal is A.D. 869. The latest date on any Maya artefact is only forty years after that. They disappeared so suddenly and so completely, vast city complexes deserted almost overnight, well historically speaking. So much of the past is still hidden beneath these forests."

He let her examine the carved stelae whilst recounting some of the conflicting theories proposed for the city's abandonment and his hope that the numerous unexcavated mounds to the south might one day throw more light on its fate.

He guided her around at a steady pace identifying the different structures and flavouring his descriptions with lurid accounts of kings such as Double Bird, Shield Skull and Jaguar Paw who coincidentally died the same day as the king of the Teotihuacan civilization was officially visiting. "You can imagine what kind of a visit that must have been!" he said.

As they toured the tombs, acropolises and ball court where the losing team were supposedly sacrificed, she realised just what a blood-soaked place Tikal must have been.

Their tour finished with an exhausting clamber up the 70 metre Temple IV, the tallest of the ancient Maya structures. Both sat quietly at the top, regaining their breath and contemplating the lustrous, green sea of trees stretching in every direction as far as the eye could see. In the silence, she decided to trust Michael with her real reason for being there.

"Can I tell you why I wanted to come to Tikal?" she asked quietly without looking up. They were now alone on the pyramid. The couple that had been at the top when they ascended were carefully picking their way back down.

"Of course," he replied.

Once more she removed the picture from its protective tube and shuffled along to sit closer to him. She decided it would take too long to describe how she had come into possession of the photograph so without further comment passed it over and waited for his response.

"I thought you said this was your first time in Tikal!" he exclaimed, looking up sharply.

"It is," she responded.

"Well, this photo of you was definitely taken here and by the look of the state of Temple 1, before I started working as a guide." He waited expectantly for her answer.

"That's why I'm here. I have never been to Guatemala or any other country in Central America. I don't know anybody in this picture and yet this woman in the photo is my mirror image, isn't she?" She looked up at him to gauge his response.

"What on earth is going on?" Michael asked as he started to take on board further details of the picture's indecipherable narrative.

"I have no idea. It looks as if my double is frightened and this man is threatening her, but more importantly, what has happened to this person covered in blood?" She pointed towards the prostrate figure. "That is why I climbed the Temple of the Masks, to try and see where the photo was taken from. Could this injured person be one of those involved in the accidents you mentioned earlier?"

"I'm not sure. We could check. There's an accident log kept at the museum. It looks to me though, as if this picture was taken from above the Temple of the Masks. The view is from a higher position than the top platform. It might be from the scaffolding they erected when they excavated the tomb or when other conservation work was carried out."

His explanation was so obvious she wondered why she had not thought of it earlier. She pressed him on the dates of such repairs, but he was vague in his responses as he had not been a guide for long and all repairs had been before his time.

"You need to talk to my father. He worked here as a guide when excavations were being carried out. If anyone can tell you about this place since...well, since the civil war, it will be him."

"Does your father still work here?"

"Most days," Michael replied. "I'm pretty certain he will insist on being buried here. He's not around today but I'm sure he wouldn't mind you calling on him at his home in Santa Elena." He finished his sentence whilst reaching into his shirt pocket and pulling out his professional card on the back of which he carefully wrote an address. "I am visiting him tonight so I could meet you there."

"Are you sure he won't mind?" she asked, concerned more with the rising crime level than his father's sensitivities.

"No. Since my mother died, he has been quite lonely and enjoys company. I recommend you use an authorised taxi from your hotel. It shouldn't cost you more than about twenty quetzals and I can arrange for another one to take you back later. You don't want to wander around the town at night. Anyway, I need to be going and you need to join up with your group before they send out search parties."

They climbed down and separated with a handshake. She headed off towards the hotel where her party was booked for lunch and had covered most of the distance before remembering she had not paid him, nor enquired about access to the accident log. She must remember to do both later on.

The hotel was already busy. She spied her group on the far side, starting to serve themselves from a lunchtime buffet and was slightly taken aback that she had not been missed. The retired English couple talked to her over lunch as if she had accompanied them throughout the morning.

After lunch, the group dispersed in line with Hernandez's instructions and independently roamed the ruins. It was awe-inspiring; the jungle seemed to be set on shrouding a city built on blood and marking the stars. At ground level, the foliage and creepers were an almost impenetrable barrier so densely intertwined were they and from above the canopy appeared solid, yet somehow the various temples poked their hoary heads above the green tide.

She wandered through various palaces and plazas before turning her attention to the less dramatic and therefore less popular complexes on the outskirts of Tikal. Arriving at Complex P, half a mile to the north of the main structure, she stopped to consult her guidebook. Centred on an altar, this edifice had, "An image on one of the walls recording a dream experienced during a ritual." The writer went on to suggest, "Such visions were probably brought on by days of bloodletting and intense dancing, without food or sleep."

Moving to a shady corner, she found a cool step where she could rest. Behind her, exotic squawks, whistles and hoots echoed from the forest that surrounded the complex on three sides. She turned to gaze into the undergrowth and closed her eyes trying to summon up visions of Tikal at its height. With her eyes closed, the forest noises intensified. They seemed to take on a strange, hypnotic rhythm and she could feel the present slipping away.

A kaleidoscope of animals, potential sources of the sounds, spun around her mind. Into the midst of this whirlwind of images, a figure emerged, running and stumbling, desperate to get away from somewhere or someone. They reached a stretch of rough grass and disappeared behind a crumbling edifice she had wandered round earlier. Reappearing much closer, it was immediately obvious who the individual was. It was the woman from the photograph, her double.

Sweat-soaked, breathless and with a camera tightly gripped in one hand, she was heading directly towards her. With a despairing glance over her shoulder, her doppelgänger dropped behind a nearby, weathered altar, sucking air into her heaving chest. Her face, a mask of fear, was streaked with droplets of sweat. Her clothes were those from the photograph, a beige t-shirt and shorts and scuffed walking boots. She was hiding from someone or something and as if on cue another group of figures emerged from the trees, fanned out and moved briskly in her direction.

As they drew nearer and became more than distant blurs, she realised these were probably the others from the photograph. They wore the same paramilitary-style costumes. Her other self muffled a panicked cry, crouched lower in a despairing attempt not to be seen, then inched back towards the cover of the forest using the misshapen altar to hide her movements, but the hunters kept on coming.

Abruptly, the vision dissolved as voices invaded her silent world and shook her from her daydreams. The Chinese group had arrived at the complex and were swarming all over the site searching for iconic photo opportunities. Though the moment was gone, the vision stayed with her. The woman, her other self, had been terrified. She was obviously hiding from the men. If she could have seen her own face from the night in Guatemala City she was sure it would have been the same look of abject fear.

Silently, she cursed the tour group's intrusion. If they had been even a few seconds later, she might have had time to make out some of the pursuers' features. She might have been able to see the person behind the shadow in the picture or maybe identify the anonymous photographer as Leonard Fosse. If the illusion had lasted even a fraction longer would she have seen the face of the man leaning over the injured body or the features of the threatening figure in the centre of the picture?

What was she thinking? This was ridiculous. It was unbridled imagination, nothing more than the product of last-minute vaccinations, lack of sleep and an interest in a forgotten photograph that was probably bordering on the obsessive.

SIXTEEN

Stripped, showered and freshly dressed, her return to the hotel soon revived her. She checked her phone now that she had a signal and disappointingly found there was still no response from Tom.

Deciding to eat at the hotel, she found Felipe manning the bar. He was proving to be a jack of many trades: chauffeur, concierge and barman. The hotel though was not a one-man operation, and two waitresses in white pinafores were busy setting tables, preparing for dinner.

It was still too early to eat so she took a seat at the bar and ordered a beer from Felipe who recommended the Dorada Azul Especial. "It is one of our best beers, Señorita," he announced, proudly presenting her with a light, frothy lager in a hurricane style glass.

It was only five-thirty but the light was already fading as dusk settled on the pretty courtyard and the lanterns started to glow. The recessed lights of the small fountain highlighted the spray cascading into the bowl below. The rhythmic cascade had a soothing musicality to it and was not yet accompanied by the frog chorus. The whole scene could have been an advert produced by the Guatemalan tourist board. Even the heat did not seem as oppressive as the previous evening and the beer tasted just fine.

"What did you think of Tikal?" asked Felipe, absentmindedly drying a glass.

"It was amazing, really fascinating," she responded, wiping the foam from her lips. "I met a guide whose father has worked there for over twenty years, since the end of the civil war."

"It is not ended," he said with profound sadness. His expression stopped her in her tracks - glass halfway to her lips.

"I thought it finished in '96?" she cautiously replied, aware of the sorrow in both his tone and his expression.

"Did you know that more than two hundred thousand people were murdered during the war? Our president ordered the destruction of over six hundred villages, whole villages crushed and burnt. In Chajul the people were forced to watch their young men tortured and burnt with gasoline. Fifty thousand *Desaparecidos* are still missing." His voice was fuelled by suppressed anger.

"*Desaparecidos*?" she asked.

"The Disappeared, kidnapped off the streets by the security forces and death squads, their bodies never recovered. Many families still hope to find their lost ones. It will not be over until the guilty pay for the slaughter of our people and we find the bodies of Los Desaparecidos and give them a proper burial." Tears glinted in the corner of Felipe's eyes and his easy-going, mañana tone had taken on an intensity that suggested an ongoing struggle with his own personal demons.

"Sorry I didn't know," she apologised, taken aback by the passion of his response.

"How could you? My father was one of the *Desaparecidos*. We lived in San Juan Comalapa, near Guatemala City. He worked on a big plantation owned by United Fruit."

He hesitated as if to collect his thoughts. "You have heard of the insecticide D.D.T?" She nodded. "They sprayed it on the crops and many workers got sick. He joined the *Central Nacional de Trabajadores*, a confederation of workers, and helped organise meetings. One day he never came home. I was only eight. I never saw him again." He paused to steady his voice. "We are the lucky ones. We found his body two years ago in a mass grave with two hundred other Maya - all murdered. We were able to give him a proper burial."

How should she respond to Felipe's obvious distress? Any apology or sympathetic words might sound hollow. "I can't imagine what you must have gone through. Why were Maya communities targeted?" She did not want to pry but sensed Felipe wanted to talk.

"The generals said they were rebels and hid communist agitators; big American companies had too much invested to allow change; well-financed death squads out of control - you choose. In 1982 the American President visited our president, Rios Montt. He called him a good man in search of social justice and gave him ten million dollars. That same ten million dollars were used to buy weapons to murder his own people, my people." He paused and took a deep breath. "It has been called 'The Silent Holocaust'. Thirty-six years of suffering have left us with so many scars." He was obviously struggling with his emotions and turned away for a few seconds to hide his distress from her.

With his feelings back under control, he continued, "They found the records of the *Policía Nacional* hidden in a warehouse. Five miles of documents in cabinets labelled *'asesinos'*, *'Desaparecidos'* and *'casos especiales'*: assassins, disappeared and special cases. They say it will take fifteen years to sort and while they do, we wait and we pray."

His harrowing description of Guatemala's recent history was interrupted by the appearance of the young Dutch couple at the other end of the bar. He moved off with a sad smile to serve them and left her sitting alone. The teacher at the airport had said it was a troubled country, but she had thought he meant just the present crime wave, not the haunting shadows of a recent, genocidal civil war.

What a tragic place Guatemala was turning out to be! The brutality of ancient Maya rulers seemed to have been adopted by modern

Guatemalan dictators. Had ancient Maya cities disappeared with the same bloody inhumanity as those 600 Maya villages destroyed in the civil war? She wondered what gods the presidents of this country believed they appeased with their bloodletting.

A Faulkner quote, she had scrawled on her course files, came to mind about the past not being dead, in fact, not even being past. She left the dregs of her beer and moved out into the courtyard to breathe in the night.

The pre-booked taxi turned up soon after she had eaten. It had no meter and she was forced to barter with the thickset, swarthy driver who wanted a hundred quetzals. Her guidebook had alerted her to unmetered cabs attempting to pull a fast one and forewarned proved forearmed. She was prepared for a confrontation. She remembered that Michael had thought it would be about twenty quetzals and quickly the discussion became heated.

In the end, Felipe stepped into the fray to sort out their altercation. He had heard the raised voices from the foyer and had come out to see how he could help. Taking the card with the address from her, he turned to the taxi driver, delivering what sounded like a short, sharp lesson in ethics. The driver shrugged and turned back to the wheel.

Felipe returned Michael's business card, calmly informing her, "He will take you straight there and if you give him a time, he will bring you back later for forty quetzals. It is better that you go with him both ways. Many white cabs are unregistered, which is not safe."

She thanked him warmly as he opened the door for her to step in. She felt reassured that Felipe knew not only where she was going but also who the taxi driver was.

As the vehicle lurched away from the curb, she glanced out of the rear window to see him helping another guest from a taxi that had just pulled up. How deceptive appearances could be. At the bus station, she had seen only Felipe's crisp white shirt, brilliantined hair and pearly white smile. His appearance and easy banter had put her in mind of a dodgy car dealer or dubious estate agent. She now gazed back at the receding figure in a very different light. She had glimpsed something of the passion and pain hidden beneath the surface.

The taxi cruised over the causeway and headed through the poorly lit grid system of Santa Elena. Turning right off Sixth Avenue and crossing over Avenue Real, they passed a Catholic cemetery dotted with tombs and statues of religious icons. Many of the tombs were thrown into relief by candlelight, whilst eternally watchful angels stood guard over the dead and seemed to shiver as the light danced on their features and stone chiselled wings.

She had spent a fair amount of time in silent graveyards, amongst the forgotten and the neglected dead; no one seemed ignored here. She could not see anyone in the cemetery, yet the place was alive with hundreds of flickering remembrances.

As quickly as the impression had presented itself, it passed. The taxi drove on through the less densely populated parts of town. Here trees dominated whole blocks as if each building plot had been hacked from virgin forest.

They passed a sign indicating they were in Barrio Candelaria and she knew they were nearly there. The taxi pulled up outside a high walled, metal-gated building and the driver indicated that she should get out and pointed at his watch. She suspected he was trying to arrange a pick-up time and responded with, "Nueva?" He nodded and surprisingly pulled away without taking any money. What had Felipe said to him? Hopefully, he had understood her basic Spanish.

Glancing up and down the poorly lit, potholed street, devoid of life except for a scabrous looking mutt, she wished she had delayed him at least until she had made sure there was someone at home.

The rusted metal gate and high walls, crowned with barbed wire, gave the place an air of a prison. She pressed a buzzer and waited anxiously. Somewhere beyond the gate, a door was unlocked. Nearby, a dog barked and then the gates swung open.

A short, dark-skinned, middle-aged man with greying hair at his temples stood facing her. He was smartly dressed in a brown jacket and trousers and a white, tieless shirt. He peered at her, removed a pair of wire-rimmed spectacles from his breast pocket, fitted them behind his ears and then hugged her to him, exclaiming in clear English, "Hera, what a surprise!"

SEVENTEEN

Disentangling herself and stepping back defensively, she stammered that she was not Hera, that he had made a mistake and that she had no idea who he was. He looked surprised and hurt. Their mutual embarrassment was interrupted by Michael's appearance. He stepped out from the shadows behind the man and quickly moved to defuse the situation.

"*Esta es la chica de la que te hablé, el que está en las ruinas, el que tiene la foto,*" Michael said, placing his hand on the man's shoulder.

"*Ella es Hera!*" the older man replied, without taking his eyes off her face.

"I am sorry, this is my father. He thinks you are someone else. I told him that I met you earlier at Tikal," Michael said. "Please excuse him."

"I don't need anybody to make my apologies for me." The man's English had the same American twang as his son's. "I am sorry if I alarmed you. You are the spitting image of someone I used to know. Please, where are my manners? Do come inside."

Exchanging glances with Michael, she assured him that she was all right and followed him into the single storey house that lay back from the road.

The mistaken identity had set off alarm bells and brought her thoughts abruptly back to the photograph. She allowed the courtesies and introductions to be made and Michael's father, Pedro, to bring them all a refreshing limonada con soda before she broached the subject of the picture.

The traditional living room, where they sat, had a highly polished table lit from above by a pendant light. Rough-plastered, mustard coloured walls added a dash of colour to the dark beams and stripped wooden floor. A large, traditionally patterned rug added the only softening touch. For the fourth time today, she unrolled the print and placed it on the table in front of Pedro.

They said nothing as the older man carefully wiped his glasses and scrutinised the picture. She watched him intently as a smile spread across his face, rapidly replaced by a look of concern. After a few minutes, he turned to her.

"This is **Hera**," he said, pointing at her image. "This is who I thought you were."

"That's what I hoped you could help me with," she replied. "Michael thought you might know who she was…is."

"What has happened here? She looks very frightened and this person on the ground does not look in a good way."

She explained that she knew nothing about the context of the picture but was hoping somebody locally might be able to throw some light on it.

"To achieve such an elevated viewpoint, I thought it must have been taken when the *Templo de las Mascaras* had scaffolding around it," Michael explained to his father whilst offering to refill her glass from the jug on the table.

Pedro excused himself and said he would only be a minute. He returned bearing a book entitled 'The Maya'. He carefully placed it on the table and opened the cover revealing a photograph. On the back, a few slanted, italicised words reminded her of her own handwriting. It read, "To Pedro, *gracias por toda su ayuda*. Love Hera." She turned it over and saw a mirror image of herself smiling at the camera, one arm around Pedro's shoulders the other clasping a tripod contraption. In the background, another pyramid-like temple, devoid of any tomb, towered over them and cast a long shadow across the subjects.

"Hera is a good friend," Pedro announced. A smile flickered in his eyes. "I will tell you what I can about her. We first met about two years ago. She looked just like you. She was working with a team of archaeologists mapping ruins. They believed that the great Maya cities such as Tikal, El Mirador and Becan had a highly advanced infrastructure to enable communication and trade and to control their empires.

"Did you know that so far over four and a half thousand Maya sites have been discovered? They thought that by mapping the infrastructures between sites it would enable them to understand how Maya society organised itself and maybe give an insight into why it perished. While they were in this area, I was hired to guide them around the Petén Basin." He hesitated, obviously recalling the areas he had covered with Hera's team. "I helped them to chart the area around Tikal, Uaxactun, Yaxha, Holmul, Naranjo, Cival and Nakum. That photo was taken at Yaxha, about thirty kilometres southeast of Tikal, on the edge of Lake Yaxha. Hera was learning to use a total station."

"A total station?" she queried.

"It's a computerised theodolite that connects to a GPS so that precise plans can be superimposed on physical maps of an area. Hera's team hoped the Maya's desire for structure, symmetry and alignment based on astronomy would allow them to use known locations and routes as geographical markers. They thought that a comprehensive survey would enable them to predict as yet undiscovered ruins, like a set of geometrical points on a graph. There is so much still to be discovered. Our forests hold many secrets!" Pedro trailed off, exchanging an indecipherable look with his son.

After a brief pause, when some darker thoughts seemed to be playing across his mind, he continued to tell them about what he knew of her double. He had spent almost two months with the team taking them around the main sites in the Petén department and unexcavated sites familiar only to locals. He had come to know the individuals in the group, but Hera was the only one he would have called a friend.

Hera Lane had been raised in North Carolina. Her parents ran a summer camp for the children of affluent professionals. Her love of the outdoors developed there, helping with the running of the camp.

"She used to say the camp was lost in misty, blue mountains," Pedro reminisced.

Her interest in classical Maya civilization arose while at Pennsylvania University, majoring in History. In the mid-sixties, Pennsylvania University had been responsible for much of the early groundwork on Maya sites and they retained all the documentation and some of the contacts.

Pedro illustrated many of the qualities he had observed in Hera with anecdotes that highlighted her curiosity, perseverance and resourcefulness as well as her innate independence. Listening to the stories, some amusing, some serious, she felt a kinship to this woman. She understood Hera's actions and responses even when Pedro described them as unexpected or unusual. Like her, Hera was a self-reliant, determined woman and when things got tough would stand her ground.

The book on the Maya had been a farewell gift from Hera when the team moved on to Belize and his job had come to an end.

Hera had been in contact a few times, the last being just over a year ago after they had left Belize for Mexico. She had phoned one evening, in a state of high excitement. By aligning their detailed plans with the Maya star charts they had discovered signs of another lost city in Campeche, which looked to be from the post-classic period. It was their first really important discovery and gave credence to their approach, uniting cartography and astronomy.

The discovery potentially meant increased funding and an extension to the project. Hera expected a lot of new interest and a new, international profile to their work. Pedro finished talking and was again scrutinising the photograph.

"This is Hera, but I don't recognise these other people," and after a bit of thought he added, "but I can tell you when it was taken."

"I told you if anyone knew, he would," Michael chimed in proudly.

Pedro smiled at his son's endorsement. "The last time they had scaffolding up on the *Templo de las Mascaras* was only a year ago," Pedro continued, obviously visualising the event. "Thunderstorms caused quite a lot of damage to some of the stonework and they shut the site for over a month whilst repairs were carried out."

"That must have been shortly before I started my training," Michael added. "There was no scaffolding then."

"But if Hera had already left for Belize before any repairs were carried out, the photo must have been taken earlier than that," she reasoned.

Pedro shook his head, "The last time any major repairs, requiring scaffolding, were done on Tikal before then would be about ten years ago."

"Could scaffolding or ladders have been used at some other time?" she asked.

Pedro just shook his head whilst Michael spoke for him, "My father knows everything that happens there. You see he is the Senior Guide in charge of the register detailing all activity and any incidents and accidents."

The reference to the accident log reminded her that Michael had mentioned it earlier, but her queries as to whether the accident in the photograph could be on record were met with further shakes of Pedro's head. He explained that during the repairs, the museum was closed and guides found temporary employment elsewhere, so no official records were kept. He had based himself in Flores for the month of the repairs, leading groups of disgruntled tourists further afield, to less popular sites.

Pedro had hardly looked up from the photograph whilst talking. His tone was tense and when he did finally raise his eyes to hers, his expression showed real anxiety.

"This picture makes me very worried, Señorita. I saw Hera deal with many things whilst she was here, from serious cuts and food poisoning to a snakebite suffered by one of the members of her team. I even saw her cope with a rabid dog that strayed onto the site, but never did I see her look as frightened as she does here." His earnest tone and dark eyes were deeply affecting and she found his concern profoundly unsettling.

"That was my thought when I first saw the picture," she responded, meeting his stare. "Have you got an address or a number where I can try to contact her?"

Whilst Pedro went to find contact details, she suddenly remembered the taxi she had ordered. Pedro returned with a mobile number, apologetically explaining that he did not think it would be of any use. He had tried it several times after her last call and the number had been dead. He did not have an address but remembered her parents' summer camp was not far from a town called Ashville.

She rolled up the picture, promising to contact him if she found any news about Hera. She left him with her number in case he heard or thought of anything new and took her leave. He gave her a hug and wished her luck before he and Michael led her to the gate. The taxi was already waiting outside, the engine still running. Michael saw her into the back of the cab, making her promise to contact him if she revisited Tikal during her stay. He closed her door and had a brief word with the driver before stepping back.

The taxi pulled away, leaving the two men silhouetted in the gateway. They were still there, shoulder to shoulder, as she turned away to focus on the pitted road ahead.

EIGHTEEN

Arriving back at the hotel it was too early to go to bed, her mind was far too active to allow her to sleep. She had only been in Guatemala for two days and already she had a name to attach to her doppelgänger and the time frame had been narrowed down to a single month. The photograph would give up its secrets - she was determined.

Ordering a beer, she took a seat at a table near the fountain, away from the couples still eating. Felipe was no longer behind the bar; instead, one of the women who had been setting up for dinner earlier was on duty. She was attentive, polite, but her grasp of English was nowhere near as good as Felipe's.

She needed time to consider what she had learnt and the implications. Her thoughts were consumed by her look-alike, Hera Lane: a graduate of **Pennsylvania University**, a summer worker for her North Carolina family camp and the capable one in an official, Maya site survey team. She now had something concrete to go on, facts that would have a digital record. Congratulating herself on choosing a hotel with decent Wi-Fi access, she retrieved her laptop from her room, powered it up and started to search.

Over seventeen million responses to "Hera Lane" were registered on Facebook, Twitter and various other social and professional media sites or referred to in a plethora of news stories. She added Pennsylvania University to her search and managed to cut the number of results to five and a half million. She changed her focus to that of summer camps in North Carolina. Once again, millions of references and even after scanning a few pages she realised that there was no reason the camp should still be operating.

What was needed was a more effective search engine and the obvious way to achieve this would be to utilise the resources of a newspaper. Did she contact Anthony at *the Gazette* or Ruth at *the Guardian*? Anthony could be trusted and as editor had the freedom to pursue whatever he believed to be of interest. Ruth was human resources and there was no reason why she should have the independence or concern to follow up her enquiry. After all, *the Guardian* did not even officially employ her, not yet. The decision was an easy one.

The UK was seven hours ahead of Guatemala and Anthony might be less disposed to help her if dragged from his sleep, so she settled for an email rather than a phone call.

Still reluctant to mention the photograph, she had the problem of justifying the search for Hera without reference to it. She baited the message with enough detail about a mysteriously missing member of a research party, apparently her double, who might link back to Fosse's work. She provided relevant details about Hera Lane and asked if he could dig up anything else. She concluded the message in bold print by suggesting that her journalistic sixth sense was tingling.

A missing person in Guatemala was of little interest to readers of *the Gazette*, but she hoped Anthony would trust her judgement and treat her request seriously.

With the message dispatched, she checked her inbox. Tom still had not replied and the phone had no other message than the "welcome to …" notification that turns up on all mobiles the moment you touch down abroad.

With a sense of disappointment, she closed the laptop down. She had hoped that the friendship and intimacy they had shared, even though briefly, might have warranted a response from him, however cursory.

Even if he had no real feelings for her, his interest in the photograph and its provenance had been only too apparent.

Pushing thoughts of Tom aside, she pulled out her notebook from the laptop bag with the intention of making some notes on her eventful journey. Significantly, the previous pages were dominated with what had sparked her quest: the details of Leonard Fosse's life, her first meeting with Tom and research on Tikal.

If she used *Gazette* resources they would expect something in return. If this was to become a newspaper story she needed to sort out the order of things and be clear on pertinent details. Where should she start? Arrival in Guatemala would make for an engaging opening, a new country, a bizarre venture and immediate misfortunes. How would that explain or incorporate the photo? No, the article had to start earlier. She flipped back to the interview with Tom. She already had several pages of notes on him and prior to that Anthony's description of Fosse. They might both be relevant, it all depended on how the story unfolded. The obvious starting point had to be discovering the photograph in the dead man's attic.

By the time she had finished writing, the courtyard was deserted, the bar no longer staffed and guests had retired to their rooms or their balconies. The frogs were her only company.

Draining the last drops in her glass, she closed her notebook and then, as she rose from the table, another thought struck her. Pedro had not recognised the other individuals in the photograph and he was certain it was taken a year ago when repairs were being carried out. Maybe the firm that did the restoration work employed the other people in the picture. Tomorrow she would contact Pedro or Michael and see if they could put her in touch with the relevant company. If Pedro was in charge of the site records, surely he would have details of whoever carried out the repairs.

Back in her room reflecting on the timeline ascribed to the photo, she was troubled by what Hera could have been doing back at Tikal? It had obviously upset Pedro. He thought very highly of her and Hera valued their friendship, so why had she not contacted him when she returned? If her group had moved on to Belize, why bother to come back? Where were the rest of her group?

She felt an affinity with the woman in the picture, not just from their shared appearance or personality similarities but something more, something intangible. Instinctively she knew that Hera Lane would not have unfathomable or incomprehensible reasons for her actions. In similar circumstances, she felt that Hera would behave exactly like her. Personally, had she returned to Tikal having worked closely with someone like Pedro, there would have been no question of not contacting him, but then she did not know the circumstances.

Hera's relationship with the others in the photograph was also troubling. The arrangement and attitude of the figures in the photograph suggested that it was not the first encounter. If they were not members of Hera's team, where had she first come across them?

Questions fermented more questions, not answers. She undressed, showered and slipped under the mosquito netting. Despite her agitated thoughts, sleep came more quickly than she expected. The last few days quickly overhauled her weary body, but further fitful dreams awaited.

NINETEEN

Even though the night had been restless, she felt more refreshed than the previous morning. Her body no longer ached and her head felt clear.

As long as she could remember, she had experienced vivid dreams. The childhood ones were often tinged with nightmarish terrors: images of loss, isolation and insecurity, with Brothers Grimm style settings. Childhood fears had given way to adolescent fantasies and more staid adult dramas where she was no longer the witch's quarry, the ogre's next meal, or lost in some strange, dark world. During the two years at *the Gazette*, many of her nighttime fantasies had related to work. More than once she awoke from a dream where she had been interviewing the dead. These though were not the frightening cadavers of childhood, just strange, dislocated spirits. As the interviewer, she set the agenda, asked the questions and recorded answers, as she felt fit.

The more recent dreams, over the last few days, were different. They had all the force and fury of childhood terrors. She was no longer in control. They swept her away into strange worlds of savagery and smothered her in the unknown and the unpredictable. Maybe the anti-malarial tablets were affecting her. She had read that one of their side effects could include hallucinations and vivid dreams. She just hoped that her body would adjust soon.

By the time she turned up for breakfast, she had the place to herself. Most of the guests had taken the opportunity to join an early morning excursion to Yaxha, another site mentioned by Pedro.

She had a leisurely breakfast, cavalierly adding the mystery dish, huevos divorciados, to the fruit platter. A plate with two fried eggs covered in vividly contrasting, red and green sauces arrived. The colour was a bit garish for first thing in the morning, but her taste buds approved. With her second strong cup of coffee ordered, she stretched, enjoying the peace and the early heat of the day.

She had brought her laptop down, but only now did she power it up. She clicked on emails and found three new ones including two messages from Anthony. The first just acknowledged her request for information on Hera whilst the second, some five hours later, was more detailed. Pennsylvania University had records of Hera Lane majoring in History, but the university was predictably unwilling to reveal any personal details. They had emailed a copy of her page in the relevant yearbook and a copy of her graduation certificate.

Hera's picture, framed in a little box, amongst a page of young, hopeful faces could have been her own from her time at university. Even the shoulder-length, shiny black hair with a long fringe was a style she had adopted during her first year.

They had also informed Anthony that any work she was doing in Central America was not under the auspices of the University. Sensitive to his request and responsive to his fears that Hera had disappeared whilst working in Guatemala, they promised to contact her parents immediately and pass on his concerns.

Anthony promised to let her know as soon as he received any further news. He also commented on the extraordinary resemblance between Hera and herself, asking a range of questions that showed he had indeed taken the seed of curiosity.

The message finished with a postscript concerning her former workplace. It seemed that the night after she had left, vandals had broken into *the Gazette* offices and trashed the place. Anthony noted that she would not be happy at the state they had left her desk but promised her a new one if she decided to return to her old job. It seemed odd items were missing but nothing of importance. They were still trying to straighten everything out. The police were very hopeful about catching the culprits as they had also smashed the single CCTV that kept a cyclopean eye on the office.

She did not recognize the address of the third email, "J-Darke@Darke.co.uk" It was from a specialist probate solicitor informing and commiserating with her on the death of her guardian.

The news took her totally by surprise. Her so-called aunt had not been old. Maybe that was what the unwelcome letter had been about. She had claimed she was ill, maybe she was attempting to put her affairs in order. Why had she not made it clearer that her illness was life-threatening? Would it have made any difference? The woman had begrudged her most things necessary for a happy childhood, so why did she feel guilty about not responding to the letter? The email continued with brief details about the nature of her death and legal arrangements.

Aunt Agnes had been suffering from pancreatic cancer, but her death was the result of a broken neck from falling down the stairs, probably brought on by the effects of the intense drug regime she was undergoing. It appeared as if she had been in a distressed or irrational state because the emergency services found her paperwork scattered everywhere as if she was desperately trying to find something while she still had time. At least her death had been quick and avoided the drawn-out agony associated with that kind of cancer. She had fallen sometime last week and been discovered by a visiting nurse.

Even if she had opened the letter when it first arrived would she have cancelled the weekend with her university friends on the strength of a few ambiguous lines from her estranged guardian? What had it said? Only that she was not well and had something important to communicate. It was hardly a resounding appeal for immediate attention. What could she have wanted to tell her? That she was dying? Did she want forgiveness for the manner she had brought up her ward, her charge, her friend's only child?

Could she have had anything to tell her of her parents? She knew all about the car accident that had killed them but so little about who they had been as individuals, how they met and fell in love or their hopes for her.

Stuck with her aunt and growing up alone she had felt as if they had deserted her. She knew it was irrational, but how could you argue with your emotions. It had been easier not to ask questions, not to try and reforge her parents' identities from a time before memories. Even if her aunt had wanted to relay some information about her parents, what was the point? They were gone and at least for her, were best left undisturbed.

The email finished by notifying her that the funeral arrangements were being organized as per instructions and that she would be alerted as to the place and date of the cremation. There was also an attachment detailing the probate process being carried out by the firm. She could not believe she was a beneficiary of any will. She doubted there was much to leave or anyone to leave it to. Aunt Agnes had lived frugally, financially and emotionally.

She drained her coffee, closed the emails and rang Pedro. He answered in Spanish. She replied in English apologizing for disturbing him and asking if he knew the name of the firm that had carried out the repairs at Tikal. Voices in the background indicated he was obviously guiding a tour group. She apologized again, but he did not sound concerned. He promised to get back to her before lunch when he had checked the records kept in the museum. She thanked him and ended the call.

How was she going to spend the morning? Flores was picturesque, truly a flower, but she had seen most of it already. She was enjoying just sitting, soaking up the heat. England was so grey and drab at this time of the year. She luxuriated in the warmth while the slight breeze from the lake dispersed the humidity that clung to the jungle. Her journalistic instincts reproachfully persuaded her to reopen the laptop and carry out some background work.

Although she felt reasonably well informed on the Maya, Felipe's description of the horrors of the civil war had left her feeling like a stereotypical, cocooned tourist - pampered and oblivious to the real country they visited. She did not want to be one of those people who travelled to exotic locations, only to return with cyclostyle pictures of sunsets over palm-fringed beaches, memories of ridiculously named cocktails and a bikini-baked tan. As the web browser trawled for references to the civil war in Guatemala, a shadow passed over the screen. She looked up to see that Felipe had paused behind her chair and was glancing over her shoulder.

"I am sorry! I did not mean to be rude. I was just on my way out and caught sight of what you are looking at," he apologized, whilst moving around her chair to stand in front of her. "I am glad you want to know about my country. Most tourists are only interested in our distant past."

She smiled, exchanged pleasantries and then asked him where he was going.

"I have to go to the market first and then I will visit my mother. You should come with me. My mother can tell you more about our country than any guide book."

The words echoed Michael's words about his father. It seemed to be a land whose recent history was locked in an older generation's experiences. Much to Felipe's apparent surprise, she accepted his offer and after replacing her laptop in her room was soon alongside him in the rickety jeep.

The market was a buzz of indigenous people shopping for fish, meat and vegetables. Felipe bought red snook and tarpon for the evening meal. The first was a sort of oversized goldfish and the second just a silver section of a much larger fish. He added to this a range of vegetables and chilli peppers and a whole branch of plantains. The array of pungent smells, bright colours and fresh produce made her feel like a small child revelling in what is considered commonplace to everyone else. It was not only the fresh ingredients and the good-natured bartering that sparked her interest but also the quantity. At home she bought bananas six at a time;

there must have been well over forty plantains clinging to the stem they had just purchased.

Felipe seemed acquainted with many of the sellers crowding the market and along the waterfront of Santa Elena, and their progress was interspersed with greetings: handshakes, hugs and slaps on the back. The whole experience was better than any official tour and Felipe worked hard introducing her to every one of his acquaintances.

An hour in the market with the occasional return to the Jeep to offload purchases, and they were ready to move on. When they settled back into the jeep, a wonderful mélange of smells from the fish, vegetables and fruit all blended in the heat of the vehicle.

Their next stop was a small house in another area of Santa Elena. In the daylight, she could see the true nature of the town. The marketplace had pulsated with life: pedestrians and cars sharing the same littered byway, carts piled high with goods, donkeys bent beneath their loads and cars ranging from battered Ford pick-ups to gleaming Mercedes coupes jostling for street space.

Away from the hubbub, in the quieter areas of town, the buildings were spread out, single-storey, painted concrete constructs. Unsealed, side roads were lined with trees and bushes. Many buildings were in the process of being constructed although no work seemed to be going on currently.

Soon they were pulling up outside the house of Felipe's mother, a modest bungalow set back from the road and framed by a pair of straggly, cashew trees.

Señora Sánchez was a wizened, old woman, dressed in a traditionally embroidered, white huipil, rectangular blouse and dark blue, woven patterned, corte skirt. She hobbled out from the dark interior to meet them at the door. Señora Sánchez greeted Felipe in a strange tongue that she later discovered was Tz'utujil, one of over twenty regional Maya languages still spoken in Guatemala. To her untrained ear, it sounded more monosyllabic and guttural than Spanish. Felipe explained that his mother could speak Spanish, but she preferred her traditional language and was not comfortable with Q'eq'chi, which was the Maya language spoken locally.

Felipe acted as a translator between the two women as they entered the rustic kitchen and took seats around a worn, wooden table. Señora Sánchez refused Michael's offer of help and insisted on making coffee before she would sit. Whilst she filtered the bittersweet brew, Felipe explained that his mother could tell her more of Guatemala's recent history than he ever could.

Over the next hour, Guatemala's troubled history was illustrated with an intensity and pathos that brought tears to her eyes. Felipe's political overview was personalised by Señora Sánchez's account of her early life in a country far too long under the yoke of big business and the military.

Her grandparents had worked on a banana plantation further south and had not really been affected by president Jorge Ubico's military suppression of farmworkers. The subsequent use of non-paid, prisoner chain gangs on the plantations though, had driven them to look for work elsewhere, nearer Guatemala City.

The popular revolt in 1944 led to elections and a new president, Juan José Arévalo. Her father's family had benefitted from some of his reforms. Prisoners were no longer used as unpaid labour and they found work on a United Fruit Company plantation, living in squalid, cramped workers' accommodation.

In 1952 they had gained a small area of land from a law called Decree 900, which ensured the forced purchase of uncultivated land from the large, mainly American owned estates. Her grandfather had been given a plot of land previously owned by President Árbenz's wife herself and they had started to keep chickens and pigs. It was then that her father had met her mother, whose family had also been lucky enough to be granted a small plot of repossessed land.

They had married and she was born soon after, just before the 1954 coup d'état when President Árbenz was deposed and the military took over. They were turned off their land, which was repossessed by United Fruit, an American company who treated workers as expendable

116

resources.

Her earliest memories were of playing in the dusty workers' compound on the banana plantation. Her mother started suffering from seizures and ever-worsening skin rashes and died of heart failure when she was only eight. They found out later it was from contact with DDT anti-pesticide. Soon after her father who had been struggling to cope with the work also fell ill, his vision deteriorated and he suffered from breathing difficulties.

She became a servant at the Estate Manager's house and managed to support her father until his death a year later. The Estate Manager had treated her well and allowed her to live in the house in the servant quarters, which is where she had learnt to read and write. She had met her husband Juan in 1975. He worked on the plantation organising the work parties. After a brief courtship, they had married and Felipe was their third child born in 1980.

When she talked about her husband and his disappearance, it was evident how fresh the pain still was. After Juan was murdered, her oldest boy and girl had to find work wherever they could, to support the rest of the family. They had somehow survived and in 1996, Alvaro Arzu was elected. The civil war ended and they decided to try to build a new life for themselves.

They moved to Santa Elena where her husband's family originally came from. With the end of the war, tourists began to return and with them a demand for accommodation. They had taken over Juan's grandfather's house and started up a budget type hostel and then bought the *Casa Maya Donna*, four years later.

It had been deserted for many years and needed major restoration work. She continued to run the hostel with Felipe's younger sister, Maria, whilst Felipe had worked with his older brother, Hortez, on restoring the new place. The hotel had been a success and with the sale of the hostel, the rest of her children had been able to marry and move away to start their own lives, leaving only Felipe and her to run the hotel.

A few years ago Felipe had bought his mother, her own place, this house in Santa Elena. Now, he ran the *Casa Maya Donna* on his own and according to Señora Sánchez had, "No time to find a good wife."

"Our worry is the violence that comes with the gangs," explained Felipe. "There are fewer visitors nowadays. News of crime and drugs frightens people away. Mexican gangs not only grow poppy fields in the north of our country but give money and guns to our street gangs. There is talk of legalising the production of marijuana and opium poppies to try and stop or at least reduce the trafficking, but I don't think they are happy about this in Washington."

Felipe glanced at his watch and then quickly rose from the table. "We need to head back. I am going to have to find a new cook if I don't get back soon." He embraced his mother and excused his hasty departure.

She went to shake hands with Señora Sánchez only to find herself warmly embraced. She thanked the old lady in shaky Spanish before following Felipe back out to the jeep. As they set off Felipe explained that his mother's physically hard life meant she found movement difficult, yet she still would not let him do things for her. "Her body may be weak but her spirit still burns bright," Felipe said with obvious pride. He wanted her to return to live in the hotel where he could look after her, but she was determined to be independent.

On the way back, the opening bars of 'Stronger' trilled from her mobile. It was Pedro who had news about the firm that had done the repairs. She typed the name, '*En Busca del Tiempo Perdido*' and a contact number into her mobile. Pedro provided the translation, "In Search of Lost Time," and she realised the firm had purloined Proust's title for their company.

She thanked Pedro and said she would be in touch before ending the call. Felipe acknowledged her explanation that she was attempting to trace a woman who had worked at Tikal but did not push her for details. And soon they were driving back over the causeway to Flores.

TWENTY

As they pulled up outside the *Casa Maya Donna*, it looked different. Her time with Felipe and Señora Sánchez had redefined the hotel. The colonial-style building with its harmonious symmetry and earthy colours, blend of ironwork and stripped wood had taken on a new dimension. The Sanchez family's heart-rending history and their labours in restoring the building had invested the hotel with both heart and soul.

She helped carry in some of the morning's purchases and thanked Felipe for allowing her to meet his mother. In return, he promised her a free cocktail for her help at the market.

Back in her bedroom, she found that she had received yet another email from Anthony. Pennsylvania University had tracked down Hera's parents. They had been difficult to contact because of a recent change of address. They still ran the camp in North Carolina, but that was when the news became more perplexing.

They had no interest in any direct correspondence with the newspaper but realised that Hera might be in some sort of trouble and were therefore "willing" to pass on the following information if it helped trace her. She noticed the distancing use of "willing" rather than "pleased" or "happy". It turned out to be a brief résumé of Hera's life.

She was born not Hera Lane but Hera Argent to mother, Elizabeth Argent, in London, on 4th October 1992. Her mother, an American working in England, had been unable or unwilling to look after the baby and a private agency had organised the adoption by the Lane Family who had no other children. She had attended Isaac Dickson, Elementary School before going on to the private high school, Ashville Academy, where she had graduated with a 4.0-grade point average. She had gone on to study History at Pennsylvania University in 2010, majoring in Latin American History and graduated in 2014 with a first-class Honors Degree.

After graduating, Hera had worked at the Lanes' summer camp as she had in previous years and it had taken it for granted that she was going to move into the family business. It was at this point that there seemed to have been some major falling out. According to the Lanes, Hera upset family plans by declaring an aversion to the business and an intension to leave home. She followed up her threat by quitting mid-season and joining a team commissioned to produce new site maps of Guatemalan ruins. Despite various, "very generous" financial incentives offered to her to return and help with the business, the argument apparently escalated and concluded with the Lanes disowning her. They had not heard from her since.

That was eighteen months ago, while she was still working in Guatemala. They specified at the end of the communication that they were concerned with finding out if she was all right but had no intention of re-establishing contact with her. "The ingratitude," she had shown, after everything they had done for her, made it impossible to renew their relationship. There was one item of postscript, the name of the organization Hera had signed up with, the Latin American Research Council.

Sitting on her bed, digesting the latest information, Shakespeare's quote came to mind, something about an unappreciative child being sharper than a serpent's tooth. What could have happened to drive a family to sever contact with the child they had adopted and brought up as their own?

With a sudden jar, she realised Hera's birthday was the same as her own, October 4th 1992. If it was not bizarre enough to come across someone of identical appearance, to also discover they were also born on exactly the same day was beyond weird.

Anthony had included a brief message at the end, hoping the information was useful and asking her to keep him informed of any developments.

Her next step was to contact the Latin American Research Council and find out if other members of Hera's group knew what had happened to her. Entering the name into the search window, she was disappointed to find no direct matches. There was a Latin American Conservation Council and various Latin America Research Programs and even a Latin American Studies of the National Research Council, but none had a remit or the finances to fund a major remapping of Maya historical ruins. Maybe the acronym L.A.R.C. should have forewarned her. Could the Lanes have got the name wrong?

Her deliberations were cut short by a knock at the door. She pushed her laptop to one side and crossed to open it. To her incredulity and delight, it was Tom. Standing there smiling, with a bunch of oversized, two-tone pink daisies clasped in his hand, as if he had just knocked at the door of her apartment, five thousand miles away.

"I thought my excuse for not bringing you flowers before you left was a bit lame. So here I am. I hope these will make amends."

"How on earth...What are you...why...?" she was lost for words.

"Have you had lunch yet, because I'm famished?" he cut in on her stuttered, confused responses. "Let's go and get something to eat and I will tell you how, what and why, while you renew your acquaintance with the English language."

She led Tom down to the restaurant, chose the same table she had taken for breakfast and ordered drinks for them at the bar, all before she had fully regained her composure. Felipe was nowhere to be seen and the woman who had served that morning was still running the restaurant.

She returned to the table with the drinks and two menus gripped beneath her arm, "I hope they're in English," Tom joked, "my Spanish runs to a few insults and some basic numbers gleaned from watching Spanish soccer teams teach English clubs how to play the game."

"You don't have to worry; everything seems to be multi-lingual here. Tourism is Flores' lifeblood. Now tell me, what on earth are you doing here? Not that I'm complaining." She smiled, looking at him properly for the first time.

When she had arrived, only three days previously, she had looked as if she had travelled 5,000 miles, slept in her clothes and been briefly kidnapped on the way. Tom appeared to have just walked off an advertising hoarding for some machismo aftershave.

"Let's order first and then I will try to quench that journalistic thirst for answers. What would you recommend?" Tom asked before scanning the menu. In the end, he ordered the same as her, the *Fiambre del Casa Maya Donna*, a house speciality salad with numerous, cold ingredients. In broken English, the waitress explained that every family would traditionally have their own variation of this recipe, customarily served to celebrate *Día de los Muertos*.

"Día de los Muertos?" *Tom* queried.

"I think it is the Day of the Dead. From what I've read it's a celebration on the 1st November and the few days leading up to it for deceased family members and friends, but it can take on quite macabre connotations," she replied, recalling something she had read in her guidebook. "It dates back several thousand years, like our Halloween and All Saints' Day. There are all sorts of ceremonies and celebrations, some involving masks of skulls and skeletons."

"One of the Bond films starts like that in Mexico City with people dressed up as skeletons."

"I think I remember. In Guatemala, their big thing is making and flying kites to encourage the dead back to earth. Families build altars or go to their loved ones' graves and prepare them with offerings to tempt the souls of the dead to revisit. My guidebook promised it would prove a highlight of any trip to Central America."

They ordered a second drink and while they waited for the hotel speciality, Tom explained why he was there. After spending so much time researching the ruins in the photograph, he had already decided to try and visit the site at Tikal, but he had not planned exactly when until presented with a fait accompli by his line manager concerning his holiday backlog and its sell-by date.

He had already provisionally booked a flight to Flores, via Cancun in Mexico, before she left, but it had not been confirmed and he did not want to mention it in case it fell through. The confirmation had arrived soon after he had dropped her off at the airport, too late to tell her but not too late to catch up with her in Flores. His flight from Gatwick had left midday yesterday and got into Cancun for about 16.30. He had stayed at an airport hotel and caught the first flight out that morning to Flores, arriving at the hotel just before midday. He had stowed his suitcase and immediately come in search of her.

"Which room are you in?" she asked. All his questions and specific interest in her travel arrangements and hotel accommodation now made sense.

"Directly opposite yours, across the courtyard. I specifically asked for the one with the view," he flirtatiously declared as the waitress arrived with the *Fiambre del Casa*. They were epicurean works of art: meats, eggs and an alphabet of salad constituents vying for attention. It seemed a pity to spoil them but far too tempting to leave untouched. They tucked in and conversation re-emerged between mouthfuls, detailing her trip so far.

She started with an account of her arrival in Guatemala and the terrifying abduction that turned out to be nothing more than a scare. Despite being upbeat in the telling, she found there was a tremor to her voice as she described the taxi driver, knife in hand, leering through the window.

Tom was all concern, taking her hand across the table. When she

123

arrived at the fateful phone call, he could suggest nothing that she had not already considered. To his mind, it sounded like instructions had been given and the lower members of the gang were just carrying out orders.

"So why did they let me go?" she asked, her hand still clasped in his.

"I don't know. I just don't know how gangs function. I suppose they are like any other hierarchy where orders are passed down a chain of command and independent action is not encouraged. Maybe the taxi driver was a lone operator after your money and he strayed into gang territory."

"He wanted more than just my money," she said, having to break off from what she was going to say in order to steady her voice. "I don't think he was working alone. I was targeted inside the airport. One of the other men, from the second car, was following me from soon after I came through customs. It wasn't a random, chance pick-up. It wasn't even the first taxi in line."

"I read that gangs often have plants at airports to identify potential victims. Travelling on your own, as you were, do you think they might have seen you as a likely mark? Could the men in the other car have been tracking your cab, hoping he would drop you off in some deserted spot?"

"I don't think so. Their car was not behind us all the way. I can't remember any other headlights when we turned into Zone 1. I remember checking behind, looking for help. That can only mean they knew in advance where the taxi was heading and therefore had to be in cahoots." She paused looking to Tom for some sort of suggestion. "If they wanted my money why didn't they just take it then and there? I don't think it was about money, it was something worse and someone stopped them, why?"

"I honestly don't know." He leant over the table and kissed her on the forehead. "Whatever happens I am going to make sure you catch your return flight without any more troubles."

She smiled at his earnest expression, disengaged her hands and leant back in her seat before continuing with her account of the trip to Tikal and what she had discovered about the photograph.

Omitting only the recent tragic history lessons and the names of those who had delivered them, she explained how the semi-aerial perspective had dated the photo. Only scaffolding erected a year before, to repair the temple, would have enabled a photographer that kind of vantage point. For some reason, she did not mention Michael or Pedro by name, just that a guide had recognised the photograph as being of Hera Lane, a member of a research group that was mapping Maya ruins. Tom's eyes gleamed at the new details. His eagerness to unearth the story was as apparent as when he had first seen the picture.

Although largely quiet and attentive to her news, his questions when they did come were not quite what she expected. He seemed more concerned in the number of staff she had questioned than any other information they might have been able to supply about the photograph.

"I only had to ask one person. Why?"

"It's nothing. It's just that I made a bet with myself that by the time I arrived you would already have cross-examined half of Flores about your doppelgänger. How did this guide who recognised Hera respond when you first approached them?"

"Very surprised and then concerned because of what he saw in the picture."

"Did he have any contact details for Hera?"

"None that are any use. Her contact number is dead and I've hit a brick wall searching for the organisation that employed her, the Latin American Research Council." Again she omitted details of Anthony's involvement in tracking down information. Later, she wondered why she had been reluctant to name her sources. Did she feel protective of them or just journalistically possessive?

Tom did not seem surprised that Hera's employers had been untraceable, claiming that many semi-charitable American organisations came and went, "With the donations of whimsical patrons."

His response to the coincidence of Hera's birthday being the same as her own and details of Hera's real mother was oddly dismissive and yet his body language was the opposite. She noticed a stiffening of his posture as if going up a gear in concentration. It was the same physical response she had noted at the bar when she first mentioned the photograph to him.

With plates scoured clean, they relaxed and discussed their options. Whilst Tom was talking, she was wondering why she had not included her vivid dreams in her accounts. Was it because he featured in them or because they were nothing more than a feverish imagination?

There was no rush. Now he was here she did not need to unload everything in one go. The fact that he had been so intent on being here with her, but had the sensitivity not to raise her hopes up too early, showed what kind of a man he was. Who knew what the next few days would bring or where their relationship was heading. Lost in contemplation, she unwittingly agreed to another trip to Tikal that very afternoon. Tom was anxious to see the site for himself and had organised a taxi before she was fully aware of his intentions. When she did realise, she insisted that they contact Michael first.

"Michael?" Tom asked. She wondered if there was a hint of jealousy in his voice?

"He was the guide who put me on to Hera." She was still reluctant to mention Michael's father and his direct involvement with Hera. Until they had some positive news about her look-alike, she was unwilling to bother Pedro. "After all his help I think it would be rude if he spotted us there without telling him of our visit."

Tom agreed and the call to Michael was answered almost immediately and despite her protestations, he insisted on meeting them later in the Great Plaza.

TWENTY-ONE

They arrived at the site well before the appointed time and she volunteered to take on the role of guide. Checking the plan in her guidebook, she calculated that if they got a move on, they had time to cover the triangle of causeways that linked the main ruins of Tikal before meeting up with Michael. Tom questioned the distance noting they only had thirty minutes, but she was confident having already walked two of the causeways.

Tikal was busy and their route along the Maler Causeway took them past a spectrum of nationalities grouped around their guides with their identifying accessories: flag, umbrella, walking stick, even a cuddly toy jaguar on a pole. She could see why tourism was so important, not just to boost a poor economy but to raise the profile of a country.

Until a few weeks ago Guatemala had been little more than a name on a map. She had encountered it in her studies as part of an ancient world ignored by Cortés in his rush to get at Aztec riches. It had cropped up again in quizzes as the place of the first chocolate bar and the creator of the instant coffee process. In a few days, it had become so much more than just a name and a few quizzing facts. She had met some of its people, experienced both ugly and spectacular aspects and been given an insight into its true identity. Never again would she pass over the name when it cropped up in the news. It was part of her world now.

She was only brought out of her reverie by a strange sensation as they passed the largest of the twin pyramids. Unimaginatively named Complex Q and R, they lay alongside each other about halfway up the causeway. More stunted than the impressive buildings in the Great Plaza and having no tombs or structures to crown them, there was no real reason for them to stand out and yet something made her pause.

The guidebook identified their significance as marking the end of twenty-year cycles that made up the Maya Long Count Calendar that went back to a mythical creation date of 3114 B.C. but had few other details. And yet the hairs stood up on the back of her neck and despite the heat and humidity, a shiver ran down her spine. Tom, slightly ahead of her, turned and noticed her odd expression.

"What's the matter? You look as if you've seen a ghost," he joked.

"I'm fine," she replied automatically, but his words had reminded her of the phrase that most clearly captured what she had just experienced; it was as if someone had 'walked over her grave'.

The weird sensation soon passed and within five minutes they arrived at Complex P, the scene of her disturbing daydream. Unlike yesterday she was glad they did not have time to loiter here. Her previous experience had left her with a deep sense of unease about this pyramid complex.

They turned left towards the sun and proceeded down another causeway. She glanced across at Tom who seemed suitably impressed by the scale and setting of the ruins. He appeared untroubled by the heat. She supposed that his experiences with fires and intensely hot atmospheres had accustomed him to abrupt changes of temperature. She found the humidity was affecting her breathing. Her whole body felt clammy and her clothes clung to her like a second skin.

They arrived at a point where the path divided. She had not been down this causeway on her last visit and instinctively felt that they should take the left fork to reach the Temple of the Two-Headed Serpent, the one that she and Michael had scaled.

Tom seemed surprised, "Surely we should be heading right?"

Uncertain of her bearings, they went with Tom's choice and a few minutes later he was proved right. The *Templo de la Serpiente Bicefalica* was spotted ahead, towering above the tree line.

Rushed for time, they hurried past Temple 4 and turned left towards the Great Plaza, where they found Michael already waiting. She had been over-ambitious with her chosen route and it had taken longer than anticipated. Tom had not only been a better judge of direction than her but had also been right to question the time it would take to cover the triangle of causeways. Although new to the site he had obviously gaged the potential distance from the first few ruins shown on the map and calculated the rest accordingly. She needed to learn to trust his judgements.

She introduced the two men and then brought Michael up to speed with her search for Hera. He was pleased with her progress but surprised that she could not trace the organisation that had employed Hera and brought her to Guatemala.

Glancing over at Tom, she had the sense that he was not relaxed about her relationship with Michael or was he uneasy about sharing the investigation with somebody else? She had not thought he was possessive about either her or the quest. It was a side to him she had not seen before. Michael sensed his reticence and mistakenly took it for shyness, kindly offering to repeat yesterday's tour for Tom's benefit.

The humidity and pace had combined to leave her feeling enervated, so she temporarily excused herself, promising to rejoin them presently when she had recovered some of her energy. Tom seemed concerned with her fatigue and unwilling to start the tour without her until she pressed him to go. Somewhat reluctantly, he joined Michael and the two men strode away down the northern side of the Great Plaza, towards the stelae in front of the North Acropolis.

The rope cordoning off the Temple of the Masks had slipped to the ground so she stepped over it and sat on a lower step, took a drink and watched the two men. Physically they were so different: the one so dark, slight and boyish, the other blond, tall and strong, every inch a man. They stopped some sixty metres away, framed by the two stones guarding the precipitous stairs to the *Templo del Gran Jaguar*. The rest of the plaza was unusually deserted; most tour parties had already decided to head back to the sanctuary of their air-conditioned hotels to rehydrate and check their cameras had caught the full experience.

Michael was pointing towards the shrine above. Tom glanced round in her direction to check if she was all right. She waved and he turned his attention back to Michael who seemed oblivious to Tom's inattention.

She withdrew her mobile to check for messages and used the opportunity to film the semi-deserted Plaza. For a moment the two men were the only people in sight. Tom, slightly blocking her view of Michael, was obviously asking a question about the burial chamber at the top as he was gesticulating towards the summit. Michael had turned to observe his gesture. She finished panning round the ruins before returning both mobile and water bottle to her daypack and then crossed the Plaza to rejoin the two men.

They continued the tour together but at four, Michael excused himself as he had a previous booking with a group from one of the park lodges. They were expecting an illustrated talk before an evening tour and he needed time to organise his presentation materials. They accompanied him as far as the hotel, where she had eaten lunch the day before. He took his leave and they decided to grab a drink.

They sat in the air-conditioned interior away from other guests. Reclining in two large rattan chairs beneath a rotating fan, they gratefully sipped their ice-cold beers and watched the sunbathers outside. The only activity was a group of children splashing around in the kidney-shaped pool.

Whether it was the beer or restful atmosphere she had no idea, but she started to tell Tom about the previous day's strange experience at Complex P. She was only planning to give a broad overview of the daydream, but Tom seemed fascinated, pressing her for details. He was not dismissive of the experience in any way, just curious.

When she had finished and answered all his questions, he took her hand and calmly reassured her, "I don't usually place much weight on psychic or spiritual connections, nor do I have much faith in telepathy, but I think it would be foolish to ignore all such possibilities. It was obvious from your impassioned response to the original photograph that your connection is more than just a physical resemblance. You also seem to have some empathic association with this woman." He squeezed her hand gently, making her feel that he wanted to share her experiences, however incredible or unpleasant. "I have a suggestion," he continued, "don't hesitate to say no, but if you are feeling refreshed and up-to-it, why don't we return to Complex P, where you had that hallucination or whatever you want to call it and try to invoke something similar?" He paused, reassuring her with a gentle smile. "Does that sound ridiculous?" he asked when she did not respond immediately.

Her earlier sense of antipathy for Complex P resurfaced, but despite a growing sense of anxiety, she agreed. With Tom beside her, she felt she could tackle most things. His self-assurance and strength buoyed her spirits. They finished their beers and headed back to the ruins. Taking the same route as before, they arrived before she had fully composed herself.

The complex was deserted. The sun, low in the sky, cast long shadows across the north enclosure. The altar stone, near where she had rested, was shrouded by the shadow of the western edifice and had taken on a distinct aura, more portentous than foreboding. Close observation revealed a faded image of a captive bound to a carved-stone altar, hands tied behind his back. Guatemala's appalling tradition of human sacrifices was resurfacing with gruesome regularity.

Tom, deep in thought, had been largely silent since they left the hotel. It was only as she stood gazing at the image did he speak, "Are you alright?" She nodded. "We don't need to do this if you're not certain." Tom's concerned tone placated her growing unease.

They clambered up the eastern pyramid to catch the late afternoon sun. There they sat, silently looking over the forest at the shining temple capstones, like luminous islands in a green sea. She withdrew the photo from her daypack but found it difficult to concentrate fully with Tom so close beside her.

After a while, she said, "I think I need to be alone. I am going to sit where I did last time." Tom reassured her that he would stay exactly where he was but all she needed to do was call.

She descended slowly, deep in thought and returned to her former stone pew near the altar, the photo still clutched in one hand.

Alone by the altar, she was not sure what she should do. She had never tried to induce her daydreams, they just happened when her mind was not occupied with anything else. She stared intently at the image of the sacrificial victim on the altar until it slipped out of focus, her eyes flickered shut and the bird noises from the forest filled the sensory gap.

Parakeets, macaws and great-tailed grackles blended with the creaking of forest vegetation. Occasional distant howls and cries punctuated the refrain, like a wild, Latin American oratorio. Its mesmerising effect gradually drew her into another realm. The light streamed through her closed eyelids and there was Hera once again, crouched, panting and sweating behind the altar, camera clasped in one hand.

It was the same as last time yet somehow different. Hera seemed just as frightened as before, but this time she also seemed distracted by something nearby. As if sensing another presence, her eyes kept darting around the complex before turning back to where the men would emerge from the trees. It was like watching a rerun of a silent film. South, from the heart of Tikal, the men appeared and yet again, closed in on where Hera was hidden.

As before, there were six of them, organised in an arc that closed in on Hera's place of concealment. On the left, a large, swarthy man, whose naked arms were smothered in tattoos, followed a downcast, thin figure. He drew nearer and she saw his face was chiselled and cruel, tanned to a leathery cinnamon colour. The close-shaven skull revealed a broad, flat forehead. His thin lips silently spat instructions or orders to the huddled figure before him. His broad shoulders and tattooed arms clearly identified him as the character in the photograph leaning over the bloody body. He wore the same paramilitary khaki outfit he had worn in the photo.

The figure that he shadowed was dressed differently, in loose-fitting, linen trousers and a matching jacket with a white shirt unbuttoned at the collar. His chestnut brown hair was smartly cut. From his shoulders dangled an array of cameras and their accessories. He stumbled and looked up and was immediately recognisable, not from her photograph but from another picture Anthony had shown her just a week ago. It was Leonard Fosse, the man whose photo had started this quest. What on earth was he doing with these men?

Three of the others were dressed identically to the tattooed giant: khaki, combat-type gear, calf-high black boots, baggy trousers with a plethora of pockets, webbed belt, jackets with epaulettes, breast-pockets and sleeves folded up above the elbow. The general impression was of a paramilitary-style force.

The character in the centre of the line and nearest to them was a squat figure with cropped black hair and dark skin. At this distance, she could not discern the colour of his eyes. His crooked nose jutted above a bushy, black beard that hid both his mouth and lower jaw. His exposed arms were devoid of tattoos but phenomenally hairy and made him look like the character in the photograph with the binoculars.

Another man, to the right of Hirsute, was the exact opposite, hairless, tall and gaunt. His face was unremarkable except for a raw-looking scar that ran from his right cheek up and over his half-closed right eye, ending in the middle of his forehead. Could he possibly be the source of the shadow in the corner of the photo?

The last character out on the far right also had his head down but was different from the others in that he had short blond hair, a black t-shirt and olive combat trousers. He was broad-shouldered and fairer-skinned. He was waiting for another figure that had just appeared from a clump of trees. He turned his head and acknowledged the newcomer. At the base of his skull was a small dark, indistinct mark, like a birthmark. It was the man menacing Hera in the photograph. The late arrival, also dressed in khaki combats, strode rapidly to catch up with Hera's persecutor.

Something suddenly dragged her attention away from the blond man and back to Hera. For the first time, the silent movie she had been watching had developed sound. It did not burst into full Dolby, stereophonic glory, but a single voice filtered through the silence. It was Hera's voice. As she inched backwards away from the altar towards the waiting shroud of the jungle, she was urgently whispering something.

At first, she thought Hera was talking to herself. It was as if she was uttering a catechism or mouthing a prayer, but as the words were repeated again and again with a fierce intensity, she realised they were for her ears and her ears only. Then just as the words had imperceptibly solidified, they dissolved and with them the vision.

TWENTY-TWO

Tom had somehow managed to book a taxi that was waiting for them when they returned to the car park. They had left the ruins soon after her apparition faded. She must have cried out when Hera spoke because on surfacing from the dream, Tom was standing over her. She caught the look of concern in his eyes and realised something must have happened to warrant such a response. She had reassured him she was all right but found that she was unsteady on her feet. With his arm around her, they slowly retraced the path to the car park.

It was only when they were driving away from the site that Tom started to question her. Hesitantly she described the vision in as much fragmented detail as she could recall. It was difficult to concentrate fully on his questions or her own responses and she kept losing her train of thought and trailing off mid-sentence. Despite her confused state, he went on pressing her specific details, especially Hera's movements, even when she could recall nothing more.

When he finally seemed satisfied that she could remember no further details, he explained that he had only come looking for her in response to some cry she had made. Although he had not been able to make out any specific words, it had sounded as if she had been in distress.

As they pulled up at the *Casa Maya Donna*, Tom was concerned that her illusory experience was still affecting her. Before leaving he persuaded her to take a rest and arranged to call back later to take her to dinner.

Alone in her bedroom, she undressed and slipped into the shower. The cold water washed away the sweat of the day and left her skin tingling and yet her mind was still miles away. It had not been the visual element of her vision that caused her disjointed narrative and lapses in concentration during the taxi ride but the aural aspect - Hera's muted prayer.

Yet again she had been reluctant to divulge aspects of her experience. For some reason, she had not told Tom that the last part of the vision was also audible. She supposed this inability to open up fully was from a lifetime's habit of compartmentalising reality and fantasy. Excursions to her inner world had rarely been shared with friends, except for her imaginary friends. But it was more than that. The hushed words Hera had intoned, again and again, might have been little more than a whisper, but their import was deafening. They had continued to reverberate through her thoughts long after the vision had faded.

Although Hera's accent was different from hers, the tone and pitch were similar. It was not their sound though that had troubled her but their meaning. Hera's urgent, repeated supplication had been, "Help me, sister. Help me! Trust no one."

She towelled herself dry and without bothering to dress, stretched out on the bed. Her mind started to function more clearly. Hera's entreaty had been an appeal to family, not sexual identity. What had literally been staring her in the face ever since she had first seen the photograph now made sense. It was not her in the picture or some photographic trick but an identical twin.

What other explanation could explain all the anomalies? The photograph, Pedro's initial response to her and the vivid dreams and visions all pointed to that one explanation. She had a sister, an identical twin sister she had never known existed, a sister separated from her at birth.

No, it was too ridiculous, something that might be conjured up on stage, not in reality. Yet what else would explain someone who looked so like her, even she could hardly tell the difference? What else could account for identical birthdays, birth cities and both of them being fostered or adopted? What else might generate the level of instinctive empathy she felt for Hera?

How bizarre it all sounded, a Shakespearian farce, except there was nothing comic about Hera's plea for help or her look of fear in the photograph.

She listened to the sounds in the courtyard, of dinner settings being organised and the waitresses chatting. She could hear Felipe's voice giving instructions in Spanish. She did not understand exactly what he said, but it slowly restored a sense of normality, a world beyond her frenzied imagination.

She pulled the laptop towards her and logged on. She had never felt the need to find out anything about her parents, preferring fantasy creations. Her guardian had told her the minimal: she was born in London on 4th October 1992, and her parents had died soon after in a car crash. Her mother, Jane Smith, was a teacher and her father, Stephen Smith, a university lecturer. That was about as much as she knew.

She had always considered nothing good would come of resurrecting her past, which was ironic as both her degree and a major element of her work was exactly that, digging up the past. Maybe her interest in retracing the lives of the dead was a substitute for her own rootless identity?

She searched through birth records for Hera Argent and quickly found she was born at 7.46 a.m. in Hampstead on the 4th October 1992, to Emily Argent and that she had a twin, but the record did not record the twin's name or even their sex. The certificate recorded Emily as having been born in Denver twenty-two years before the birth of her daughter. Her occupation was listed as a full-time student. No father was recorded. Had she been an American student over at an English University and found herself pregnant? Was that why she gave her children up for adoption?

Where next? She sat rocking slightly, struggling to take on the full implications of what she was uncovering. She entered her name and date of birth into the search engine. No record could be found. If her birth was not recorded where could she look? Surely it was a legal obligation to record all births? Suddenly she realised how stupid she was being and changed her surname to Argent and searched again. There she was, born in Hampstead at 7.50 a.m. to Emily Argent on 4th October 1992, and she was one of twins. No father was recorded.

The missing pieces of the jigsaw puzzle suddenly fell into place. She had an older sister, a twin! Her real surname was Argent, not Smith. Stephen and Jane Smith had adopted her and given her their surname but kept her first name true to her birth certificate. Aunt Agnes had taken on the job of fostering her as an acquaintance of Jane Smith, not her mother. Maybe that explained her inability to show any warmth for the child in her care.

Suddenly it struck her, Emily Argent, her real mother might still be alive, in fact, she would only be in her early fifties. Did she ever think of her children? In a matter of minutes, the whole foundation for her existence had been reduced to tinder and shakily reassembled anew. She had a family! It was too confusing to know how to respond, whether to shout and laugh or rage and weep. She had a mother and a sister - a twin.

She had a mother who had rejected her at birth, a sister who probably had no idea of her existence and maybe even a father who had deserted them before birth: laugh or cry, cry or laugh? She wanted to do both at the same time.

Why had her guardian not told her? Maybe that was why she had sent that last letter. With death knocking at the door, Aunt Agnes had felt obliged to tell her something of her real identity. Had she been lied to or protected? So many of her childhood make-believes involved fantasy family members. She sat, oblivious to time and surroundings, one thought chasing the next, one question hatching another.

She remembered that the first time she had searched for Hera on the

Internet, the Queen of the Gods had been amongst the first web pages that had appeared. As the wife of Zeus, she was the Greek goddess responsible for women. A linked site had briefly opened, but she had only scanned it. What had made it memorable was that her name had been attached to Hera's. She had thought nothing more of it at the time but revisiting her search history she re-opened the website to find Juno was the equivalent goddess for the Romans as Hera was for the Greeks.

The Romans had taken nearly all Hera's traits and transposed them to their Queen of the Gods, Juno. Even their statues were identical. In the eastern side of the Roman Empire the two goddesses were interchangeable – more than even twins, they were the same identity.

Emily Argent had named her twins after classical clones, doppelgänger goddesses. Not any old goddess either, but the Queen of the Gods. Had her mother been studying classics or Ancient History at a British university? She had bonded them at birth with the names of the ultimate, classical female gods. She had forsaken the role of mother, yet loaded her twins with the names of the goddesses of motherhood- bloody hell, what an irony.

A knock on the door dragged her back to the present and she realised she was still naked. She quickly wrapped a towel around herself and answered the door. It was Tom, freshly showered and dressed in cream trousers and a navy polo shirt. She apologised for her state of undress, claiming she had fallen asleep and promised to join him shortly.

Tom's departure sobered her up. The past might be another country that needed exploring, but it was the present she must deal with now. She caught sight of herself in the mirror and realised why Tom had seemed so distracted, the towel, hastily wrapped around her, hardly covered her modesty.

As she dressed she considered how much to share with Tom. She was not ready to admit that she had a new identity, another mother and a long-lost sister. Like an unexpected and perplexing gift, she wanted to keep it to herself for a while in order to decide what to do with it.

She was not ready to discuss whether Smith should be ditched for

Argent. As a child, she had dumped the second syllable of her first name. Was she ready to reclaim it? As for Smith, she had no strong feelings. It was about as bland as they came and had even fewer connotations now she knew the couple who had died in a car crash when she was only a few months old were not her flesh and blood.

If she was indeed named after an immortal Greek deity, the supreme goddess, it needed to sink in. Juno or D'you know was no longer a childish taunt, it had status, it even sounded different. It was so long since she had encouraged anyone to call her Juno she had forgotten what it sounded like. In comparison Ju sounded curtailed, more of an exclamation or vocal tic, something to be blurted out, not the name of a promising journalist. "Juno Argent, Juno Argent, Juno Argent," she said out loud. It had a ring to it. Wasn't argent something to do with silver?

She had to tell somebody. Maybe if she told Tom, she would know how she really felt. It was only then that she recalled Hera's fearful words "Help me!" and, "Trust no one!"

She removed the curled photo and stared at her sister's image. Something had led her to find and save this picture amongst thousands of others, to impetuously seek out the location, and directed her to the one person connected to Tikal who knew Hera. Something was filling her daydreams and nightmares with images of her sister. Hera was depending on her and had warned her about sharing confidences.

The picture curled up as she let go of the edges, hiding her twin from her. She rerolled it tightly and slid it back into its protective tube and placed it next to the laptop that was flashing a low battery warning. She closed it down and pushed both items to the foot of the bed.

TWENTY-THREE

She joined Tom and despite feeling her world had been turned upside down managed to compose herself. She was determined to stay focused. While they ate, their conversation retraced the events of that day. Tom's professional skills as an investigator were all too evident in the manner he again picked over every aspect of her vision, anxious to isolate specific details. The barrage of questions kept reminding her of what she was keeping from him.

In the end, rather tetchily, she told him that she did not want to discuss it any further. Tom looked slightly taken aback but accepted her wishes without further question. She knew it sounded as if there was more to divulge and she was not being entirely honest, but she was tired and could feel emotion welling up inside. The conversation lapsed temporarily and it was some time before either spoke again.

"Where do we go from here?" Tom eventually asked leaning back in his chair and staring up at the clear night sky.

"I think that we need to visit Yaxha," she responded after a moment considering possible options. "Michael showed me a photograph of Hera taken at Yaxha. Perhaps someone there will remember her and be able to say why she returned to Guatemala after leaving for Belize."

Tom agreed and left her to check whether there was an organised trip the following day. He soon returned, holding two balloon glasses with measures of a brown liqueur, declaring he had booked a tour for the following morning and that he wanted to toast their progress.

"Ron Zacapa,_Guatemalan rum," he announced raising his glass and congratulating her on how much she had discovered so quickly.

His compliments made her feel ashamed at what she was hiding from him. She sipped at the rich, heady alcohol tasting of burnt caramel and brown spice. With all, she had been through during the day the rum soon blurred the world's harsher edges.

At some point, Tom must have ordered refills, but she was oblivious to him doing so, or to the drinks arriving. All she was aware of was that at some point her glass only had a treacly residue and next time she looked, it was full again.

When she finally attempted to stand, her legs were unwilling accomplices and she ended up sprawling backwards into her chair. The empty courtyard spun around her. The frogs and fountain sounded as if they were being played through invisible headphones, so loud and immersive had they become. Tom was still talking to her, but the words were not making sense; those damn frogs kept drowning him out. She stumbled out of her chair and someone caught her. She giggled at her inability to co-ordinate anything. Even words seemed to be too much of a struggle. Her facial muscles felt as if someone else was controlling them. She saw Felipe glide across from the bar, a strangely worried expression on his face and then he was gone.

The arms that had steadied her were suddenly propelling her forward. With surprise, she realised they were Tom's arms. Her feet did not seem to be moving and yet the building's ochre walls were passing her on both sides. A door loomed ahead, but someone seemed to have removed the handle. A hand reached around her and mysteriously found a handle and then she was sprawling on a bed, enmeshed in a mosquito net.

She giggled, or thought she did, at the image of herself as a giant fish trammelled in a net. She pulled at the netting and found herself even more entangled, then she was being lifted, gently turned, carefully unwrapped and suddenly she was free.

Strong arms sat her up like a puppet. They seemed to belong to Tom. She laughed at the thought that they belonged instead to some giant fisherman. She looked up at Tom. His mouth was moving and the voice was his, but the words made no sense. Was he doing frog impressions?

Her blouse somehow had come unbuttoned and slipped off her shoulders. Her shoes also seemed to have disappeared. The arm that supported her relaxed and she flopped backwards. She was now gazing up at the ceiling fan, spinning slowly but making no noise. She felt a slight pressure on her stomach and then it eased and something was pulled from beneath her. The hand passed in front of her eyes holding her belt. That was strange, what was it doing there?

The hands slipped beneath her hips and she was being lifted. Fingers pulled at the edge of her skirt, easing it down over her thighs and knees and then her legs were free. What knickers was she wearing? She could not remember. Had she even bothered to put some on? She wanted to check but did not have the strength to lift her head. She felt the arms beneath her near-naked body, lifting her like a rag doll.

TWENTY-FOUR

Her head was pounding and she felt sick. Where was she? Were her eyes open? She thought they were, but everything was so dark.

A crack of light materialised to her left. Her eyes must be open. She carefully eased herself up. She was on the bed. Her legs tentatively took her weight as she stood up and stepped unsteadily towards the light. She reached towards it. Wooden shutters swung back and moonlight flooded in. It was still her room and at first glance, she appeared to be alone. She stumbled back across the room and made the toilet bowl in time to be violently sick. Despite feeling drained, her insides continued to churn. When the overwhelming sense of nausea finally eased, she opened the bottle of still water provided by the hotel and washed out her mouth before forcing herself to drain the bottle.

What on earth had happened to her? She remembered Tom had plied her with a glass or two of local rum, but surely it could not have been that strong. She had never been a big rum drinker, but from what she could recall it had never affected her like that before. She had been wasted several times at university but never totally wiped out. The discordant throbbing in her head had eased and she sat on the wicker chair by the window to catch the night breeze. A breath of air from the lake stroked her flushed face. On the opposite side of the courtyard, Tom's room was shrouded in darkness. Unlike the windows on either side of his room, his shutters were closed. He had brought her back to her bedroom and apparently undressed her! She looked down at herself. She was still wearing her underwear, white lace knickers and bra. Tom must have put her to bed and left.

The world span every time she closed her eyes so she remained sitting by the window staring out into the darkness and concentrating on not feeling sick. Her eyes started to close again and the room spiralled away from her. She needed to focus on something to stop her eyes from closing and forestall the accompanying waves of nausea. She searched around for her laptop. It was no longer on the bed where she was certain she had left it but on a chest of drawers next to the door. Tom must have moved it when he put her to bed.

She logged on remembering she had left it very low on power. She was on the point of searching for the cable to recharge it when the screen lit up and the battery showed a thirty per cent charge. She must have been mistaken. There were no new emails, although she could not remember having opened the last one from Anthony. It asked her how she was getting on and reported that the offices were back to normal. The police still had no news on the vandals.

Her eyes were getting increasingly heavy and the nausea seemed to be ebbing. She decided to recharge her phone and download the Tikal videos and photos onto the laptop, before risking lying down again.

She found she had taken about twenty pictures and only one video. The first were those from the top of Temple of the Masks, attempting to recapture the angle of her sister's picture. The last shots were taken that day and the final brief video clip was of Michael and Tom in front of Temple of the Jaguar.

She downloaded the images and quickly flicked through them until she arrived at the video. There was something about the clip, panning round the Plaza, which made her feel she had copied it twice. She played it through again. No, she was mistaken, there was only one clip taken that day, but it was accompanied by a sense of déjà vu.

She played it again at half speed and suddenly realised what had struck her. Freezing the video halfway through, the camera had framed a shot of Michael and Tom against the temple pyramid. Tom was gesturing up to the crypt whilst Michael looked at him apparently without comprehension. The shape, actions and positions of the two figures were remarkably similar to the central tableau in Fosse's picture. Although taken from a much lower vantage point, the coincidence was too striking to ignore. Michael's slight frame was surprisingly similar to Hera's while Tom was of almost identical build to the aggressive male figure.

She opened up the document library to look at her saved pictures and was unable to find a copy of the photograph. She tried to find the original email that she had sent herself from *the Gazette* with the picture attachment but that had also disappeared. She checked the trash folder, but it was not there either. She hated technology when it did not do what you expected it to do, or did something extra and unrequired. It was not the first time her emails had mysteriously vanished. One day she would have to find out why that happened. She retrieved the hard copy from the cardboard role and compared the two pictures.

She was right; the images had obvious similarities. Apart from standing almost exactly where Hera and her persecutor had stood, it was the shape and interconnection of the two men that drew her attention. They were posed in a manner that superficially resembled her sister and tormentor's pose. Michael faced the camera, partially blocked by the body in front and looked surprised, with large eyes and mouth slightly agape, which at a cursory glance resembled her sister's pose.

It was Tom though who seized her attention. His stance, leaning forward with a raised arm and one foot slightly off the ground mirrored the character in the picture. Although it was difficult to judge, considering the different camera angles, the shape and size of the bodies appeared almost identical when measured alongside the stelae on either side. The broad shoulders, narrow waist, muscled forearm and the blond hair colouring were remarkably similar. Only the contrasting clothes and length of hair differentiated them. The mark beneath the cropped-haired figure in Fosse's composition was also missing from her video, but the similarities invited comparison more than the contrasts discouraged it.

This was ridiculous; she was being paranoid. How could she suspect Tom? A man she had approached, five thousand miles away in her own home town, a man who had done nothing but help her, a man who had proved himself a true gent, however old fashioned and corny that sounded. She pushed the absurd thought aside only for it to be replaced by her sister's warning, "Trust no one!"

As a final action, before returning to her bed, she emailed Anthony asking him if possible to check out the fire officer, Tom Webster, the man who she had interviewed. Her feelings of disloyalty grew as she typed the brief message and only intensified as she hit the send button. Returning to her bed she felt weak, exhausted and ashamed at doubting him.

TWENTY-FIVE

Some animal kept tapping at the woodwork. She opened her eyes and listened intently. Sunlight flooded in through the open-shuttered window. The noise was coming from outside the door. Someone was knocking. She struggled out of her net and wrapped the towel around herself. Her head fired off little discharges of pain with every step. She opened the door to find Tom standing there with a coffee pot and cup.

"I thought you might need a restorative," he said. "How are you feeling?"

"I'll let you know when they stop playing the Anvil Chorus in my head. How much did I drink last night?" she asked, carefully taking the tray from him.

"I'm not sure, three, four. It's definitely more potent than I'm used to. Anyway, I wouldn't have disturbed you yet, but do you remember we organised a trip to Yaxha today? The bus leaves in half an hour. If you're not up to it, don't worry."

"No, I'll be fine. Give me twenty minutes and I will be a new person or at least fake an impression of one." Tom turned to go as she remembered to add, "Oh and thank you!"

"What for?" he turned back, inquiringly.

148

"Well for one, the coffee and secondly for last night, for looking after me."

"*De nada*," he replied with that broad, closed-mouthed smile that had so attracted her when they first met. "Our transport leaves in thirty minutes. Let me know if you change your mind."

She still did not feel one hundred per cent when she met Tom, twenty-five minutes later, but at least the anvils now had woolly covers. Daylight was too bright and conversation too loud, but she was going to survive despite her stomach bulking at the thought of breakfast.

Tom explained that he had reserved places on another hotel bus because the *Casa Maya Donna*'s tour was fully booked. Both buses left at the same time from the road outside the hotel. Despite what Tom had said, the *Casa Maya Donna*'s bus was only half full, but she supposed, as with her previous bus journey, that it would call at other hotels on the way out of town. Their bus, a new Mercedes with tinted glass and high backed, reclinable seats, was much larger and occupied mainly by Spanish speaking tourists.

She dozed for much of the journey, opening her eyes only occasionally. The route set off in the same direction as Tikal, but at the eastern end of Lake Petén Itzá continued in an easterly direction towards Lake Yaxha.

She awoke fully only as the bus was pulling into a makeshift car park. An organised tour was included in the cost of the excursion, but as the bus was full of Spanish speakers that became the primary language of the tour. By the time they arrived at Plaza A, overlooked by twin soaring pyramids, she felt a bit like a second-class citizen and persuaded Tom to continue on their own.

They found some shade and sat awhile waiting for their group to move on. She scanned her guidebook to find that Yaxha was one of the larger sites in Guatemala. Although not on the scale of Tikal, it was more than enough for her suffering body.

After a while, she felt up to tackling the vertiginous steps of the highest temple at the east end of the plaza. They climbed slowly as the heat was already building. The view from the top was phenomenal. Below was the acropolis, beyond the forest and then the blue-green lagoon. Yaxha was built on a ridge overlooking a scenic lake.

Far fewer people were milling around below them than had been at Tikal. She remembered that Hera's photo with Pedro had been taken at the foot of this temple, unimaginatively named Structure 216. They descended to the base and she stood where Hera would have posed for the photo but could sense nothing of her sister's presence.

"What do you want to do?" Tom asked

"I'm not sure. Let's wander around and see if anywhere triggers a response. We can ask any guides we come across whether they remember a girl that looked like me."

They wandered around the site that was generally in a worse condition than Tikal but had similar structures: acropolis, ball courts, temples, stelae and plazas. It seemed to be modelled on Tikal and again felt lost and deserted even though it was popular with tour groups. The scale made it possible to escape from other visitors and much of their personalised tour was so shaped, angling away from potential encounters except when they chose to confront guides who looked as if Yaxha was their regular haunt.

Those guides they approached were initially puzzled by her questions, but she explained that her look-alike had worked there for a while. It seemed strange not to openly acknowledge the existence of her twin, but she was still not quite ready to let Tom in on her new status. One or two of the guides remembered a survey team from the previous year with a woman just like her but obviously had not known Hera well. They commented that the party had brought in their own regional guide and had been fairly self-sufficient staying at the campsite by the side of the lake. She assumed it was Pedro they were referring to.

By late morning she was feeling dispirited at the lack of any progress and weak from the lack of any sustenance. Tom produced his second surprise of the day, responding to her hunger with the news that he had asked the hotel to pack lunches for them. She had wondered what he had stored in his daypack, as he had not yet removed a camera, guidebook or any sort of water bottle.

He seemed far more resilient than her to the heat and humidity but was concerned for her welfare. He suggested they follow the causeway down to the lake where it would be cooler and find a picnic spot. After four hundred metres the wide path reached a grassy stretch on the lakeshore. Various other tourists had the same idea, sitting around sunbathing or eating lunch.

To their left was a rough camping site, probably where her sister had stayed. It was deserted except for a single, two-person tent that a couple were in the process of packing away. It looked as if it was going to be a very quiet night at the Yaxha camping grounds. They wandered along the edge of the lake, past a sign warning of crocodiles, to find a more secluded spot.

After ten minutes they were out of sight of the lunch parties. The rough grass had been superseded by forest, which crept ever closer to the water. The broken, stony shore gave way to a thin strip of sand, not suitable for a tropical island but good enough for a lunch venue. Trees hemmed in either end of this makeshift beach making it feel like a cove. Behind them, a trail cut a clear path through the undergrowth away from the lake and in front, the water lapped gently at the sand and pebble shoreline.

They moved back into the shade of the trees and Tom unpacked the picnic. He refused any assistance and she was forced to sit and watch him carefully lay out the food: a pile of corn tortillas, guacamole, cheese and salsa and then a range of fruits including sweet pineapple rings, cantaloupe crescents, pink papaya spears and peeled bananas. A flask of pink fruit juice completed the buffet. The hotel had even provided paper plates, cups and napkins. She began to salivate before half the items were even on display.

As they ate, they were aware of activity in the trees nearby. High above in the canopy, a troop of monkeys with long, spindly limbs and prehensile tails were busy doing whatever monkeys did. The smell or sight of the lunch drew them closer and discarded remnants of fruit tempted the braver ones down to the ground in brief sorties. The guidebook identified them as Geoffroy's spider monkeys. Once the lunch was gone, their aerial antics and quick forays soon stopped as the troop excitedly swung off in quest of new pickings.

The gentle lapping and occasional exotic birdcall were nature's lullaby and her eyes felt leaden. In the shade of a ceiba tree, she lay back so that her head rested in Tom's lap. The sun's heat penetrated beneath her skin. She allowed her eyes to close as the sense of peace seeped through her. Thoughts of her new identity slipped away on a breath of air from the lake that caressed her body before disappearing into the depths of the forest.

TWENTY-SIX

Shaken awake, she sat up abruptly feeling light-headed. The sun had dipped in the sky and she was no longer lying in the shade. They must have fallen asleep and been oblivious to the passage of time. Tom was rapidly gathering up the plates and cups.

"We're late, the bus is leaving in fifteen minutes. We need to get a move on. They may wait for ten minutes or so but no longer." His tone had a sense of urgency that dragged her to her feet.

"There's no way we can get back to the car park in a quarter of an hour," she said. She could hear the anxiety in her voice.

"This track through the trees probably cuts off a corner, it's heading roughly in the direction of the ruins," he reasoned, gesturing towards the path that led off behind them into the forest. She remembered his innate sense of direction at Tikal and deferred to his judgement despite having qualms about heading off on a new path into dense jungle.

Five minutes down the winding trail and she was utterly disorientated. Tom seemed assured of the direction, but time was against them. She stopped briefly to catch her breath.

"I don't think we are going to make it at this pace," Tom said, waiting for her to catch her breath. "Shall I run on ahead and delay their departure? I can be back as soon as I stop them from leaving. You shouldn't be on your own for long."

Caught between two fears, that of being stranded at Yaxha overnight or of being on her own in the forest for a brief period, she opted for the second, reluctantly agreeing Tom should go on ahead. He immediately dropped the picnic daypack and set off at pace, deeper into the already darkening tangle of trees.

Within seconds, he had disappeared and soon after his pounding footsteps had also been swallowed. The speed and thoroughness with which the forest concealed his existence was alarming. She recalled Pedro's enigmatic words about the jungle and its hidden secrets.

Standing there, immobile, the silence crowded in on her. It was not the gossamer-light, restful tranquillity experienced beside the lake but a dark, oppressive overcoat of stillness. There was no point just standing here and feeling sorry for herself. She picked up his bag and set off after Tom. There was only one path, how difficult could that be?

After ten minutes she was apprehensive, after twenty she was seriously worried and by thirty she was panicking. Something had gone seriously wrong. Her initial thoughts were that she had missed a trail junction although she could not remember any route alternatives. It had all seemed so straightforward.

Retracing her steps, she quickly felt she was not on the same path. She did not recognise anything; the trees appeared different and the undergrowth even denser. Surely, it was just an optical illusion caused by looking from a contrasting direction and the effect of light and shadows?

Another change of mind and she turned again and wandered back in the direction she had originally been heading to see if it felt familiar. It was like an Escher picture, the harder she looked the stranger it appeared, the shadowed areas seemed to be transforming in front of her eyes.

She stopped, listened intently and then tried shouting for Tom. A fit of coughing cut off her clamour. A swig of water from her flask eased her throat and calmed her enough to think clearly. Tom must be looking for her right now. Why hadn't he heard her? She grabbed her phone to call him, but there was no signal.

Her safest bet was to head back to the lake and return the way they had walked earlier, along the shore. It was much further, but at least she could not miss the camping ground or the broad causeway that led back to the ruins.

Hitching her arms through Tom's daypack and wearing it in front of her as a balance to the one on her back, she set off, forcing herself to remain calm. The layers of trees were so impenetrable she could not get a bearing on the sun and even if she could, the path twisted and turned so frequently she was not sure it would have helped.

Walking for what seemed far longer than her journey there, she reasoned that caution had replaced speed. She wished she had taken regular time readings so that at least she would have some idea how far she might have travelled. Checking her phone once again for a signal she realised that she had been walking for over an hour. The bus was supposed to have departed at four, it was now 5.10, and the light was fast fading.

While it was still light, she needed to use her head, force herself to think calmly. Once dark, she would be totally lost and it would not be safe to move. She had never been a girl guide, but avaricious reading of childhood adventure stories had left her with various bits of spurious knowledge related to survival in the wild.

The cries and calls around her were growing in volume. Although loud, the avian choir was playing second fiddle to the howler monkeys. Their deep, guttural growls drew ever closer, building to a deafening crescendo, like some enraged monster hunting her down. And all around her, twisted shapes, streaks of light and shadows were the stuff of nightmares.

She had to keep her imagination in check. Tom knew she was missing. He would find her. She needed to think calmly and logically. Even if Tom failed to find her, the hotel would know there was something wrong when she did not return. But then she remembered that

Felipe had not been involved in the trip. Tom had not booked with the hotel so no one was expecting her.

With the last dregs of daylight, she rummaged through the two bags until she found her small torch. By the time she started to examine Tom's bag, the torch was required to see clearly.

By now the howler monkeys' throaty calls were almost directly above her, although she could not see their movements. They sounded as if they were bellowing warnings to her, reverberating howls and shrieks, urging her to run. She crouched beneath the onslaught, hands over her ears in a vain attempt to deaden the uproar. Gradually their noise abated as they moved on to proclaim another part of their territory.

She stood up, breathed deeply and tried to regain some composure before continuing her search of Tom's bag. It offered up a few items of use including a cigarette lighter and a penknife. She had not seen him smoke and briefly wondered why he carried a lighter.

Her path through the forest was becoming ever more oppressive as the light vanished and the trees crowded in on her. She needed to find somewhere to rest. Blundering through these forests in the dark was sheer madness.

However frightening the howler monkeys had sounded, they were not the real danger. Her guidebooks had made it perfectly clear that night brought its own threats with the emergence of nocturnal hunters. Her fear of snakes was second only to that of spiders and the diamond headed Fer-de-Lance, a venomous pit viper growing up to two and a half metres in length, had struck her as particularly horrific. According to her guide, it was extremely quick-tempered, rearing up and attacking at lightning speed. Its jaws opened 180 degrees to free up its viciously curved fangs.

With morbid fascination, she had flipped through the section on reptiles discovering details of over one hundred types of Guatemalan snakes and then with shock noted there could up to another six hundred types alive and active in the region's forests. The dead tree mulch under her feet was the potential home of the Coral Snake, smaller and less aggressive than the viper, but only the Black Mamba was more venomous.

If snakes were not enough, the forest crawled with her worst nightmares, arachnids. There were tarantulas and spiders by the thousands, such as the highly poisonous fiddleback that grew larger than a dinner plate. Their list of aggressively suggestive names said it all: black widow, jumping, wolf, dart, and even one called a bullet spider that spat acid at its victims.

She had researched some of the venomous creatures online and seen the effects of reptile and spider attacks. Gruesome photographs illustrated puncture wounds surrounded by swollen, red skin. Later shots of the untreated bites revealed gangrene as necrosis enveloped the tissue and spread to infect the surrounding areas. She had to avoid any contact with these creatures and the places where they hunted. At least the guidebook had stated they would leave her alone if left undisturbed, but there were other creatures that would not.

In the feline world, only the tiger and lion were larger than the jaguar. This solitary predator was capable of crushing a caiman's skull with its jaws. They also hunted at night, often near water, ambushing their prey from dense undergrowth. Gruesomely, her guide noted that they were not averse to human meat, allegedly eating the face and neck first. When she had first encountered details of the savagery within these forests she had found it stimulating reading; facing them in the flesh was a gut-churning reality.

TWENTY-SEVEN

Edging along the path, the torch cut an elliptical beam between the tightly woven shadows. She retrieved a dead branch and tested her footing ahead of each step until she came to a point where the path broadened. Although not quite a clearing, the undergrowth was thinner at this point. A towering kapok, the sacred tree of the Maya, dominated the area. Its solid trunk, some three metres in diameter, soared up through the canopy. The forest floor beneath was carpeted with oversized, wilting leaves piled high around a spreading root system.

Raking up twigs and leaves that carpeted the path she cleared a circle of damp earth, two metres across. Hopefully, this would create a no-man's-land, which would discourage any venomous creatures and where she could spot any movement. She turned her attention to the pile of leaves and twigs at her feet, making a small tepee of the driest, flimsiest elements, before applying the butane lighter. With relief, a flame flickered out over the edges of the dead vegetation. Within seconds, the leaves were smoking and a few gentle breaths enticed a flame that soon licked up round the twigs.

Rapidly her whole stash of kindling was alight and she suddenly realised she had not gathered any larger pieces of firewood. Hurriedly she pulled at fallen, dead branches just beyond the cleared area. She was in the process of building a pile of wood to burn through the night when a swift movement made her freeze in horror.

Caught in the firelight, a flattened, diamond-shaped head reared from where the last branch had rested. Its coiled, triangulated body quivered with hostility. The black, vertically elliptical pupils stared malevolently at her, as the forked tongue stabbed the air, sensing her vulnerability, preparing to attack. Its tail, raised from the coils, vibrated and rattled menacingly. She had invaded its space and it felt threatened. The head swayed from side to side and the sinuous body below curled tightly on itself, tensed for a deadly strike.

She was petrified, her basic knowledge of snakes useless. Should she move or remain motionless? What would antagonise it least? Suddenly to her left a branch on the fire cracked and a glowing ember shot out. The snake's head whipped round to confront the new threat, curling back into an S-shape.

The spark not only drew the snake but also released her limbs. She tumbled away from the imminent attack and then half crawled, half dragged herself so the fire was between her and the Fer-de-Lance. As she fell, the snake struck, viciously fast, at the space where she had stood only an instant before. If it had not been for the briefest of distractions from the fire, it would have pierced her and the venom would already be pumping through cells and blood vessels, poisoning and paralysing.

It swiftly recoiled ready for the next attack. Unable to get off the ground, incapable of fleeing, she was at its mercy if it struck again. It hesitated, its head twisted away and slowly it unwound and slithered back into the darker undergrowth, revealing its full, two-metre length. The soundless, serpentine movements were soon lost to her view.

The fire sputtered as she unsteadily climbed to her feet. The whole attack had lasted only a matter of seconds, but she felt as if she had just passed through hell. Her hands were shaking and she had started to cry. Subconsciously she grasped her lucky charm cradled against her pounding chest. One way or another she was going to get through this. Calling on untapped, internal reserves, she busied herself with keeping the flame alive, knowing that she had to remain active to keep her fear at bay.

She returned to collecting fallen twigs and branches but with far more caution, tapping everything with her stick before gathering it in and using it to form a wall around the clearing. When she judged there was sufficient to keep the fire burning throughout the night, she huddled as close as she could get to the crackle of the fire and its glowing heart. She was still shaking, but at least the tears had stopped.

Parched from the exertion, she started to gulp from the water bottle. Several large swigs and she hesitated, aware of the need to preserve what little remained. She bitterly regretted the remnants of fruit they had so carelessly discarded for the monkeys. Apart from a few crumbs and two small containers, with dregs of salsa and guacamole, nothing was left of the food prepared by the hotel.

In her own bag, she found a solitary packet of chewing gum and some mints. Searching the deeper recesses of her bag revealed the anti-mosquito spray, which she applied generously to every inch of her exposed skin, aware of the increased activity of swarming insects silhouetted in the firelight.

Time passed and her trembling eased. She started to listen more attentively to the forest around her and consider the night ahead. Without any perceptible breeze, the smoke from the fire trailed up into the branches above. She added some damp moss scraped from a dead tree trunk in an attempt to discourage both biting insects and any arboreal creatures such as tree snakes from being drawn to the heat. The fire began to billow as the flames licked at the fresh moss.

The Howler Monkeys were now silent and the insects' white noise filled the void with clicks, hums and vibrations. She imagined eyes watching her from beyond the tracery of branches illuminated in the firelight.

She needed to fill the time until dawn - sleep was not an option. Pulling her guidebook from the daypack, she reread the flora and fauna sections. Chapters she had merely skimmed became essential reading. The pages on snakes provided no sense of satisfaction in finding she had correctly identified her assailant as the Fer-de-Lance. Carefully she read the chapter on reptiles before turning to the pages on mammals. She was appalled to see that not only was there a risk from Jaguars, but cougars were also residents. Although traditionally mountain cats, they could adapt to most habitats and had become another nocturnal predator in the Petén forests.

Replenishing the fire, she arranged the daypacks behind her, leaned back and listened to the cacophony of night sounds. Staring into the fire, she began to reflect on what had happened earlier, whilst the hypnotic flames danced before her eyes.

How had she got so badly lost? Why hadn't Tom found her? Where was he? If the roles had been reversed, what would she have done? She could not imagine returning to Tikal without him, but what could one do without help? Was it unfair to think that he knew her sense of direction was not good and should not have left her? Maybe that is what Hera had meant by, "Trust no-one."

She had a few more sips of water and finished the mints. The insect noises continued unabated, interspersed with occasional, distant calls and cries that fortunately came no closer. The flickering flames and exertions of the day started to do the inevitable and try as she might she could not stop her head from drooping and her eyes from closing.

When she woke, she was no longer on her own. A group of people wound their way below her, single file, tracing a path through the forest. She seemed to float above them without any physical effort. There were about fifteen individuals. Those at the front and the back were dressed in the same khaki outfits worn by the people in her previous daydreams.

At the rear of the party, she recognised the squat and hairy Neanderthal-looking character from the photo. Near him were two others that she did not recognise, dressed almost identically. Unlike previous visions, she had time to register specific details. They were all carrying packs and guns draped over their shoulders. Strapped to their backs were machetes sheaved in leather scabbards. They marched at a regular pace, eyes ahead and silent.

Towards the front was a smaller group wearing contrasting, stained expedition-style clothing. In the middle of this group was the man with the tattooed arms and beside him the blond individual with the scar or birthmark on the back of his neck. He was dressed, as in her last vision, in a black t-shirt, olive combat trousers and ankle-height boots. He had no obvious weapon just a large, faded daypack.

Drifting on ahead she turned to scrutinise the blond man's face. The recognition was like an electric shock. To her absolute horror, she realised it was Tom. The hair was shorter, the skin more deeply tanned but the strong features and gunmetal eyes were unmistakable. His inscrutable expression revealed little and there was no way she could guess at his emotional state.

As well as Tom the unarmed group consisted of two women and four other men, all looked dirty and tired. They were paler skinned than the armed characters that escorted them. They stumbled along, heads down, oblivious to their surroundings.

Her attention moved to the woman near the front of the group. It was her sister. Hera's clothes were dirty and her arms and legs below her shorts were scratched and covered in insect bites. Her face was streaked with dirt. The man ahead of her staggered and she reached out a supporting arm. He turned briefly and gave a pained smile. Hera seemed oblivious to her presence above or maybe she was scared to show any signs.

At the head of the line were another four, armed men led by the bald man with the vicious scar. The other three were hard-faced, skinheads swathed in tattoos, like human stelae; inscriptions and emblems covered every visible part of their bodies. Certain designs were repeated on all of them including a gothic-styled MS carved prominently into their foreheads or chests. She remembered the teacher's frightening description at the airport of *Mara Salvatrucha*. Were the MS symbols of gang membership?

One of these intimidating figures had his machete sheath strapped across his chest and only the top of the M and S were visible. It formed the same double and single ridge she had seen beneath the t-shirt of the man following her at La Aurora airport. She had thought it was an M and an A but now realised the style of the S gave it the same ridge as an A. From the moment she arrived in Guatemala, she had been targeted by members of *Mara Salvatrucha*, and here they were again with Hera and her colleagues as apparent captives.

As with previous visions the group moved in silence. At times the khaki-dressed characters addressed each other, but to her, they were mute apparitions. After a while, the forest thinned and they approached a clearing alongside a body of water. A narrow pier, painted the same sea green as the lake, ran out ten metres over the water and a small, amphibious floatplane, bobbed at the end.

Alongside the lake, tucked under the cover of trees, were several wooden huts that merged with the forest beyond. Above them and amidst the trees was a platform some thirty metres high and level with the tallest of the surrounding trees. She noticed an aerial and a satellite dish attached to the tower. Both were painted the same forest green as the leaves of the trees. A bearded man dispassionately stared down at them from the viewpoint.

The party crossed in front of the first few roughhewn huts. One of the doors was open revealing unmade bunks inside. There was a small uniformed group down by the lake that had acknowledged the party's initial appearance but soon resumed some kind of dice game, otherwise, the place looked deserted.

They turned between two of the huts and re-entered the forest. Ahead was a larger, windowless warehouse with metal doors and next to it a solid looking cabin. The scarred man at the front of the line slid back the bolts that secured the cabin door and swung it open, silently barking orders at those around him.

Sound re-emerged as the image faded. The deep throaty bark came again as if the man who had been issuing commands was clearing his throat. Her back ached and she woke to find she had been lying awkwardly on the backpack beside the smouldering vestiges of the fire.

The flames had died and the embers glowed weakly. Only a thin wisp of smoke showed any real sign of life.

She sat up stiffly. Cautiously she retrieved more branches from her stockpile and placed them on the fire. Another cough reverberated from beyond the rekindled glow. Surely the man in her dream could not be here. The fear she experienced at that thought was nothing to the absolute terror that surged through her in the next instant.

The source of the deep throaty cough stealthily emerged from the forest only spitting distance from her, a massive black cat almost three metres from nose to tail. The black panther paused and sniffed the air, its stocky, muscular body and thick chest an embodiment of power. It was in no rush and untroubled by the rekindled fire. It turned and glared at her with reddish-yellow eyes that mirrored the embers.

She remembered having read that their name originally meant, "he who kills with one leap." Her breath snagged in her throat expecting the sleek, black killer to be on her at any moment. It yawned, exposing savage incisors as long as her fingers and transforming the elegant, feline features into a mask of savagery, an image from the underworld, one of the pitiless Maya gods. The jaws closed and the face relaxed. It slipped past her, so close she could see the rosettes that dappled its black coat. It padded out of the light and was instantly lost to sight; a deadly, silent shadow cloaked in the forest night.

Slowly she let out her breath, still not believing the jaguar had really gone. After several minutes, without any further movement from the undergrowth, she forced her muscles to unlock. She busied herself with the fire and only stopped to consider her dream when the flames once more licked at the darkness above.

There could be no mistaking that the blond man in her dreams was Tom Webster. How much should she trust her dreams? She had dreamt of Tom before but never in these terms. She knew deep down that just as she had recognised herself or rather her twin sister in Leonard Fosse's photo she knew that the character appearing to menace Hera was Tom. His size, hair colour and shape were all identical. Neither t-shirt nor fitted shirt could hide those broad, muscled shoulders, strong arms and powerful chest. Even the distinctive hands were the same.

If it was him, why had he lied? Why the charade of not knowing Hera, not knowing the place? What was he doing there? In the original picture, the character appeared to be threatening Hera or even inflicting violence, yet in her dream sequences, he was differently dressed to the *MS-13* gang members and unarmed among the rest of the captives.

Although she had not heard anything or witnessed any violence or direct threat, Hera's dejected group had to be hostages. The weapons carried by the men in combat gear and the dirty, dishevelled state of Hera's party suggested as much. If Tom had also been held hostage why hadn't he told her?

After raking through all the things he had said to her, wondering what other lies he'd told, her thoughts turned to other aspects of the dream. What were the camouflaged buildings, seaplane, aerial and satellite dish doing hidden in the middle of the jungle? Where was the lake she had seen in the dream? Was it Lake Yaxha? She did not think so; the water was far greener than here and she had seen no sign of any pier or buildings from the Yaxha campground. So had the armed men been travelling around with Hera and Tom's group? It might explain why she had thought Hera had encountered the *MS-13* members before the photo was taken. It still did not explain Tom's involvement and the web of lies he had told her.

The wind picked up and the fire sputtered. Another gust and a foul odour began to permeate the air around her. Something on the fire must have produced the stench, but it was distinct from the smoke that fanned intermittently in her direction. She picked up her torch and aimed it into the branches high above. The sight was surreal, the tree fluttered with large, black leaves.

As the beam cut a swathe across the leaves, they dissolved into hundreds of giant bats and like a cloud, rose in a thunder of leathery wings. Her heart raced as the colony swelled, rose as one giant form and dispersed into the night. The previously dark branches now boasted dozens of pink and white flowers from which the rank stench seemed to drift on intermittent gusts. It was as if she was still dreaming, stranded and alone inside a nightmare with no way out.

A distant, guttural howl snapped her attention away from the tree. She stiffened and listened intently. The cry was repeated louder and nearer and answered by other hoarse cries. She relaxed; it was not the Jaguar returning, but the howler monkeys signalling the return of dawn. Their gruff calls, minute-by-minute growing in volume, were welcome harbingers. Their roars would soon herald the first streaks of daylight and with any luck her exit visa.

She realised the white noise of the insects had eased but was unsure when. She helped herself to a piece of gum, hoping the chewing would at least temporarily deceive her empty stomach. Her water bottle treasured the last few drops of water. She carefully sorted out the backpacks, stuffing one inside the other and as day's early rays penetrated the foliage above and fell in hazy shafts, her spirits lifted.

The howler monkeys' calls dwindled as the light thickened and the glorious exotic bird chorus rose in exultation at another night's terrors survived. She pushed around the last few smouldering sticks and kicked loose earth over them to snuff any cinders.

Recovering the branch she had used as a snake prod, she stood at the centre of her two-metre world gazing around at her bivouac. There had to be a way out. The thought of surviving the day with just a couple of pieces of gum and a few sips of water was distressing, but the idea of coping with another night was unthinkable.

The path behind her and the direction the Jaguar had vanished was slightly downhill. It had to make sense to go that way. The lake should be at the lowest point and the Jaguar was probably looking for water. She knew they were crepuscular, with much of their activity at dusk and dawn, so assumed that was when it would need to drink. She took a last look at her impromptu campsite and remembered how she had turned her nose up at the rough, lakeside campground. Never again would she be so condescending about rustic camping facilities.

Hoisting the pack onto her shoulders and with the staff probing the path in front of her, she set off down the trail, relieved that she was moving again but wary of every step.

TWENTY-EIGHT

The trail wound through the forest and moving slowly, watching where she trod and what was around her, she began to notice the diversity of plants that initially had appeared to be one solid, green mass. Some trees soared to over forty metres while others squatted, shrub-like. Some majestically stretched out to the sun with broad, straight branches while others twisted towards the light allowing loose tendrils to trail down and across the forest floor in search of nutrients.

Similarly, the forest that had looked uniformly green from Tikal's highest temples now revealed a spectrum of colours that far exceeded her vocabulary. She could name certain shades of green: moss, pine, avocado, fern, teal, olive, myrtle and mint, but the blends and intensities of the hues quickly exceeded her vocabulary; however, the forest spectrum was far broader than just greens. The trunks of the trees, some smooth and erect, others gnarled, pitted and kinked, covered a colour range from intense blackish browns through to silvery whites. The fruit, berries and flowers provided further shades to the range.

Shapes and textures were another accumulation of possibilities: elliptical, round, rosettes, lobes, and spear shapes textured with silky smooth, sandpaper coarse, small spiked and deeply rutted surfaces and then there were the aromas. The fetid leaf and mud mulch mixed with the sweet and bitter scents of flowers and an array of spices such as cloves, black pepper, nutmeg, and cinnamon enriched the compound fragrance.

Bolts of vivid colour shot through this sensory-rich world as kingfishers dissected the shafts of sunlight. Parrots, toucans and parakeets fluttered and chattered above and hummingbirds hovered momentarily in pools of shimmering light. Frequent glimpses of intermittent movement revealed how alive the forest was, never still, never silent, a sensual patchwork.

She had made it through the night and thankfully it had remained dry. The stories she had read about tropical storms were far better experienced as stories than in person.

Her measured, quiet progress was rewarded when she became aware of a snuffling ahead. It continued unabated neither increasing nor decreasing in intensity. She crept towards a vast mahogany that blocked the path. Claw-like roots clutched at the ground to support the massive trunk above. Concealed from the trail ahead. She risked a glimpse over the buttressing roots towards the source of the sound.

Ten metres away, a strange-looking beast snuffled at something in the mud. The creature looked like a small hippo with longer legs but with an extended fleshy nose or stunted trunk. Its hair was of a greyish hue and cream-coloured markings flecked both face and throat. About a metre tall and two metres long, it was a bizarre mix of other animals. Its actions were similar to those of a pig and she knew how dangerous they could be in the wild, so she continued to watch and wait.

The animal finished whatever it was working at and then pushed on slowly through the undergrowth. Checking her guidebook she realised the odd-looking creature was a tapir, Baird's Tapir and auspiciously it tended not to stray far from water.

Sure enough, the trees soon thinned and the light became less dappled and more constant. The trail ended abruptly on a slight rise overlooking the lake. Her sense of relief was profound, although it was not a section she recognised; she now had a shoreline to follow.

To her left, the lake curved gradually and in the distance, she spotted the campground below Yaxha. She must have strayed at least a mile from a direct path to the ruins. Her phone still could not get a signal so without rushing, she worked her way along the lakeshore, occasionally cutting back into the forest when the route became impassable. Never were her diversions more than was absolutely necessary for fear of losing her lake lifeline.

On one of her forced detours, she was faced with the bizarre sight of the path moving in front of her. On closer observation she realised it was hundreds of thousands of leafcutter ants in a wide ribbon, trailing up a mahogany and flowing like a river across the path and into the jungle. The ceaseless torrent of brown bodies, clasping leaf bits in their serrated mandibles, was too wide to cross and obviated the use of that trail. She returned to the lake and searched for another detour that would bypass the inexorable current.

By mid-morning, she had reached the deserted camping site. Groups were starting to descend from the Maya ruins to view the lake and soak up the sun. She felt like an explorer who had been away for an eternity, trailblazing new routes, witnessing natural wonders, yet nobody responded to her arrival. To them, she was just another tourist who had merely gone for a stroll.

The anti-climax and accompanying deflation suddenly brought home to her just how tired, hungry and thirsty she was. Her boots, covered in mud, felt too heavy to lift. She dragged them back along the causeway and still no one spared her anything but a cursory glance.

Wearily she made her way to the car park and was fortunate enough to find a taxi that had just dropped off an American couple. The young driver, apparently oblivious to her state, calculated he had time to run her back to Flores before returning to pick up his fare, so by early afternoon she was safely back at *Casa Maya Donna*.

Even the woman at the hotel reception only spared her the briefest of looks as she handed over her key and a litre bottle of still water. The signs of her night in hell should be scrawled in indelible marks across her appearance, but back in her room, the mirror revealed the same person who had stared at her reflection only yesterday, a few more bites, mud-spattered and unkempt hair, but not someone who had passed through purgatory.

Still unable to contact Tom, she opted to leave a message on his phone. During the return journey, she had worked and reworked a dozen different scenarios for when she was reunited with him, from outright accusation to grovelling apologies. For now, she was too tired to dwell on it and peeled off her clothes and stood, immobile under the shower. The night's horrors replayed in her mind as the streams of water ran down her body.

Dressed in fresh clothes, she descended to the restaurant and despite the hour ordered the breakfast omelette, reasoning it would be one of the quickest items to prepare and while waiting downed several large fruit juices. The large folded omelette, tacos, black beans, salsa and fried banana arrived - manna from heaven.

Washed, watered and fed she did not want to stir. Her body had taken on an inertia that she was not sure she could overcome. With a determined effort, she pushed herself out of her chair and made her way back to her room, encountering Felipe on the way. He was carrying a large pile of clean sheets and towels and was obviously tackling another of his roles, one of room service. He was the first person to greet her with any concern and pleasure, welcoming her back with a gleaming white smile. He had been aware that neither she nor Tom had returned last night but imagined that they had chosen to camp over-night with the tour they had taken. It was not common for guests to camp at Yaxha, but the call of the wild seemed to tempt some to spend a night under canvas. She considered telling Felipe what had occurred but was just too tired and put it off till later.

She re-entered her room and only then did she register Felipe's parting words, "You should have come with our group, there was plenty of space and they were lucky enough to hear a Jaguar."

It was not the irony that she had done far more than just hear a jaguar but the fact that there were spare places on the Casa's minibus despite what Tom had told her. The range of possible scenarios with which to confront Tom immediately contracted to just two, both accusatory.

Back in her room she lay on her bed with her laptop and opened up her emails. There were a few awaiting her attention. She ignored them all except for the one from Anthony. The slightly jokey tone concealed his underlying concern. He opened with an enquiry as to whether she did background checks on all the men in her life? It continued in a more serious vein. No such person as Tom or Thomas Webster was registered with the fire services.

Anthony was troubled by what she was getting herself in to. He had even gone as far as visiting the local fire station to see if anyone knew anything of the uniformed officer at the recent house fire. None of the regular firefighters had seen him before. They had just accepted the rank denoted on his uniform. They recalled him asking questions but had just thought he was a regional officer who lacked the courtesy to introduce himself. The two senior fire officers at the blaze had both thought their partner had dealt with the stranger. Anthony's message concluded with an entreaty for her to look after herself.

She closed the emails and opened a search engine, typing in Tom Webster. She was not surprised to find over thirty-seven million references to that name. She scanned a couple of pages without success and realising it was a futile task, logged out. Who was Tom Webster? Not the man he claimed to be. He had lied to her. Had he also intentionally left her to the mercies of the jungle?

TWENTY-NINE

It was already dark when she awoke with a start to find Tom standing by the side of the bed. His presence was a shock and she was about to shout, scream, or something, when she realised the state he was in. If she thought she had looked a mess on her return, he looked worse. He was mud-spattered and dishevelled and his clothes torn and smeared with dried blood.

Before she could say anything he was holding her and whispering, "Thank god you are alright. I have just spent the longest day of my life searching for you." She held back on her accusations and listened to his story.

Although he had run all the way back to the car park he had just missed the bus and decided to return to where he had left her. Initially, he had been surprised that she had not progressed any further along the trail but realised something was wrong when he finally retraced his steps to the lake. He had carried on round the lake and back up the causeway to Yaxha but without any sight of her.

Nobody had seen her back at the car park and he waited there until the last vehicle had disappeared. As the day faded he had walked back down the entrance road to Yaxha, recalling a series of buildings several kilometres towards Santa Elena. The family in the second house he tried were extremely helpful. Not only had they provided torches, but both the father and oldest son had returned with him, despite the late hour, to carry on the search. After several hours searching the ruins they had left him, promising to return at first light.

During the following night hours, he had retraced their original path from the lake, time and again, scouring every inch for evidence of where she might have left the trail. Thoughts of her lost and alone had haunted him throughout those hours.

Just after dawn, the locals had been as good as their word, returning with five others. A more systematic search had been organised, starting from where they had lunch and fanning out from there. The sense of relief felt by every single one of them when his phone picked up her message was immense. He could not understand how she could have walked back through the campsite and ruins without anyone spotting her, despite the general alert he had put out.

He related all this, sitting next to her on the side of the bed. His concern and obvious distress at losing her temporarily placated her misgivings, but as he finished speaking, the nightmare visions from the jungle and his pretence of being a fire officer forced her hand.

At first slowly and then ever more rapidly she unloaded her fears. Why had he pretended to be a fire officer? Why did she see him in her visions? If it was him in the photograph why had he not told her and what was he doing with Hera? Did he know that Hera was her twin sister? If he had lied so completely why should she believe anything he said now?

She had intended to be angry even furious but as the accusations accumulated, the words began to gush out accompanied by tears and then sobs. Like a dam breaking, trickles turned into rivulets, forcing their way through the protective wall, cracking the facade. Finally, torrents of pent up emotion burst forth, until there was nothing left.

He just sat and listened, making no move to comfort her or to say anything in self-justification. Her outburst subsided and eventually ceased. Breathing heavily, emotionally drained, she stared at him warily.

"I owe you an explanation, but not here or now, it's far too complicated and needs time. If you are prepared to listen to me I will do my best to explain. I need to clean up, but can I suggest we talk over dinner. If you are happy to hear me out, I will be in the foyer at seven." With that, he turned and left, without waiting for a reply or even an acknowledgement that she understood what he had proposed.

It was not the reaction she had expected, but then what had she expected? She really did not have an alternative. However much she mistrusted him, he was still the closest connection to her sister. What on earth could he say to even start to justify all his lies?

THIRTY

The short walk to the restaurant, Vista al Lago, passed in uneasy silence. The tables, under large, thatched sunshades, stood on the hotel terrace overlooking the lake. Strings of coloured bulbs draped between ornate metal stanchions, cast reflections in the dark water below. The crescent moon that had initially guided them through the streets had been devoured by storm clouds seeping out of the night sky and overwhelming the horizon. An eerie stillness, the forerunner of the approaching storm, mirrored the tension between them.

As they were guided to their seats the first stab of white light, forged in the heavens, slashed the far side of the lake and illuminated the intense blackness of the towering mass of clouds. For an instant the horizon was thrown into sharp relief: a single, skeletal Ceiba silhouetted like a bony hand raised in surrender, a small, isolated boat anchored amongst choppy, white flecked waves and a barren, rocky outcrop struggling to stay above the angry water.

She ordered without much thought or consideration for the menu and only then, without preamble, did Tom begin to enlighten her.

"My real name is Tomas Webster, without an h. My mother was Swedish. She married an American teacher and I was raised in a small town in Vermont."

She looked at him in disbelief. All those things that he had told her about his family and their influence on his career choice were lies. All those personal details that had so endeared him to her were fabrications.

He pre-empted her next thought. "If everything I've told you so far is a lie, why should you believe me now?"

When she did not respond, he withdrew his wallet and pulled out a photograph of a blue-eyed, blond woman with pale skin standing next to an attractive man with neat, brown hair and tanned skin. Both were informally dressed and held each other's hand. In front of them stood a little boy with the same hair colouring as the woman, wearing jeans and a matching, child-size, denim jacket. He stood grinning, chest puffed out, revelling in the moment. He was probably only five or six years old, but there was little doubt that he was the man across the table from her as a child. The background to the picture was a white clapboard house with a small porch, a typical New England style building.

"That was taken on my sixth birthday. We were going out for the day."

Sure enough, the little boy had Tom's gunmetal grey eyes and even then a sense of physical solidity.

"Because my father was a language teacher at the local high school and my mother spoke Swedish, especially when she got frustrated with my father's slipshod habits, I excelled at languages. I ended up doing Hispanic Studies at Liverpool University in England, where I studied Spanish and Portuguese along with Latin American Studies. You can find me on their list of alumni graduating in 2001. One of the options I chose was Quechua, a language spoken in the central Andes and that was my introduction to pre-Colombian languages."

"How does this relate to my sister?" she interjected sharply, as another fork of lightning speared the far side of the lake and a trailing clap of thunder reverberated over the water. For the moment, the storm seemed to be content raging above the distant shore.

"It was the reason I was in North Carolina and where I first met your sister. I was there as a post-graduate, studying Yucatec Mayan at North Carolina University and..." he broke off as he saw her look of incomprehension. "It's the Mayan dialect spoken on the Yucatan peninsula. Anyhow, I needed to support myself so I picked up a temporary job at the Lanes' summer camp.

"I first met Hera there. She was working as a counsellor. I was in charge of Pack Out, organising their camping equipment and setting up their overnight camps. We became friends and it so happened that when she started her History course at Penn State, I was based nearby in Virginia. She stayed with me during one of her vacations and an affair started. It was passionate and intense but short-lived. Unfortunately, my work took me south and we made a mutual decision to go our separate ways."

Their meals arrived as he announced this and Tom paused his account while they were served. Both oval plates bore grey fish that had lost any glossy sheen. A startlingly bright salad in a large ceramic bowl was placed between them, probably as a distraction from their drab fish dish. She could not remember what she had ordered but followed his example, removing head and tail and filleting it, in preparation for digesting the unappetising fare.

Tom's account continued during the meal, accompanied by the dramatic storm that still raged at a distance, regularly illuminating the forested shores but reluctant to cross the water.

"Hera and I remained friends and it was the reason I suggested she would be ideal for the Latin America Research Council project. A suggestion I deeply regret."

"What! The organisation that employed Hera? I thought you knew nothing about it!" she demanded.

"I said, I was not surprised you could not find details of it. It was a front. They approached me about three years ago to help on a project in Guatemala and Belize. They needed someone trained in various Maya languages. There are about thirty different dialects or languages derived from an original Proto-Mayan language spoken some five thousand years ago. Anyway, this so-called charitable organisation wanted to map the infrastructures of Maya ruins and needed an expert in local dialects.

"Six months into the project, we lost one of our team to some family tragedy. Regrettably, I suggested that Hera would make an ideal replacement. I knew she had finished her course and had completed an extended dissertation on Maya civilization and was looking for work. Also, as a seasoned camper, she was not averse to roughing it for a few months."

By now, they had finished their meals. She had not registered what the fish had tasted like and her plate looked as if she had butchered rather than consumed her meal. In contrast, Tom's plate was surgically clean. And still there was more to tell.

Every statement elicited another question. As each lie was exposed a new narrative emerged - another deception or at last the truth? They refused a dessert and sat looking out over the lake towards the receding storm, nothing more than distant rumbles. Broken, cascading clouds offered up irregular glimpses of the moon. A gusting wind had ousted the uncanny stillness and driven most diners from the terrace.

"So when was the photograph taken? What was going on between you and Hera?"

"I'm coming to that," Tom replied calmly, staring down at his fleeting reflection in the water below. The wind gusted stronger and churned up the image.

He continued, "The organisation which employed us turned out to be a facade and when the man in charge of our team confronted the official we normally dealt with, a Mexican called Senior Ramirez, everything changed.

"We were mapping Chicanná, in Campeche, Southern Mexico and the causeways that link it to Becan, about two kilometres away. Bill, our team leader, who was also our resident archaeologist specialising in Maya history had various concerns that had arisen from some of the bizarre instructions we had received. He organised a meeting with Senior

Ramirez, our contact from the L.A.R.C. in Chetumal, one of the nearest cities in Mexico. He failed to return that evening and the next morning we were awoken by the arrival of a group of armed men.

"As I said before, I don't place much faith in visions or revelations, but I think your dream, with us being marched through the jungle to a lake, was probably of that. We were kept in a place very like your description, with a small dock and a range of camouflaged huts. Our temporary prison was a hut, set back in the trees."

He stared out over the water as if he was talking to some invisible being. Tom's account was taking on the form of an extended confession, and at times she was not sure whether it was for her sake alone.

"Did they tell you who they were or why you were being held?" she asked. Her tone had softened. She could tell that Tom was not finding it easy to unload his memories. It was the first time she had seen him hesitant, concerned to find the right words, determined to keep his emotions in check.

"No, nothing. We thought initially they were soldiers because of what they were wearing but then realised they must be some kind of paramilitary, guerrilla group. Various insurgent or terrorist factions are operating in this part of the world and we thought we had been taken by one of them."

"Were they connected to the organisation that hired you?" she asked.

"I don't know, maybe, although I never managed to find out. I assumed their plan like ours, was to discover and chart the ancient routes linking Maya cities. We hoped it would enable further discoveries they seemed to want to find ancient trails to hide their movements and criminal activities. Why they took us I have no idea. I can only think that Bill must have said or confronted them with something that they were not prepared to deal with."

"Did you see Bill again?" she asked, knowing the answer before Tom replied.

"No. I've looked for him since, without any luck. He has no family that I can find."

"How long were you kept imprisoned? How did you get away?"

"If you don't mind I need a drink." She nodded her acceptance as he caught a waiter's eye and ordered a bottle of Chilean Shiraz. "We were kept in that hut for a couple of days. Our captors were not inhumane. We were fed and allowed the opportunity to leave the hut to go to the toilet and to stretch our legs, and we had proper bunks, but we had no idea why they were keeping us. There were six of us and most of our discussions were about what was going to happen. Were we being held for ransom, or would we be released when they had worked out that we were not a threat? Nobody mentioned that we might be executed, although I knew it was at the forefront of all our thoughts."

He paused and poured a glass of wine from the bottle the waiter had brought. He pointed at her glass and she decided she could also do with a drink. He filled her glass and then continued, "After several days and for some reason I have never fathomed, they divided us and flew Hera, myself and Andrew, a cartographer, to Uaxactun, a rundown site north of Tikal with a dilapidated airstrip. We were locked in another hut next to the runway where we spent most of the night. I suspected they were either planning to fly us out or were expecting someone to arrive by plane, but their plans changed and early the next morning we were picked up by a truck and driven to Tikal."

She grew tense. Finally, the story behind the photograph of her sister was about to be told.

"The site was closed for repairs and although there was scaffolding on various monuments, none of the workers were around, maybe because it was a public holiday. There were other armed men already there and they had brought a photographer with them; a man I later found out to be Leonard Fosse, our mystery photographer. It seemed they wanted a pictorial record of their presence and achievements. I never found out whether he had been paid or was there under duress.

"We were largely ignored whilst photographs were being taken of the armed gang members posing in front of various temples. After about an hour some of the men left and while the others were distracted, Andrew made a break for it. I warned him it was foolhardy and that his escape would impact on Hera and myself, but he would not listen. He fled into the forest near Mundo Perdido, The Lost World Complex. Within minutes they realised he was gone and soon tracked him down. The person in the corner of your picture, prostrate on the ground and covered in blood was Andrew." He paused and looked at her. The past tense he had used to refer to Andrew revealed the poor cartographer's fate. "The photograph was taken soon after they dragged him back. They insisted Fosse get a shot of it.

"Hera was distraught at what they did to him and had become frantic. I'm afraid the photo caught me just after I slapped her." He looked sincerely contrite as he mentioned the fact that he had hurt her sister. "I knew if they were prepared to beat Andrew to a pulp in front of us then the same fate could and would be ours if we did not play along. I was desperate to stop her from becoming too hysterical and forcing their hand."

"Explain to me what I saw at Complex P, then?" she interrupted.

"Despite what had happened to Andrew, Hera was desperate. She asked if she could go to the toilet and instead ran. They went after her and took me with them. That must be what you saw in your apparition. They told me that if I did not help find Hera, she would die, but not before they had made her suffer.

"She headed out past where you had the vision but was soon tracked down. I pleaded that the men should not hurt her. They brought us back to Complex Q and bound us. From what I could pick up they were angry at the inconvenience we had caused them and were arguing over what to do with us. What I was certain about was that part of their disagreement was over who could have Hera first. They left us guarded by just one man, whilst they disappeared to use the radio back at their truck. Fosse went with them.

We knew that our fate might be sealed when they returned, so somehow we managed to wriggle free from the ropes and slip away from the guard whilst he was taking a piss. We had to get as far away as possible and thought that by heading north, back the way we had come, it would confuse them.

"It was about half an hour before the first vehicle, a jeep, came in our direction. We hid and it passed without spotting us but returned a few minutes later. They must have calculated how far we could have got in the time. Although we were concealed they must have had trackers, because they stopped where we had entered the forest. That was the last time I saw Hera.

"I knew they would catch us if we stuck together so I tried to distract them by crossing the road behind their jeep and setting off into the trees in the opposite direction. I think my plan worked, as they pursued me deep into the forest. I can only hope that Hera used the distraction to make good her escape. When I felt I had drawn them far enough away, I hid until they gave up searching.

"It took me a day to get back to Santa Elena, where the police were of little help. When I finally persuaded one of them to drive out to Tikal, there was no sign of any of the armed men and the place was full of workers from a restoration company.

"I tried the embassy in Guatemala City, but they said it was a Mexican issue as that was where we were taken hostage. The Mexicans proved even less helpful. They are still supposedly looking into it." He drained and refilled his glass as if the very act of retelling the story had exhausted him.

"Do you mean you have no idea what happened to my sister? And what the fuck were you doing playing the fireman at Fosse's place?" Her pent up frustration finally found vent. "Why the hell couldn't you have told me all this at the start instead of all the lies?" Tom was unfazed by her sharp, accusatory tone. He wiped his mouth with the napkin and carried on.

"Your sister is why I was in England. Over the last year, I followed up every possible lead I could to find Hera. The Lanes were moving house and knew nothing of her whereabouts, nor wanted to know. None of Hera's friends that I could trace had any news. I even paid a weighty bribe to local officials to be notified of any unidentified, young female corpses matching Hera's description that might turn up in the morgues around the region. I hit the same dead-end with inquiries round the hospitals. My search for any other members from the original L.A.R.C. team also came to nothing. Your sister seemed to have vanished into thin air. Leonard Fosse was my final possible lead.

"I tracked him down to the UK and his death notice brought me to your town. I decided he might have records of the group that had kidnapped us and visited his house a few weeks ago and that is when I first caught sight of you. It was only a glimpse through the kitchen window, but I instantly knew you had to be related to Hera. You left so quickly I did not have a chance to introduce myself.

"When she first stayed with me in Virginia, Hera told me that she was born in England and adopted, but she had no idea then that she had a twin sister. She only learnt that by accident and quite recently. She stumbled over the information a few weeks before she took on the job down here. It was one of her deepest desires to be reunited with you and was the main reason for the tension with her adoptive parents and the estrangement. For some reason, they had kept your existence a secret. Hera discovered that a British family had adopted you but the Lanes would not or could not provide any more information. Immediately I saw you, I knew you were that sister. It was providence."

"It was you that scared me, that day in the house," she said.

"It must have been. I'm sorry I didn't mean to. I was not aware of making any noise. I was outside waiting for you to leave in order to get a better look. I went around the back to try and get a better view and that was when you fled."

Tom continued to explain how he had returned to the house on Sunday night to see what he could find and had arrived soon after the fire had caught hold. He knew it was too late to stop the conflagration and needed an excuse to poke through the embers in case anything had survived. Before returning, he had "borrowed" a uniform to give his presence credence and then she had turned up again. He took this as the second providential act. He had considered telling her everything when they met later that day but was uncertain of her response.

"I soon realised you'd had no contact with Hera and that you were oblivious to her very existence, but when I saw both the photo and your reaction to it, I knew you were my best hope. Your journalistic training and intuitive genetic bond were the only way I could imagine tracing her. Your response to the photograph was so intense and so instinctive, I decided to go with it. I'm sorry, I realise I should have been upfront from the start, but I was desperate and we both wanted to find Hera, even if you did not then know who she was."

As Tom explained his strange behaviour she found her pent up anger and sense of betrayal seeping away. So many of her fears and questions had been defused: the Spanish curse at the near-collision in London, why he had not wanted his name in her article about the fire service, his ability to order a taxi in Tikal from someone unable to speak English, his knowledge of distances and directions at Tikal, and why he was not troubled by the heat and humidity – he was used to it.

"It was unforgivable, deceiving you as I did and it is why I was so reluctant to take our relationship any further despite how I felt...feel about you."

Thoughts of their first, less than passionate kiss, and the missed opportunity the night he had slept over, sprang to mind.

"I have been searching for your sister for a year and I had just about given up hope. That connection you have with her is something I believe is shared by many identical twins. Your psychic link or intense empathetic sensations are, I believe, our best chance of finding her. I have no more avenues open to me. We were once very close and I feel responsible for her, not just that I recommended her for the job, but that I had to leave her in the forest. If for some reason she does not want to be found because she has adopted a new life or just gone to ground, it will be hard, but I'm prepared to accept that. I just need to know that she is all

185

right."

There was a tremor to his voice and she realised that the quest he had followed, like hers, was emotionally draining but had started a long time before she had started looking for her sister.

"I will understand if you can no longer trust me and want nothing more to do with me, but could I ask that if Hera does contact you or you find her, that you let me know." He looked at her pleadingly with those gunmetal eyes no longer a cold steely grey but a cloudy shadow blue.

THIRTY-ONE

Afterwards, she remembered the evening as two separate events, so different were the start and end. She began embittered, suspicious and hostile and ended tender, forgiving and transfixed.

The pivotal moment was Tom's final appeal and the intense sadness in his eyes. She took his hand over the table and just held it, this time his fingers locked in her grip. She did not need to say anything the contact was the most eloquent of responses. They drained their glasses, paid and returned to the *Casa Maya Donna*.

The town looked and sounded different on their return. The storm had never fully materialised and the wind had subsided. The narrow, cobbled streets were now enchanting, where earlier, they had been an annoying hindrance. Dormant, whitewashed houses, balconied and shuttered, were interspersed by aromatic restaurants spilling out onto the streets. They crossed picture-postcard piazzas set around burbling fountains, where shops were gathering in their touristy trinkets before closing up for the night. The streets were emptying and peaceful except for the occasional sputtering, three-wheeled, red and white taxi rattling over the cobbles.

Their conversation, now relaxed and easy, was mainly about Hera and what she was like. She still had so many questions. Tom's memories of Hera were not the quirky, remarkable tales Pedro had recalled when describing her sister but everyday incidents and mannerisms she recognised in herself. With every action and attribute recalled she felt a growing bond with her sister.

The *Casa Maya Donna* was already tucked in for the night with only a night duty receptionist responsive to the bell on the desk. Tom asked for their keys and they headed for her room. At the door, she refused to let go of his hand and backed in drawing him over the threshold. He did not resist and her retreat across the room ended abruptly at the bed. She kept on pulling until Tom was pressed against her. She needed more than just his words.

Grasping his hair she raised her mouth to his. Momentarily he tensed, then relaxed. The first kiss was passionate and liberating and felt so right, so different from before.

She pulled back breathless and flushed and without pause took hold of the bottom of his white polo shirt. It slipped easily over his tightly muscled lower abdomen and then clung to his chest. He took hold of her hands and dragged the shirt over his head and off his shoulders. She freed her hands and ran them down the carved torso, hard and smooth beneath her touch. His arms curled around her and slowly slid the zip down her knee-length dress. It slipped off her shoulders and she dropped her arms for a moment to allow it to slide to the floor.

She had not dressed for passion but did not spare a thought for her choice of underwear. She drew him to her and felt his solidity against her skin. Their mouths met again until heady with the contact. She pulled back from him, her bra now unhooked, and his long fingers stroked the straps off her shoulders before lifting her effortlessly so that her breasts were there for his lips and tongue.

She shook off her sandals and locked her bare legs around his waist, abandoning herself to his mouth. Her neck, shoulders and breasts were smothered with caresses from his lips. His teeth slowly closed on her left nipple, the slight sharpness an exquisite contrast to the soft moistness of his lips. She shuddered, lifted her head, grasped his shoulders and pushed him away.

He let her body unhurriedly slide down his. Her hands reached for his trousers and without breaking eye contact she unfastened the button and loosened the zip. She bent to ease them over his arse and thighs. He stepped out of his deck shoes and trousers revealing the same snug style boxer shorts she remembered from the night he had spent in her bed. She grasped his bum and pulled him to her so that his growing erection could be felt through the thin cotton of his boxers and her flimsy knickers.

Gradually he laid her back on the bed and eased off her underwear before removing his own. She was moist and needed him inside her. He stood there looking at her, his agile fingers massaging her thighs, gradually working inwards to the baby-soft skin. Her body shuddered as he slowly traced the folds of the labia round to her clitoris.

Her muscles seemed charged, a surge swept up and down her body as if her blood had suddenly come to life. His fingers slid away and she heard herself demanding more, her voice hoarse with desire. His hands fastened either side of her waist and slowly she was being pulled across the bed towards him. She clamped her legs round his arse and took his penis gently in her hand. She could feel it, engorged and hard in her grip. She stroked the smooth tip back and forwards across her vagina, each stroke a little electrical charge. He cupped his hands under her bottom and lifted her closer. The exhilaration increased until she could wait no longer and guided him inside her.

She had not felt empty before but it was as if she was being filled with something that was missing. Her legs clenched tighter dragging him deeper inside. His weight bore down on her as she felt him pressing on further, deeper and deeper then slowly easing back until she felt only the lightest of touches. His hands grasped her waist and she was lifted on to him again. The sensation stole her breath. The movement was repeated, rhythmically, passionately, building from a smouldering fire to a sense of blazing urgency. Her back arched with each new thrust.

An intense heat spread inside her as if she was going to detonate or blossom. She was only vaguely aware of her rapid breathing and moans of pleasure. She heard herself cry out as the build-up of desire and all the tension of the last week erupted and met his own explosion: deep, intense and fulfilling.

Their lovemaking did not end there. The first orgasms were a relief valve for them both. After he slowly withdrew, he climbed onto the bed beside her and gently stroked her flushed skin and this time, when he grew hard and re-entered her, it was slow and languorous. There was no sense of urgency just a desire to stay locked together.

He eased himself off the bed so that his body only just touched hers. His hands pinned her wrists to the bed and she was totally at his mercy. There was more to athletic men than their pleasing physiques, their staying power should not be undervalued. This time when she was near to climaxing he eased off. He could sense her exquisite pleasure, her growing excitement and knew when to press and when to ease off. Her stimulation became almost painful waiting for the final release.

When he allowed her to come, the orgasm was deep, lasting and intense, it left her drained and panting. They drew apart, their perspiring bodies gleaming in the moonlight that washed through the un-shuttered window, and filtered through the mosquito netting.

She awoke sometime later. The sweat had dried on her and a cooler breeze whispered through from the courtyard. She felt dehydrated and carefully detached herself from his arm and slipped to the bathroom.

In the heat of passion, her teardrop charm had worked its way round her neck so that it hung behind her, blind to the path she chose. She drew the moonstone back round to hang near her heart, splashed water on her face and returned to find the moon had been all but hidden by high clouds.

In the dim light, she could make out that Tom, still lying on top of the covers, had rolled on to his front, his v-shaped torso angling down to two, bite-worthy buttocks. She slipped under the netting and leaning on her elbow gazed down at the body that so recently had given her so much pleasure. His blond hair was tousled exposing the hairline on his neck and a black birthmark that had been one of the early features that she had spotted in the picture.

The clouds parted again and Tom's sensuous body was instantly washed in a silvery light. The birthmark emerged from the shadows, taking shape and form. The blur of a suspected birthmark became the defined shape of a tattoo. A gothic style "z" lay exposed below the hairline. Too tired and gratified to wonder more, she eased into his heat and drifted off.

THIRTY-TWO

Morning came with a yawn, a luxurious stretch and a sense of wellbeing that only follows great sex or a really good night's sleep, she'd had both. She felt no sense of recrimination or anti-climax that usually attended first nights, just a sense of relief.

Hera had not been found, but she had an ally in her quest and a lover, someone who did not leave expectations unfulfilled. It was the first time she could remember feeling that way. Sex with him had been everything she could have hoped for, physically and emotionally.

Tom had already disappeared leaving a tray with a single, pink tiger flower, fresh fruit juice and a message. The brief note, in the neat controlled style she recognised as his, said that he had something he needed to check. He had not wanted to disturb her but promised to wine and dine her that evening if she had "no other prior engagements." It was signed with a single kiss.

She smiled, slipped out of bed, showered and dressed then checked her email. There was another message from Anthony. Traces of a fire accelerant had been found at Fosse's former house and the police no longer believed it was an accident. Investigations were still ongoing.

Progress had also been made on the break-in at the paper. The police had also changed their mind on that case. Various surveillance cameras, covering the approach to the newspaper's offices, had been disabled just before the break-in. It was too much of a coincidence for it to be considered an unpremeditated act of vandalism.

The investigation had revisited the damage report and found most of the destruction to be very superficial as if to cover the real intent, which looked as if it might be linked to the newspaper's computer system. Somehow it had been accessed during the raid, despite a strict password regime, although for what purpose was still a matter of conjecture.

She was relieved the fire was not caused by an electrical fault. Surely that let her off the hook. The light she had left on in the attic was not to blame. She remembered thinking the place would soon be bulldozed, but why would anyone want to risk being charged with arson? The place was a long way from any other dwelling and off the beaten track. Maybe it was pure vandalism or an insurance claim by the owners?

She closed down her laptop and went down to the restaurant. She had missed breakfast but caught Felipe clearing the tables. He greeted her warmly and offered to rustle up something from the kitchen if she so desired. She settled for a coffee and asked if he had time to join her. He seemed pleased as he had already done the market run and checked on his mother.

He brought out two strong, sweet coffees and they sat out in the courtyard in the shade of the main building. She wanted to ask about the gangs that had kidnapped Tom and her sister but was uncertain of how to begin. They sat for a while in sociable silence before she said, "Felipe, I wonder if you can help me?"

"I will try, Señorita," he said with that gleaming smile that had drawn her attention when he had picked her up at the bus station.

"I am trying to find some details about one of the gangs in Guatemala," she announced.

Felipe looked taken aback. His relaxed posture had stiffened and his smile had vanished. "It is not sensible to ask such questions. These people do not like you knowing their business and it is difficult to know who to trust."

"I realise that Felipe, but I need to find out where a friend of mine might have gone." She looked at him for some kind of response, but he was waiting for her to continue. "She was last seen with a group of armed men in the forests near Tikal. They wore khaki paramilitary-style clothes and some of them were heavily tattooed. Most looked Guatemalan."

Felipe's face took on an expression of deep concern at her brief description. Before answering he looked round the courtyard, crossed and closed the doors to the restaurant and then returned and pulled his chair closer to hers.

"This is not good, Señorita," his tone was tense and muted. "If they carry guns and wear the type of clothes you say, they may well be connected to *Los Zetas*." The final words came out almost as a sibilant whisper.

"The who?" The name struck some distant chord, but no specific details came to mind.

"I am surprised you have not heard of them. They are one of the most powerful drug cartels." He continued quietly to explain who *Los Zetas* were.

It seemed that originally they had been a group of Mexican soldiers who had deserted to become the bodyguard of the head of the Gulf Cartel, the lead exporters of Colombian drugs. Their influence had grown, recruiting ex-military from the country's death squads, men who had been trained by Israeli and American Special forces in guerrilla and anti-guerrilla warfare.

They brought their murderous skills and ruthless means to bear on inter-gang wars with beheadings, torture and indiscriminate slaughter. Unlike some other gangs who supported and invested in local communities, creating a symbiotic relationship, *Los Zetas* were pure parasites, obtaining co-operation through fear.

Eventually, they split from the Gulf Cartel and dominated much of both the drug trade and people trafficking through Central America.

"They are extremely dangerous and it is not safe to talk of them," he anxiously whispered, his eyes betraying real fear. "If your friend is involved with them, you can do nothing. If you start asking questions they will know."

She was surprised at his alarm, alone as they were, in the sanctuary of his home. "Where does the name Los Zetas come from?" she asked quietly, sensitive to his fear.

"Originally the Z stood for the Federal Judicial Police in charge of a city. Now the name is so feared that it is enough to cut it into trees with messages such as 'we are watching you' to keep people fearful and obedient. They sometimes cut a Z into the abdomen of their victims as a warning to others. In some places, children are so scared they dare not use their name, calling them only, 'The Naughty Ones.'"

She suppressed a giggle at the moniker realising just how serious Felipe considered the issue.

"The tattooed men you talk of could be members of *MS-13*. They are heavily tattooed street gangs that might have become *Los Zetas'* foot soldiers. The MS tattoos are the devil horns worn as a badge of honour."

Her guess about the nature of the MS tattoos had been right. *MS-13* gang members, potentially working for *Los Zetas*, had taken Tom and her sister hostage. She had been trailed from the airport by a member of that very same gang and released on orders from someone higher up the chain. Could that person have been someone connected to *Los Zetas*? Were the two events any more than a coincidence?

She was suddenly aware that Felipe was still talking. "You should not ask questions about these people, it is not safe. You cannot trust anyone." He trailed off, looking at her earnestly hoping for acceptance of his advice.

His final words ominously echoed her sister's warning. She was aware of his beseeching gaze, but her mind was elsewhere. His mention of tattoos and *Los Zetas* had recalled Tom's hairline Z. The MS tattoos were big, in-yer-face, symbols of gang identity. Tom's delicate Z, hidden by his hair, was surely nothing more than a Beckham-style self-adornment. She would have to ask him about it over dinner.

She left Felipe, thanking him for the advice and promising to be careful. Back in her room, she immediately went to her laptop and searched for information on *Los Zetas*. Felipe's information had been accurate but did not even start to communicate the scale or obscene violence of the cartel. Key facts, she jotted down in her notebook. The majority of items were newspaper reports highlighting their atrocities: 49 bodies without feet or heads dumped on a busy road, corpses hung from city bridges, bombs, assassinations, torture, the list was sickening. One article estimated they were responsible for thousands of deaths in the last five years.

Felipe's warning had been no melodramatic plea. They had supposedly infiltrated every level of the Guatemalan judicial and prosecution system. He had also been correct about *Los Zetas* not having any mutual dependence on locals unlike some other cartels such as *Sinaloa*, *Los Zetas* main adversaries.

Each article expanded the search parameters and her notes increased at a pace. *Sinaloa* seemed to be *Los Zetas'* rivals in trans-Guatemalan drug operations. They ran one route down on the Pacific coast whilst *Los Zetas* ran a central and northern route that, sure enough, went through the Petén district. Not only was it a major thoroughfare for Columbian cannabis, but Guatemala had also become a prominent centre for methamphetamine production. The relationship between the two rival cartels was strained, to say the least, and hugely fluid as alliances were continually made and betrayed.

It was when she turned her attention back to *MS-13* and their involvement in rival cartels' activities that another alarm was triggered. They originated in Los Angeles as heavily tattooed, skinhead street gangs. Their moral code was based on merciless retribution. Originally the *Sinaloa* Cartel recruited them to counteract *Los Zetas's* ruthless intimidation. They expanded rapidly and their membership was now vast and their loyalties lay with their own interests. They worked alongside other gangs on their own terms. One article reported a major trial in Charlotte, North Carolina, of twenty-six *MS-13* members. North Carolina? Tom had met her sister in North Carolina. Coincidences were beginning to accrue.

The suspicions she thought had been laid to rest, crawled back, leeches of doubt sucking at her sense of security. She unfurled the photograph that had started the whole journey. Was she looking at drug smugglers? If these were members of *MS-13*, what did they want with Hera's team? Was it just as Tom thought, they needed new routes for their drug smuggling? Was there anything more sinister to the delicate Z tattooed into Tom's neck? Surely he would soon clear that up. And yet why had he organised a trip to Yaxha with another company and lied to her about the lack of places on the *Casa Maya Donna* bus? She had forgotten to ask him about that.

Had he been telling the truth about searching for her? He certainly looked as if he had. What secrets could they have after last night? Supposedly, he had also been a hostage, yet in both the photograph and her dreams he did not give the impression of being a frightened captive. True, he had not carried a gun or been dressed in the same khaki fatigues as the kidnappers but neither did he look dazed and fearful like the other prisoners.

If Tom was connected to *Los Zetas*, God forbid, why was he looking for Hera? It made no sense. If it was one of these sickening gangs who had taken Hera, what hope was there for her? None, according to Felipe, yet the visions and dreams were so intense. Surely her sister was still alive and trying to contact her.

Recent articles on the gang's activities seemed to be dominated by people trafficking, often for the sex trade. Vast numbers were being moved through Central America and Mexico up to the American border. She could not even bear to consider that as a possibility.

Tom claimed he and Hera were taken and held at Uaxactun, not far from Flores. Should she believe him? Was it worth a visit? It was only twelve miles north of Tikal. She could go that afternoon. Maybe Michael could be persuaded to go with her. She left a message on his phone and continued to research gang activity.

Whilst reading another news story, suggesting *Los Zetas's* possible splintering with lead members' arrests and deaths, Kelly Clarkson started up again. It was Michael on the phone. He would be free from two and seemed pleased to have the chance to show her Uaxactun. The road there ran past Tikal, so she organised to pick him up on the way through.

With the call finished, she packed away her notes and went to find Felipe. He booked her a taxi for later but was surprised at her desire to see Uaxactun.

"Señorita it is not so special. We have better ruins."

She assured him that she would consider some of the more spectacular sites tomorrow, but it was fine for a half-day trip. At his concerned look, she tried to reassure him that she had taken his advice to heart. She wondered if Felipe believed her when her words sounded hollow even to her own ears.

THIRTY-THREE

As the taxi pulled into Tikal parking area, Michael was waiting for her, sitting in the shade of a Caribbean pine. He greeted her with a hug like an old friend and as they set off down the single track, unmetalled road that cut through the forest, he gave her some background on Uaxactun. Its ancient name meant, "Born in Heaven" whereas its modern name meant "Eight Stones". So deeply was it buried in the jungle, it had only been rediscovered in 1916.

It was supposedly one of the longest occupied of the Maya ruins, largely used for astronomical observations and probably the birthplace of the highly complex Maya calendar. His subsequent explanation lasted the majority of their forty-minute journey and went into the ridiculously complex cycles of differing lengths that made up the Maya calendar, from a 260 day *Tzolk'in*, to a 365 day *Haab'* and a 52-year circular calendar that all interconnected to record celestial and worldly events. By the end, she was confused and hugely appreciative of the Gregorian calendar.

Uaxactun was a squat, sleepy, straggle of low-rise, corrugated roofed buildings to either side of a rough landing strip. The Maya ruins were set back in the trees. They left the taxi and walked past young children playing in the dust at the side of the road and mangy dogs lazing in the heat or scratching listlessly at persistent irritants. Poorly dressed farmers were carrying xate palm leaves and allspice from the forest. A woman with a blanket-engulfed baby on her back worked at a vegetable patch. The occasional cow and a few thin horses wandered freely along the paths between the fenced properties, nibbling at scrubby grassland.

Michael explained that the ruins were in a worse state of repair than Tikal because they found it difficult to encourage those who visited Tikal to extend their visit to here. There was a basic museum to keep artefacts from being removed and plans were afoot to attract more tourists, but as yet they were no more than plans.

Despite the uninspiring first impressions, Michael's enthusiasm piqued her curiosity, but for much of the tour, her attention was on the huts and houses either side of the old airstrip, not the ruins.

At times, they wandered off into the forest to view other insect-infested sites of "historic interest," but it was the runway that galvanised her. Tom had spoken of a hut next to an airstrip.

Most of the buildings near the runway were incapable of holding captives, lacking bolts or locks to secure them, but towards the northern end of the runway, they passed a solid, stocky, shed-like structure with blacked-out windows no larger than air holes. It stood apart from other buildings in a surly, self-sufficient manner. The solid ledge and brace door was secured with a large, heavy-duty hasp and staple. There was no padlock and nobody close by.

She knew she had to look inside. Could she tell Michael the truth? What had both Hera and Felipe warned her? "Trust no one!"

She asked if they could sit for a moment or two, took a gulp from her water bottle and decided she had to trust Michael. Briefly, she updated him on the photograph. The news that she had discovered that Hera was her twin sister, adopted at birth by an American family, elicited a really joyous response from him and showed just how important family was in this part of the world. She continued to explain how she thought a local gang had kidnapped Hera but avoided any mention of *Los Zetas* having seen the fear it stirred in Felipe and ended with her speculation that her sister might have been held nearby.

She explained that the hut opposite was the only one she had noticed in the village that looked secure enough to imprison anyone. She left out any reference to her dreams and visions being a major source of her information. It was vital that he believed her sufficiently to want to help, or at least not hinder her search and references to her sources being daydreams and nightmares was hardly likely to inspire confidence.

To her surprise, he did not seem surprised or question her account and with a genuinely concerned manner, suggested she look inside the hut.

There was no one nearby and even those at a distance showed no interest in them. Michael suggested that he remain outside, to stand guard. She agreed and with one last, furtive glance up and down the abandoned airstrip, slipped inside.

The sweltering heat was the first thing that registered followed by a musty smell. As her eyes adjusted to the fragmented light, filtering through the cracks between the boards, she became aware of a stack of empty, fibreboard shipping drums. Fumbling in her pack, she retrieved her small torch. It had proved a godsend over the past few weeks. Then with her nail scissors, she prised the top off one of the drums and noticed a yellowy white residue. The smell and colouring of the drums suggested ephedrine or pseudoephedrine.

A year ago she would have had no idea about the colouring or smell of any particular drug, but her background reading for a story on drugs in schools had provided a sound, basic knowledge. Her research for the article included investigating how synthetic drugs were manufactured and had detailed the use of ephedrine or pseudoephedrine as precursors in the synthesis of methamphetamine, the highly addictive crystal meth or one the forty street names it went under. Although in the UK this drug was still mainly restricted to urban, gay communities to fuel so-called chemsex parties, the epidemics in Australia and America had placed it firmly on the radar.

The drums in front of her were key to the large-scale production of crystal meth. Her fears about Hera being caught up in some gang, heavily involved in the drugs trade, looked even more probable. She replaced the lid and continued to examine the walls and floor for some sign that her sister had been there.

As she searched, she continued to register the sounds outside. Every noise put her on edge. She had stumbled across evidence that would make her intrusion highly unwelcome, to say the least. She had no idea what drug dealers would do if they found her here. It was not something she could afford to contemplate.

Kneeling behind a drum to inspect a fragment of paper on the floor she suddenly heard male voices outside. Michael was talking to someone. She froze, masked the torch and listened. A drop of sweat dripped down her brow on to the bridge of her nose. She swallowed and waited, not daring to move or even breath. The tiny droplet of sweat broke free and splashed into the dust at her knees. More words were exchanged and then the voice moved on. She breathed out slowly and listened to the silence.

She returned to her search, picking out some marks on the boards that ran behind the containers. Partially concealed by the drums, thin white lines had been scratched onto the board abutting the floor. Whoever had made them had been lying or crouching.

Awkwardly she dragged the empty drums away from the wall. She pressed herself in behind them and squatting, examined the scratches. Faint, narrow white marks ran back towards the corner. She moved more of the drums and squeezed herself into the gap. The torch picked out indecipherable lines scratched into the wall. She brushed the rough plank with her hand and blew away the dry dust and dirt that coated all the walls. Further interconnecting marks appeared. She tilted her head and realised they were crude letters scored into the rough boards. The letters formed two words, "HELP ME". The words she had seen in her dream were carved right there in front of her.

Imprisoned in that space, Hera had scratched a plea for help. So small and concealed were the letters, so dark the hut, nobody would have found them if they did not know where to look. Who did Hera think would find them, hidden in a dusty corner of an isolated hut in a backwater of

Guatemala? Was it just a vain hope or did she have some inkling of a kindred spirit, a twin sister's search, of her quest?

As quickly as possible she dragged the drums back into place making as little noise as possible and then moved to the door. She stood, ear pressed to the crack, alert to any sounds. Easing the door open, she quickly slipped outside. Michael was waiting for her and looked relieved that she had delayed no longer.

They hurriedly moved away from the hut before any words were exchanged. At a ruined observatory, near the end of the airstrip, they stopped and rested in the shade while she described what she had found.

At the point of telling him about replacing the drums as she had found them, they heard a vehicle rattle in their direction. A pickup truck bounced up the grass strip and drew up outside the hut she had just searched. Their position in the shadow of a ceiba tree concealed by the buttress roots, allowed them to watch unobserved.

Two men swung themselves out of the battered, mud-streaked truck. Both wore tattered jeans and cut off t-shirts with crude logos splashed across their chests. The passenger was a skinhead, whose body was an aggressive collage of dissecting tattoos: words, images and symbols. Even his face was smothered in designs that at a distance resembled primaeval war paint. But it was the driver who drew most of her attention. His leathered face and flattened forehead, shaved scalp and heavily tattooed arms instantly identified him as one of the men from Fosse's photograph.

Neither of the men paid any attention to their surroundings and were obviously accustomed to stopping here. She noticed that several farmers originally working in the vicinity of the hut had judiciously moved further away and turned their backs on the activity. It was obvious that the locals might not be directly involved with the drugs, but they were complicit in its trade.

Suddenly Michael was pulling at her arm and she realised that he was trying to press her further into the shadows. He looked seriously frightened and had not taken his eyes off the scene unfolding before them. The men sauntered round the back of their pick-up and folded back the cover, revealing yet more drums. They strained to lift each container off the back and through the door. The effort involved revealed the weight within each of the dozen drums. Empty drums were then carried out and the door secured with a padlock they had brought with them.

The men hardly spoke a word, and the whole process had a sense of routine and familiarity. Within ten minutes the pick-up was reloaded and departed without any sense of urgency.

Michael breathed out audibly and immediately turned to her. "We need to leave. These men are extremely dangerous. God knows what you have got yourself into!"

"But they have gone now," she replied, trying to sound reassuring as Michael hurried her away from where they had been hiding.

"Those *MS* tattoos on their arms mean they are members of *MS-13*. They are notoriously violent and will disfigure or kill you if they think you are poking about in their business."

They had already recovered half of the distance back to the waiting taxi, and still, Michael urged her forward. The reputation of these gangs seemed to conjure abject fear. Both Michael and Felipe's responses to *MS-13* involvement should have been enough to send her running back to the airport and she would have done had it been just herself to consider, but now she had a sister to think about.

Back in the taxi, he seemed to relax a little and once he had found that the driver understood minimal English, tried to explain his fears. Much of his description of gang activity retraced ground already covered by Felipe, what he found strange though was that members of *MS-13* were operating in this area.

"Although their mantra is 'we work for nobody', in the past, they have been recruited by the *Sinaloa* Cartel. This area though is *Los Zetas* territory, which means either *MS-13* is working with *Los Zetas* or the *Sinaloa* Cartel is muscling in on the supply routes here, which could mean a bloodbath." She listened horror-struck as he unfolded his fears.

"The Petén area has been *Los Zetas* territory ever since they recruited members of the *Kaibiles*."

"Who are the *Kaibiles*?" she interrupted.

"Not people you would ever want to meet. They were set up as a commando force but quickly developed into a jungle warfare brigade. Their name comes from a sixteenth-century Maya warrior who fought the Spanish Conquistadors. Their motto is, 'If I advance, follow me. If I stop, urge me on. If I retreat, kill me,' which is not some hyperbolic bullshit. The *Kaibiles* slaughtered thousands during our civil war. In Dos Erres they tortured, raped and murdered all two hundred villagers, men, women and children, even though not a single revolutionary was found there."

He paused again to check whether the taxi driver was listening and when satisfied he was not, carried on, "Their training is legendary; only sixty-four enter the programme every six months, of which no more than ten ever qualify. They are taught hand-to-hand combat, survival techniques, special weapons, demolitions and emergency medical training. The final ordeal is to be stranded in a hellhole for two days, without sleep, up to their necks in stagnant water. The training involves eating everything and anything, even biting the heads off live chickens. Some say they are even intentionally wounded and have to perform field-surgery on themselves."

She must have looked sceptical because Michael continued with, "These are not exaggerations. The *Kaibiles* are truly fearsome. Since the civil war, some of them have been employed by the United Nations, ironically as peacekeepers and to counteract the drugs trade, but others have found much more profitable employment with *Los Zetas*. It is rumoured that they run secret training camps deep in the Petén jungle for recruits, maybe after what we have seen that includes members of *Mara Salvatrucha*."

His description of gang atrocities in Guatemala and especially the development of people trafficking, using the same supply routes forged for drug running, lasted the rest of the journey to Tikal. It was a cruel and evil underbelly to a world that repulsed her and throughout the description of *Los Zetas*' vile activities, images of the "Z" tattooed on Tom's neck kept forcing their way to the front of her mind.

They arrived at Tikal and Michael quickly climbed out, but before allowing the taxi to leave, he entreated her to abandon her search, "Please ask no more questions. These people think nothing of hurting, mutilating or destroying anyone that gets in their way and anything or anyone you might love."

With this shocking warning, he turned and was gone. Only when the taxi was on its way again did she realise that he had not asked her to stay in touch or to contact him again. Did her search mean she was persona non grata? Did these gangs instil that level of fear?

THIRTY-FOUR

Once back at the hotel, she paid the driver and retreated to her room. She was so confused. What should she think about Tom? The concern he had shown for her being lost in the forest was real enough, as was the passion he had shown the night before. Yes, he had lied to her, but his reasons made sense and surely he would be able to explain away the questions that still bothered her. She could not believe the man who had touched her so tenderly and held her so closely could have any connection with violent crime.

Neither Felipe nor Michael had suggested that members of *Los Zetas* used tattoos of the letter *Z* as gang insignia, despite important members of the gang claiming individual *Z* numbers. The *Z* on Tom's neck was nothing. It was *Mara Salvatrucha* who utilised tattoos as gang insignia, not *Los Zetas*.

Pushing these troubling thoughts aside, she remembered she had planned to contact the firm that carried out the repairs on Tikal. She found the number and phoned. A secretary, with reasonable English, passed her on to the manager, Señor Grasit, who was happy to help. He acknowledged that they had dealt with the repairs.

"It was quite a feather through our hat to win the contract for Tikal," he announced proudly, pressing a misshapen metaphor into service.

When she announced she was trying to track her sister through a photo taken there at that time, he assured her that no members of the public would have been permitted on-site during renovations because of health and safety issues. She explained that Hera might have been there in a formal capacity and that there were others in the picture she did not recognise as Hera's friends and wondered whether they might work for his company and if so whether he would be able to identify them.

The call ended with Señor Grasit suggesting that she email the picture to him and he would check them against his staff, all of whom he knew by sight. She thanked him and immediately took a picture of her photo and emailed it to him, with a brief covering message.

Despite Michael and Felipe's warnings to her, she was not particularly worried about her latest inquiries. She reasoned her low-key search for her sister could hardly attract anyone's interest. She was no threat to international or local gangs.

Whilst waiting for Señor Grasit's reply she updated her account of events in her notebook and finished just as the expected email arrived in her inbox.

The message stated that he did not recognise any of the people in the picture and was concerned with the injury to the person on the ground. He had checked his files and found that they had been on site for a month, but no one had been there between the 31st October, and 2nd of November, because of a public holiday for *Día de Muertos*. He could only assume that the photograph was taken then and that his firm had no liability for any injury during that time as the whole site had been cordoned off, and signs forbidding entry were clearly displayed, She acknowledged receipt and thanked him, before signing off.

She had only arrived in Guatemala six days ago and in that time she had discovered a mother, a sister, a lover and a culture permeated with suffering and sacrifice. She had survived a night in the jungle, a snake attack and a close encounter with a jaguar. Her search had revealed a world of unspeakable, drug cartel atrocities and a proud, persecuted people in a land of ancient cities lost in primordial jungle. It would be a colossal understatement to claim the adverts for Guatemala she had perused just a week before, had failed to do it justice!

She lay back on her bed, beneath the slowly rotating, mesmeric fan, and tried to be objective about what she knew and what she only feared or suspected: the photograph was pinned to one of three days, Fosse took it from scaffolding above the Temple of the Masks, and at least one of the individuals in the picture was a member of *MS-13*, a vicious criminal gang. Was Leonard Fosse there of his own volition? Why would he have this photo otherwise? Was that the last time Hera was seen? Tom's determined hunt for her would seem to indicate this was true. What was Tom's full involvement and could she believe everything he had claimed?

What next? She had less than four days left in Guatemala to find her sister. What could she possibly do in less than four days? Maybe as Hera had not been seen in Guatemala for a year she might as well continue the search from home. Who knew what *the Guardian's* resources might allow her to do?

She had no more leads here so what next? Most of her leads had arisen through dream world experiences; maybe, she should pursue that course of action however capricious and intangible it proved. After all, it had not only led her to identifying Tom but also to discovering Hera's concealed message at Uaxactun and finding one of the tattooed men from the photograph. The problem was that apart from her visit with Tom to Complex P at Tikal her spectral insights were not of her own volition. They seemed to need some external stimulus.

According to Tom, he had been held hostage with Hera at a lakeside settlement. She had also dreamt of this place and had little reason to doubt that it was where Tom claimed, Chicanná near Becan, in Mexico. Would it be worth travelling there and could she do it in the time still remaining? Maybe Chicanná would incite further visions? What other options were open to her?

Her deliberations were cut short by a knock on the door. She recognised the rhythmic sequence as characteristic of Tom and crossed to let him in.

Their greeting was intense and physical and concluded some thirty minutes later, hot and breathless, in the shower. But it was different from the night before. This had been a release where her body was fully involved but not her emotions. She had spent so much of her life compartmentalising aspects of her existence and unintentionally she was doing the same with Tom. Last night had been all-consuming, where the physical and the emotional, the desires and the needs had been as one. When they had made love, it was an epiphany. She had felt as if all pretence had been stripped away, emotions and desires laid bare. It was not a sensation she had ever experienced before. Today was different. Today the sex was an escape, a temporary respite for her doubts, but pretty damn good all the same.

They washed and dried each other. She dressed in fresh clothes whilst Tom sat on the bed with a towel draped modestly around his waist. He watched her dress and spotted her unusual teardrop pendant. She explained it was a good luck charm supposedly from her mother. Even while she was saying the word "mother", she wondered whether it had been her real mother's gift or that of her adoptive parent and did it make a difference?

"Does it bring you good fortune?" Tom enquired quite seriously.

"Well I found you didn't I?" she quipped.

"The ancient Maya placed huge store in gold and silver jewellery. They would have appreciated a teardrop encased in silver. They believed that silver was the tears of the moon and gold the sweat of the sun."

"That's both sad and beautiful," she replied. Her thoughts turned to her mother, Emily Argent. Had the name Argent anything to do with the pendant? Could a silver teardrop have been her mother's attempt to keep both her name and the heart-wrenching nature of her decision alive?

She finished dressing and began to recount her trip to Uaxactun and the discovery Hera's message but decided to refrain from mentioning the visit of the two tattooed men or the drums of yellowy white sediment.

Tom was initially reluctant to speak of his day. She pushed and he admitted that he had been to the Belize border, to Melchor de Mencos, the biggest of the border towns. He had gone to identify a body in the morgue. He had not told her where he was heading in case it was Hera. It was not. It was a girl in her twenties who superficially resembled Hera and whose body was found floating and bloated in the Mopan River. Tom's financial inducement with various Petén mortuaries for information on unidentified female cadavers was obviously still ongoing.

"What did she die of?" she asked, feeling guilty at distrusting Tom's actions and motives.

"They are not sure yet. They were going to carry out an autopsy later. Initial thoughts were a revenge killing. There seems to be a lot of tension between the Guatemalans and the Belizeans living there, with regular beatings and revenge killings, even though they have lived side-by-side for years."

Picking up his clothes and moving towards the door, Tom announced, "We need to talk about where we go next. I'll get dressed and if you like, we can try another restaurant. I promise it will be better than last night's. I provisionally booked us a table for eight." He blew her a kiss and left, wearing only his towelling loincloth, his clothes tucked beneath one arm.

She watched him through the window and the glances he was attracting from female guests savouring more than just their apéritifs. Her thoughts though were elsewhere. Tom had been to Melchor de Mencos, a place that had also cropped up more than once in her research. It was a recognised location for training *Kaibiles*, the elite military force recruited by *Los Zetas*. She roughly brushed her hair, annoyed at her pervasive doubts.

THIRTY-FIVE

Tom's chosen restaurant was set in a picturesque square dominated by colonial arches, towering, central kapok and a squat, twin belfry of a yellow washed church.

They chose a table outside in the square. Softly lit by a candle and the light from the open-shuttered, restaurant windows, it offered a view of the church where an evening service was drawing to a close. The congregation slowly filed out. Muted conversations, dark formal clothes and veils layered the steps in front of the church, while ranks of votive candles flickered in the subdued light beyond the open church door. The crowd mixed for a while then seeped away through different passages leading from the piazza: roads, alleyways and doors.

Only muted restaurant sounds and the harmonious chatter of diners remained, occasionally punctuated by the irritating, insect-like whines of scooters and three-wheeled taxis. Lulled by the atmosphere, her doubts seemed ridiculous, but she still did not ask him about the letter tattooed on the back of his neck.

Unlike the night before she was able to savour both the romantic setting and the meal. They joined other tourists ordering the Guatemala Taster Menu, an expansive array of small dishes. They stuck with the local beer, Gallo, and in contrast to the previous evening, luxuriated in the experience. The enchanting atmosphere seemed so at odds with her experiences earlier that day. It was hard to believe both were real.

They ate, drank and talked about themselves for the best part of three hours. Tom's previous revelations allowed him to chat freely about his childhood. He also told her about his current employment with Texas University in Austin. He had persuaded them to grant him a year's sabbatical from the Latin American Studies course, nominally to prepare a new course on Maya history. He was supposed to be doing the groundwork for future, field-study expeditions to attract potential undergraduates.

She felt ridiculous remembering how she had taken on the role of a guide at Tikal when he obviously knew the place far better than she did. It also explained how he had swiftly matched the image in her photograph to Tikal. Her questions and concerns were gradually being answered without any need to confront Tom directly and risk ruining their relationship. What she had with him was something special and needed to be nurtured.

She chatted about her upbringing and reflected on how different it might have been if she had not been separated from her twin sister and whether she should search for her real mother. Tom showed concern for her lost family and even extended his sympathy to her estranged guardian and the unfortunate nature of her death. It was only later that she wondered when she had told him that her so-called aunt had died from a broken neck. He had read the letter back in her flat and knew of her poor health, but she could not remember telling him that her aunt had actually died or the violent nature of the death.

Over the vividly coloured desert, containing such unknown fruit as nispero, zapola mamey and jocote, she explained her desire to travel to Chicanná. Half expecting an outright rejection, considering the distance involved, she was surprised by his positive reaction. Like her, he also believed it might act as the catalyst to her psychic connection with her sister.

He calculated the road trip was getting on for three hundred miles either way and would be difficult to tackle in a single day. The bus option would initially skirt the forest before heading out east through Belize to the Caribbean Sea and then north towards Belize City and a change of buses. From there they would cross into Mexico and probably have yet another change at Chetumal on the Yucatan Peninsular for the final seventy miles west to Chicanná. The long, tedious journey would involve delays at borders and every bus depot. They did not have enough time.

As an alternative, he suggested that they flew from Santa Elena directly to Chetumal in Mexico and then he could hire a car for the last stretch to Chicanná. Although there were no regular flights between the two airports, he knew that there were a number of small planes that could be chartered for a reasonable price. She was uncertain about the expense, but he put her mind at rest informing her that he would cover the cost, or at least his university would.

They chattered until the restaurant was almost deserted and the waiters hovered nearby anticipating their departure and a tip reflective of their length meal. They seemed pleased with whatever Tom left and were chatting animatedly as she and Tom pushed their chairs back, rose, and arm-in-arm left the square.

By the time they reached the hotel, it was too late for any travel arrangements to be made and they immediately retired to her room.

The sex was no less passionate than before but tender and languid. Slowly and sensually they undressed each other, touched, stroked and explored each other's body. He thrilled her with his tongue: probing, flickering, warm and soft, building her desire. She then took him in her mouth and drew him to full firmness, moistened him and then sitting astride, drew him in.

Their mutual, shared rhythm was slow and easy. She allowed her body to gently rise and fall, feeling him inside, an essential part of her. When they came together it was drawn out and triumphal and afterwards they lay, folded together, the fan above cooling their heated bodies..

THIRTY-SIX

Yet again, Tom had disappeared before she surfaced. She wished they could have shared the morning, waking slowly together, but knew he was anxious to sort out their flight to Chetumal.

She showered, dressed and decided to wait until his return for breakfast. Sitting outside her room, she logged on to her laptop. Wondering what Tom's public persona was like, she typed in Texas University and searched through lecturers until she found his name, Tomas Webster, lecturer in Latin American Studies. Unfortunately his profile, unlike other staff, did not have an accompanying photo. The site stated that he was on sabbatical. She changed her search to check the distances they were planning on covering today and the route. Tom had been spot on with both his estimation of distance and the road connections.

It was eight o'clock and still no sign of her man. She checked her email and found another message from Anthony. She noted, unlike previous correspondence, he was using his personal email account and not that of the newspaper.

The message was disturbing. Anthony had confidential news. The police had made progress with their investigation into the house fire. It was definitely arson, started sometime on the Sunday night, employing an unusual fire accelerant that was difficult to trace. The fire patterns had not originally suggested arson, with no irregularities to the burn pattern, but they had sent off samples for gas chromatography-mass spectrometry analysis. The presence of an advanced toluene-based accelerant, with none of the usual paint thinner smells or typical fire patterns, indicated a professional job. Use of this particular accelerant had alerted the Security Services.

It was when their investigations connected the fire with Leonard Fosse that alarms first started ringing and the reason they had revisited the cause of the fire for detailed scientific analysis. He was already on their yellow list for involvement with an international crime syndicate. Two years ago he had been recorded, by the CIA, attending a meeting in Nuevo Laredo, Mexico, with leading figures of the *Los Zetas* cartel.

The email continued to include various disturbing details about *Los Zetas* that she already knew. They had managed to trace a foreign account, belonging to Leonard Fosse, which held a considerable sum of money. This in turn had been traced back to an account in Mexico.

Their latest thinking was that his death might not have been an accident and there was a request to exhume his body for a detailed autopsy. The fire at his house might have been to dispose of some form of evidence, potentially photographic, considering the nature of Mr Fosse's profession.

Anthony explained that the newspaper was given access to this information because it was considered advantageous to release specific details in the hope of eliciting further information about the secretive Mr Fosse. The Security Services believed that it might jog local memories about Fosse's more recent activities or people he might have been seen with.

The Mexican bank account seemed to explain Fosse's presence with *MS-13* at Tikal but not why a successful photographer with an apparently strong moral compass, considering his photographic history, allowed himself to get involved with such people?

Another line of enquiry, they wanted to pursue was to trace a man present at the scene of the fire, calling himself Tom Webster. This was the main point of Anthony's private communiqué and the subject of his concluding lines.

"I explained to two very courteous gentlemen that you had thought Tom Webster worked for the fire service and that he had escorted you to your leaving do. I also mentioned that for some reason you had asked me to check on him. I don't think there is anything to worry about, but they would like to have a brief chat with you when you return. Try not to worry and enjoy the rest of your holiday."

There was no mention of the story she had told Anthony she was working on. He obviously expected "the courteous gentlemen" would be checking his correspondence! Disturbed and perplexed by the new development, she signed off.

As she closed the screen, Tom was crossing the courtyard towards her, his characteristic closed mouth smile signalling positive news.

She considered telling him about the email but did not want to worry him. There would be time to deal with that later. She only had three more days in Guatemala and was determined to do her best for Hera and make the most of Tom before she left. They had not talked about what would happen to them when she returned home. Her life was changing and she could not see how Tom, with his job at an American university, could fit into it, yet she was not prepared to just walk away and leave it like other holiday romances.

She watched him approach, linen jacket hanging off broad shoulders, crisp, white shirt, neatly pressed chinos and matching deck shoes. The immaculate impression could, once more, have materialised from an advertising billboard. She had never felt about a man as she did about Tom. How she would love to flaunt him at one of those university reunions.

Surely when one met someone who made you feel the way he did, aroused you the way he could, someone who made you laugh and who was strong when you felt weak, such a man was worth serious time and effort. It was an odd sensation but she felt complete with him by her side.

Her romantic thoughts were curtailed by Tom's arrival with the news that he had sorted out their transport. It was ready to take them as soon as they could get to the airport.

They returned to their respective rooms and she quickly packed the things needed for the day: passport, water bottle, mosquito spray and a change of clothes for any hiking they might do. They met down in the foyer where Tom was picking up a packed breakfast he had ordered earlier.

Outside, a pre-booked taxi waited. She was continually impressed with his organisational abilities. With his linguistic capabilities and range of contacts, there seemed very little that he could not organise at the shortest notice. As if to confirm this judgement he let her know on the brief journey to the airport that he had already sorted out a car from Chetumal airport.

They pulled up opposite departures at Flores' airport, Mundo Maya International, a low, metal and glass structure. Belize's national airline, Tropic Air, ran daily flights from Flores to Belize City, but they did not connect to Chetumal, the nearest Mexican city to Chicanná, just over the Mexican border. Tom's idea for a direct, private chartered flight would therefore save time, bypassing Belize altogether and any cross border regulations that would have dragged out their journey time even more.

Mundo Maya was an international airport and so there were passport formalities to undergo, but they proved surprisingly cursory for a private flight. Within half an hour she and Tom were boarding a disconcertingly small, 9-seater plane, which according to the pilot was a Cessna 208 Caravan. The faint shadow of FedEx's two-tone logo attested to its previous incarnation. She had never flown in something so small and had never even dreamed of hiring a private jet.

A glance from the plane's steps to the northeast, the direction they were heading, was not auspicious. Storm clouds were gathering in the distance.

By ten they were airborne and flying over Lake Petén Itzá. The teal coloured shallows washed into a Prussian blue as the lake's increasing depth absorbed more light. From the air, the lake's outline resembled a cowboy-style moustache with Flores a crumb near the bottom of the right-hand droop. She spotted a range of pleasure boats and working vessels, differentiated by their paintwork.

Then they passed over the opposite shore and were flying above fields: cut, burnt and claimed in oblong blocks from the jungle. Stretches of intensely green forest that had survived the incursion of farms, stood out clearly against the khaki, camouflage slabs of cultivated ground. Right angles and straight lines dominated the geometry of the earth below, while off-white, thread-like tracks squirmed between the cultivated areas. Intermittent dwellings dotted the human landscape, small square dots in vast oblong fields, providing some sense of perspective.

The farmlands reluctantly gave way to the jungle, which she noticed was not a uniform colour. At altitude, the forest took on various hues, but not the panoply it did from ground level. The fern green was mottled with darker, hunter green blemishes that might have indicated valleys or watercourses. Strange, small bald spots marked their passage, some were steep, rocky outcrops devoid of trees and others were inexplicable instances of forest alopecia.

Tom returned from discussing their flight with the pilot and interrupted her aerial appreciation of the landscape. "I'm afraid we're in for a bumpy ride. The pilot says there's some turbulence ahead. There's a storm brewing. We need to belt up and it might be an idea to lay off the breakfast until we're through." He smiled reassuringly and took the seat across the aisle from her. She reached across taking his hand and turned back to the window just as they approached Tikal.

The pilot was making a point of flying close to the ruins to give them a superb view of the scale and situation of the Maya temples. The main plaza dominated by the two towering pyramids and perimeter structures were clear of trees. Vegetation encroached on all other monuments. A number of other ceremonial buildings thrust through the greenery from within the confines of the forest, revealing the scale of the site. The straight lines and symmetry of human design, so loved by the Maya, was clearly evident from their bird's eye perspective.

They flew on over the vast green realm, climbing and turning away from the road linking Tikal to Uaxactun. She started to gain a sense of the lost worlds Hera had been trying to reconnect. This 150,000 square kilometre eco-region, spilling into three different countries, hid the most awe-inspiring flora and fauna, archaeology and history, and if Michael was right, *Los Zetas* training camps and supply routes.

The plane was still climbing, attempting to rise above the storm that loomed ahead. The towering cumulonimbus was a mass of dark grey clouds spiralling up above the forest to an anvil of intense blackness. Their flight path soon submerged them in cloud cover. As with the colours of the lake, the lighter shades were soon engulfed and devoured by the darker ones. The cabin lights came on as day was snuffed out and the plane began to be buffeted like some child's toy.

The rain came not as intermittent drops, gradually increasing in intensity, but in a torrent battering at the windows and fuselage. Sheet lighting briefly illuminated the billowing menace barring their way, whilst fork lightning slashed between cloud masses, creating a stroboscopic effect. She had never seen so much lightning, so close together.

It was as if the Gods of the Ancients were warring in the heavens; deafening thunder shook the small craft. Her grip on Tom's hand tightened. She could not believe this flying tin can could survive such monstrous, firmamental rage.

The plane dropped, tilted, climbed and then plunged again and with it her stomach. Thunder drowned out the struggling whine of the single-engine. Lightning flashes streaked the sky ahead like veins, revealing a bulging head of ink-black ferocity. It was the face of Huracan, the Maya god of storms: angered, omnipotent and terrifying. His roar drowned out her very thoughts.

She closed her eyes and felt the plane smash into the tomb-black mass, a speck of impotence confronting unbelievable dark forces. Her closed eyelids were merely tracing paper to the spikes of lightning trying

220

to spear the plane and her body, doll-like in the hands of a careless child, snapped back and forward as the plane was flung to and fro.

And then, as abruptly as they had confronted the storm, it was gone. The plane, remarkably still airborne, was steady on its course and the engine's regular hum once more provided a reassuring soundscape. She opened her eyes and the skies outside were clear. She felt Tom disengage his hand and turned to see him rubbing red weals where her nails had cut into his palm.

"Our pilot wasn't kidding," he laughed. "Let's hope we don't have to go through that on the way back. Are you ok?" She nodded not trusting herself to answer quite yet.

THIRTY-SEVEN

They landed to the south of Chetumal under clear skies. Hugging an expansive bay, the city appeared fairly modern, a result of a 1950s hurricane, inoffensively named Janet. They descended from the plane along with the pilot who seemed unperturbed by the storm they had just passed through. At the terminal they left him, slipping unchallenged through passport control and out of the airport.

A cadaverous looking man was waiting for them with the keys for their hired vehicle. Tom explained that the rental agency he used was not based at the airport, so cars were delivered upon your arrival. The vehicle was a four-wheel drive, Jeep Wrangler in pristine condition. He exchanged some hurried words in Spanish with the gaunt man, before taking the keys. They left immediately without checking the vehicle or filling in any paperwork.

As they sped along the airport access road towards the highway, she questioned the transaction. Her experience of car hire was limited, but she knew that typically you checked the vehicle for scratches before departing and then you signed a contract. Tom explained that his university had an arrangement with the rental company to allow for quick pick-ups. She accepted the explanation and settled down to enjoy the journey and as her stomach was settling, to catch up on breakfast.

It was an uneventful drive on a straight, two-lane highway cutting across scrubby wasteland, past occasional, unremarkable settlements. Traffic was minimal and the seventy-five miles was covered in little more than an hour. A right turn to Becan signalled they were approaching their destination. Nearby a small hotel and restaurant, the first they had seen for a while, were obviously angling for the passing tourist trade.

The left turn to Chicanná quickly became a single, rutted track and after only five hundred metres ended in an uneven, deserted parking lot. As they pulled up near the entrance to the complex, Tom explained the name Chicanná meant House of the Serpent Mouth. The central building of the complex boasted a doorway resembling the open mouth of a giant snake and had given rise to its name. The elaborate entrance had supposedly enabled priests to enter the underworld to conduct their grisly rituals.

They locked the jeep and walked through the deserted ruins towards the eponymous temple. As they drew near, two glaring eyes carved into a lintel stared at them from above stone fangs. Tom removed a detailed map from his backpack and they sat on the low steps in front of the doorway considering their options.

He thought the armed men had escorted them out to the west but was not certain. He calculated the lake where they were held was within an hour and a half march. Accordingly, they set the radius for their search at five miles. Considering the winding nature of trails, it was more likely only half that distance had been covered in any single direction.

The map was scattered with various bodies of water of differing sizes and shapes. Only those within the radius and large enough to land a seaplane were left in the mix.

The road from Chetumal running east to west and a route from north to south intersected six miles to their east and split the forest into quadrants. Tom had not crossed a road during the forced march, which meant their search was restricted to the southwest quadrant. Within that area, there were about twenty bodies of water of which only a handful appeared of sufficient scale to land a seaplane. They excluded the nearest lakes and those near cultivated land and the choice became easier.

One lake stood out from the rest, being far larger and more immersed in the forest than the others. The nameless lake, complete with island, was a few miles directly southwest of them. She felt that once on route, she would instinctively know if it was the path Hera had taken.

Ultra wary, after her last nightmarish excursion into the jungle, she double-checked they had all the necessary provisions and then changed into her walking gear. Tom took a reading from a compass and then they were ready.

Their path ominously set off directly through the snake's jaws, the entrance to hell. The serpent's unblinking eyes watched them climb the steps and approach its gaping mouth. They passed beneath the fangs and out into the jungle beyond. The trail formed the snake's body extending from the head and twisting back into the trees.

The jungle soon closed around them and the continuous soundscape of insects and birds disconcertingly recalled her time alone near Yaxha. She stayed in Tom's wake, two steps behind, concentrating on the path in an attempt to stave off her fears. From time to time he stopped to see if she was all right or to have a drink from their water bottles and to check on their bearing. At certain points the track forked and Tom was careful to take a reading at each junction, calculating how far they had come.

Despite the thick undergrowth either side of the track, their path was relatively clear and they made steady progress arriving at the lake in just over an hour. Neither Tom nor she had recognised anything on the trail. The heat and humidity were getting to her and starting to make her feel they were wasting their time. Finally, they emerged from the trees to be confronted by a large stretch of water. The lake, with a small, forested island, was devoid of both huts and pier.

They stopped, examined the map and debated which way to continue. She felt they should continue north around the head of the lake, where they might be afforded views down its full length. Tom thought they should turn south, as that was the side they would have approached, from

Chicanná. He prevailed and they followed a rough track around the eastern edge of the lake.

The gap between the shore and island closed to not much more than throwing distance. It was definitely not the expanse of water she recalled from her dream. As they continued, the trees on the island thinned to reveal the full width of the lake, some two hundred metres. It was as if curtains had been drawn back and a vista exposed, one that she recognised.

Tom suddenly stopped and pointed out a structure still some distance ahead. A jetty protruded from the shore into the lake. Chameleon-like, it merged with the water beyond. She felt her pulse quicken. There was no mistaking the place now. Even though they were approaching from a different angle, the mottled green jetty jutting from a stony shoreline was the one from her dream. Any buildings, pressed back into the trees, were still concealed from them.

The enormity of their actions and possible consequences suddenly struck her and she stopped dead. Tom was ahead of her and did not realise until he had gained some distance. He turned, saw she was not moving and returned at a run, thinking something untoward had happened.

"What if the kidnappers are still there? They might have already seen us coming. We can't just walk into their camp," she spluttered.

"I don't think we need to worry," Tom replied calmly. "As the plane has gone, I would think it's deserted. The place is too close to Chicanná to be a permanent base. Look, if it makes you feel easier I will go on ahead and check."

She refused to be left alone again and they warily continued together. Hesitating in the tree cover at the edge of the open ground, they scanned the apparently deserted camp. They could now see the half dozen huts and the lookout tower set back into the trees. The tower no longer had the antennae or satellite dish and the whole place had a sense of abandonment. The lakeside setting had returned to nature.

A flicker of movement between two of the huts caught their eyes and both froze. A reddish-brown stag tentatively broke cover. Broad, branching antlers swished the air as he sensed their presence. He turned towards them, black nosed and black-eyed, stock still, testing the air, alert to any threat. Tom took a step forward and the majestic beast turned, flicked his tail to expose a white stripe and bounded for cover. The deer's presence was the clearest indication yet that the camp was deserted.

Cautiously they worked their way around the huts, which contained little more than rough bunks, basic tables and chairs. The only sign of inhabitants were the spiders' webs. Their search of each cabin was cursory until they moved deeper into the forest and found a corrugated iron warehouse with padlocked door and a solid, wooden building, bolted from outside. Tom tried the door. It opened easily.

The dappled sun of the forest streamed in revealing four sets of bunks, a trestle table and stools. The boarded floor was stained and knot-ridden. Unlike the other huts, there were no windows, shelves or cupboards. The only light, apart from what streamed through the door, were narrow bands penetrating the pencil-thin cracks between the horizontal plank walls. Tom acknowledged that this was where they had been held before suggesting that she might do better left on her own as at Tikal. He would be close by, checking the warehouse.

Alone in the gloom, she peered at the walls. The whole place was about five metres square and smelt fusty with disuse. She found her torch and explored the walls, then the bunks, tables and stools just in case another message had been left for her to find. There were no signs, no marks, nothing of any interest. She sat on one of the stools, back to the door, closed her eyes and tried to recall her dream. This was the hut. She remembered it clearly from her dream but nothing materialised. Outside she could hear Tom moving around, trying to gain access to the warehouse she supposed.

Ten minutes passed and the noises outside had ceased. She sensed the presence of people having been here, but that was all. There were secrets here but something was protecting them or were they protecting her from

226

the secrets?

Frustrated she gave up and left the hut. Tom was nowhere to be seen. A surge of panic welled up inside her. She closed the door and hurriedly made her way back through the trees. There to her relief was Tom, sitting on the dock, looking out over the lake. He seemed to be talking into his phone, but as she approached, he moved it away from his head and held it in different positions as if attempting to get a signal.

"It's useless. I wanted to contact our pilot to say we are on the way back, but I can't get a signal," he said as he climbed to his feet and came to meet her on the shore. "Any luck? Did you sense anything?" he asked. At her negative response, he seemed nonplussed. "I hoped this place would stir some kind of psychic memories for you."

His voice seemed to have taken on a negative quality, a slight derisive edge she had not registered before. They were both tired and frustrated, that was all.

"I thought you'd be able to sense something," he repeated, before turning and starting for the forest. "We can't spend any more time here if we want to get back tonight," he said over his shoulder, continuing to walk away from her.

She was reluctant to leave so quickly. Hera had been a captive in that hut for several days and would have left some kind of clue or warning. It was just too indistinct, nothing more than a vague tingling at the edge of her consciousness. Fearful of being left alone, she jogged to catch up with Tom who had already reached the edge of the clearing.

THIRTY-EIGHT

He was quiet and unresponsive during the hasty walk back through the forest and by the time they arrived at the Jeep she was gasping for a drink.

Tom drove quickly and still did not seem to want to talk. She supposed that, like her, he was disheartened. All this way and for what? She knew Hera's group had been held by the lake, so why no signs, no visions, no messages? There had been something there, something she was supposed to understand, but what? She sat back and contemplated the road as they ate up the miles.

Tom's mood had darkened from when she found him with the phone on the jetty and did not seem to improve with the journey, despite all her efforts to lift the atmosphere. To make things worse, about a third of the way back, the Jeep started to pull to one side. Tom stopped, climbed out and swore. She supposed it was swearing, just not a word she knew. It crossed her mind to wonder whether Latin American invective was a module on the course he taught.

The lesson in exotic bad language continued as Tom vainly looked for a jack. His final abusive words returned to English, possibly for her benefit. "That arsehole has forgotten to reattach the jack to the roll bar. The brackets are there but no fucking jack." She had not heard Tom swear before, well not in English and it had a surprising effect. It was not that the words shocked her but his use of them and the anger in the delivery. Like seeing a kind-hearted person do something spiteful, it made you wonder what else were they capable of?

"There's a small town, Nicholas Bravo, not far ahead. We can change the tyre there," he informed her as he climbed behind the wheel. They limped on for the next mile while she envisioned the sorry state the tyre would be in by the time they arrived but knew better than to say anything.

The town, built on a grid, was relatively quiet. They painfully drove over mountainous speed bumps, down the tree-lined, central avenue. The road sank below banks on either side, whilst a formal guard of white emblazoned trees marked their uncomfortable progress. Brightly painted, single storey, concrete buildings lined up behind the trees. An expressionless old man, in a checked shirt and straw hat, sat on a stuffed sack at the side of the road and watched them pass. They bumped along towards a military statue lording it on a plinth in the centre of a traffic island.

"One of our heroes, Nicholas Bravo, he fought both the Spanish and the Americans," Tom distractedly noted, his eyes scanning the road ahead for garages.

They had almost driven through the sleepy town when they spotted a gas station. Tom pulled the clunking vehicle over, away from the pump area and went to see if they had a jack. She removed her water bottle from her pack and in frustration found it had been lying in the sun. Although there was adequate water, it was lukewarm and had developed a brackish taste.

Tom returned with a jack and immediately got to work. She climbed out. The tyre, as she had imagined, was wrecked. Her offer of help brusquely rejected, she stepped over to the small store attached to the garage to see if she could find something cold to drink.

The shop, cooled by two ceiling fans, had several rows of shelves scattered with sweets, crisps, drinks and assorted tins and packets. Glancing around, the store appeared deserted. The wooden counter with the cash till was unattended. She found the shelf with a muddled assortment of hyper-vivid soft drinks. Unfortunately, they were not chilled, but they had to be more palatable than the water in the car. The cans and bottles filled two shelves and she squatted down to see what exotic concoctions might be hidden further back. She was aware of people entering from a door at the back of the shop but did not stand up. Her eyes were locked on a solitary, clear bottle tucked behind the colas.

The two people she heard emerge were behaving strangely. She could overhear them, near the front of the shop, a man and a woman whispering intently. They spoke rapidly in Spanish and the tension in their voices was palpable. She felt embarrassed to reveal herself now, in the middle of some marital dispute. The more she listened the more distressed the woman seemed to become while the man sounded increasingly het up. The woman kept repeating, "*Es él!*" The man seemed to agree, but his anger did not abate.

She peered around the shelf and noticed they were arguing about something outside. The middle-aged couple were short, dark-haired and dark-skinned. They stood in the shadows at an angle from the window, so as not to be seen from the forecourt or the road. She was right; the woman seemed distressed and was repeatedly gesturing at something outside. The man grabbed her shoulders and drew her further away from the window as he spat out a rapid stream of words.

The altercation made no sense to her, although odd words were within her limited Spanish vocabulary and occasional phrases reminded her of recent conversations. She picked up various pronouns, prepositions and conjunctions but was lost with the verbs and the adjectives, although, "*Guate*" and "*policía*" seemed to play significant roles in the exchange. The man finished with a tone that brooked no challenge. She ducked down again as the two retraced their path, down the aisle next to hers, to the door at the back. Their exit provided her with the opportunity to stand up, additive-soaked drink in hand.

Tom entered the shop. "It's fixed, we can be on our way. Have you got what you need?" She nodded, holding up the bottle and whist Tom tried to find someone to take the jack and to pay for her drink; she stared out of the window. What had the couple been looking at? The petrol station was deserted. Three lonely looking pumps parallel with each other stood under a shiny, metal canopy in the middle of a large forecourt. The road was devoid of vehicles and on the other side was an unmetalled pull-off with an empty bus stop. Maybe they had seen someone get on or off a bus? Their Jeep, now roadworthy again, was the only vehicle in sight.

Tom returned with the man she had seen arguing. The man had lost his passionate intensity and now seemed timid. His eyes were cast down and his voice was a muted monotone. He took the jack refusing any payment. She tried to pay for the drink but only had pounds and quetzals. Fortunately. Tom managed to dig out a fifty Peso note. The man fumbled some change and they were soon back in the Jeep.

Tom's mood had lightened. The delay had not been long enough to warrant a stopover in Mexico and as they reached the outskirts of Chetumal he was on his phone again to the pilot, organising a departure time. The jeep was left in the parking lot, with the keys hidden in the glove compartment. The flight was pleasantly uneventful and they were back at Flores soon after dusk.

She realised as they walked into the hotel just how hungry she was. A late breakfast had been her only proper sustenance and she was not aware of Tom having eaten anything. They both felt an early dinner was called for and decided to freshen up and return to the same restaurant as the night before. At the top of the stairs, they kissed, arranging to meet downstairs in thirty minutes.

THIRTY-NINE

She knew something was wrong as soon as she saw Tom. He was at her door well before the half-hour had elapsed. Freshly showered and dressed he looked ready for their evening together, but his face told a different story.

Another call had come through from the morgue at Melchor de Mencos. Another dark-haired, Caucasian girl of about the right age, without any id, was lying unclaimed in their freezer. He was expected there in ninety minutes. He tried to persuade her that it was unlikely to be Hera, but his anxiety was evident and his abrupt, unsmiling departure was ominous.

Left to her own devices she decided to eat at the hotel. She felt resentful: her usual table was already occupied, Tom had deserted her and the day had proved a waste of time. Somehow she instinctively knew the body would not be her sister's and therefore did not feel overly concerned on that score and neither did she feel guilty for not insisting on accompanying him to the morgue.

She sat in the corner of the courtyard and ate without much thought for what she consumed. Why had Chicanná and the deserted lake camp refused to offer up any clues? She finished her meal but remained at the table, deep in thought. She turned away the waitress who came to see if she wanted a dessert and sat, cradling a beer, listening to a conversation nearby.

An American couple were arguing about politics and the election of their local Congressman. She picked up that the two-year electoral cycle was coming to an end and there were two candidates in the running for their district, their current member of the House of Representatives and a newcomer, a decorated general. The discussion became quite heated round the premise, 'better the devil you know'. The articulate lady was all for the experienced, resident Congressman despite his dubious financial dealings. Her verbally taxed partner wanted the new boy on the block, justifying his choice with, "He's a man of action and one of our country's heroes."

The discussion continued, but she had stopped listening. She knew something had been bothering her and now she realised what it was. It was that phrase, "one of our country's heroes." She had heard it earlier today, but where? Then it came to her. It was when they had driven through Nicholas Bravo and had passed the town statue. Tom had said, "One of our heroes." It was not the choice of noun, "heroes" which perturbed her but the use of the possessive pronoun "our". Tom had called the Mexican general, Nicholas Bravo, "our". Surely his Latin American Studies had not made him feel that possessive about famous Mexicans? She returned to her room and logged on.

Tom's use of the possessive pronoun recalled the strange experience at the filling station. She had initially thought the furtive couple was discussing someone getting on or off a bus because there was nobody in sight when she glanced through the windows. This though would not have been the case. When they were busy arguing there would have seen someone outside. They would have seen Tom. He had been replacing the wheel directly outside their shop window.

She recalled some of the man's tense words including, "*Guate*" and "*Policía*" and started to search. It turned out *Guate* was the locals' name for Guatemala City. A number of the websites she had come across previously, reappeared. At last, she found the one Felipe had mentioned, The Guatemalan National Police Historical Archives, abbreviated to

233

A.H.P.N. Discovered in 2005 in an abandoned, munitions depot, they spanned one hundred years and were over eighty million pages in length. Not all had been digitalised but much had. She started to search for the most recent records.

Her phone rang and disturbed her research. The call was from Tom. He sounded frustrated. The morgue was closed by the time he had arrived and would not open again until the following morning. He was going to stay the night and return as soon as he could gain access tomorrow morning. He had an idea but wanted to discuss it with her personally. They exchanged hushed intimacies, involving mutual desires and then rang off.

Whilst Tom had been arousing her with his words, the laptop had carried on searching the A.P.H.N. site and it had now finished. Her search for Tomas Webster had come up with a number of hits. She opened the first one and to her absolute horror, the man she had just been whispering sexually provocative entreaties to, was staring out from the screen.

His photograph was in the top corner of a police registration document for membership of Guatemala City Police Department. It showed a younger, stony-faced Tom. She ran the document through Babel Fish and the translation revealed Tom's age, physical statistics, educational background and nationality. He had joint American/Guatemalan citizenship. Most of his background details, merely listed here, accorded with what he had told her: born in Vermont in 1985, a degree from Liverpool University, post-graduate qualifications from North Carolina. The other details seemed to be test results, scores and his official police number.

The next few hours were some of the most painful she could remember. Tom's career with the police force had obviously flourished. His name appeared in various glowing reports detailing typical police cases involving violence, theft, rape and murder but then started to turn up on less common assignments: dispersing rallies, pursuing political insurgents, dismantling anti-government movements. His career seemed to have moved into covert operations.

She worked into the night, slowly sifting through each file and reference, tracking Tom's clandestine career: every reference a denial of the man she thought she knew, each case file another laceration to her overwrought emotions. The man it painted was not the one she knew. Physically he was the same, but the things he had done were the actions of someone she did not recognise. The last file that the search engine traced was the most troubling. It was a file reporting Tom's successful passage through the *Kaibiles* training at *El Infierno,* Hell, in the municipality of Melchor de Mencos. A proud picture of him in maroon beret and camouflage combat gear dominated the page. She felt sick. The bile rose in her throat and she rushed to the bathroom and threw up.

Her world made no sense. What was happening to her? She had no idea what to feel or believe. Almost overnight she had gained a mother, sister and a lover. The first had deserted her, the second could not be found and the last was a lying stranger! The world span and she vomited again.

It was sometime later before she was able to move away from the toilet and stumble back to the bedroom. Huddled at the open window she stared out at the slab of darkness over the courtyard. She would not let circumstances crush her. Why should she be the victim? She was in a country whose history was full of victims, but she was only a visitor.

Retrieving the bottle of water from beside her bed, she took a large mouthful and returned to the bathroom to splash cold water over her face. The cool water washed away some of the self-pity. She returned to the window and the slight breeze to try and cool her over-heated thoughts.

The couple at the petrol station had obviously recognised Tom from their past. Their use of the locals' expression for Guatemala City seemed to imply they had once lived there and whatever role Tom had performed at that time, they were still in fear of him.

She opened up her notebook and started to jot down key points and questions, a process that had always concentrated her mind:

1. Hera was her identical twin and had disappeared a year ago, whilst

mapping Guatemalan ruins. Was she still alive and hiding? Tom evidently thought so.

2. Tomas Webster, of dual American/Guatemalan nationality, had been searching for her sister ever since. Why? His protestations of guilt at having involved Hera no longer seemed a plausible cause for his hunt, therefore he needed to find her for something she had or knew.

3. Tom qualified in Latin American Studies and then enlisted with the Guatemalan Police force, and specialised in covert operations before qualifying for the *Kaibiles*. He was remembered and feared from his time in Guatemala City. Was he still a registered *Kaibil*, deep undercover, or had he sold out to a crime syndicate?

4. He was listed as a lecturer at the University of Texas yet there was no picture of him. Was that a real job? A cover story? Was it even him?

5. Leonard Fosse, apparently hired by a Mexican drug cartel, had recorded Tom and Hera together at Tikal. For what purpose?

6. The repellent individuals in Fosse's photograph included members of *MS-13*. What did this notorious gang want with her sister? And why had they kidnapped her and then let her go? How was Tom connected to them?

7. The Petén district was traditionally *Los Zetas* territory. Was *MS-13* working for *Los Zetas*? If so did her release in Guatemala City have anything to do with *Los Zetas* instructions?

8. Leaders of *Los Zetas* were designated specific Z numbers. Did Tom's Z tattoo mean anything? Did it implicate him in that organisation or was it part of a disguise for an undercover operation?

She went to find her cardboard role with the copy of the original photograph, but it was gone. She had left it lying on the bedside table and it was no longer there. She could not even remember when she had last seen it. Had it been there that morning or the previous night? At least she had the original copy back at her flat and the scan saved on *the Gazette* hard drive.

Then she remembered the break-in and vandalism. Anthony had said they were not sure of what was missing but that the computers had been tampered with. She knew, without a doubt, the digital copy of the photo had been the target. The image had been wiped from *the Gazette's* records, scrubbed from her laptop and any copies incinerated at Leonard Fosse's house. She guessed that when she arrived home, her flat would also have been broken in to and the original photograph stolen. Only the copy she had emailed to the restoration company remained. Tom knew of the different copies and could have accessed them all, either on his own or with help. Did that mean he was also the person behind the arson attack? The police believed it to be a professional job and surely that was an element of the *Kaibiles* extensive training.

All the facts were pulling her in one direction. Tom was trying to destroy any evidence that linked him or Hera to the gang members caught in the photograph. His success in the police force had been with covert operations. If he was still undercover, it might explain the patchwork of lies that he had stitched together. Was his involvement with gangs that of an agent infiltrating their sordid world? The secret services in England had information on Fosse's involvement with Mexican crime syndicates. Did Tom have anything to do with that?

Were all the lies and deception essential in extricating himself and Hera from some kind of undercover operation? If Michael was right, gang vengeance would target not only Tom but also everyone he cared about. Hera might be in as much danger as him if he was ever uncovered as a traitor.

It was a possibility, but not the only one. However intense her feelings for Tom were, she had to remain objective. Just as likely was the scenario that Hera had or knew something detrimental to *MS-13* or *Los Zetas* and Tom was working for the cartels to regain or destroy that evidence.

As he was still searching for her sister, it was self-evident Hera had not yet been found and gave ample reason for her disappearance and concealment. Only an organisation with considerable financial resources, few scruples and an alternative agenda would pursue Hera in the ruthless manner Tom had. Therefore Tom must be working for some organisation other than Texas University. What kind of games was he playing and exactly how dangerous were they?

A wave of self-pity welled up again as she thought of how she had been duped. No wonder he was fit and not affected by the heat and humidity, not because he was a fireman, neither because he revelled in the outdoor life, but because he had been trained by one of the most extreme, specialist military forces in the world. He was able to organise planes and cars at the drop of a hat, because of his contacts.

He had shown he was prepared to pursue any means to find Hera. Was that what she had sensed earlier at the lake, but had been unable to pin down, Tom's real agenda? Christ, had he spiked her drinks the night her emails vanished? Shit, he had even known about the nature of her guardian's death, surely he could not have been involved with that? Yet, she remembered how he had delved for details about her background and had even commented on her aunt's address. Had he visited her aunt in search of clues to Hera's whereabouts? It would explain why her papers were uncharacteristically scattered around the house as if she was desperately being forced to search for something.

No, that was ridiculous. If he had deleted her emails he would have read about her aunt's death and anyway a trained killer and experienced undercover operative, which is what she now had to accept Tom was or had been, would not need to resort to violence with an old lady. The professional manner in which evidence at Fosse's house, *the Gazette* and on her computer had been eradicated without risking anybody getting hurt showed that was not his game. But then she came back to the same question. Exactly what was his game? Just because he had left a shocking part of his history untold did not make him a monster or did it?

Who was Tom? According to Michael and Felipe, her life might depend on the answer. Was he deep undercover in some official role as his police training suggested, infiltrating the cartels or was he one of the *Kaibiles* who had found more lucrative employment with the Mexican crime syndicates? Were his lies for everybody or just for her?

All the anomalies so far could be harnessed in support of either narrative. What of his distress at her being lost in the forest? The relief at finding her alive and unharmed had been real enough. Was that merely a response to losing her as a potential conduit to Hera? What of their passion? Their lovemaking had been just that, lovemaking, so much more than just sex.

The answer lay in finding out who Tom really was and for that she could only rely on herself. It was as Hera had told her, "Trust no one!" She would not consider asking Felipe or Michael for any further help. It could be disastrous for them and their families if she involved them in any way. She could fly home and seek official help, maybe from the Foreign Office. They were already interested in Fosse, but what could they do and how dangerous might that be for Hera?

If Hera was safe in hiding then the less official fuss was made, the longer she was likely to stay that way. It was more than she could deal with. She had to be thinking clearly when Tom returned. If he was working for *Los Zetas* and his care and passion for her was just an act... If, if, if, how could she ever know? She lay down, fully dressed, not expecting to sleep.

FORTY

Out of the clear, painfully bright sky swooped the king vulture, his vast, white wings tipped with black, like some regal mantle. The savage hooked beak, long stately neck and black neck ruff all adding to his grandeur. Red-ringed irises scanned the ruins below for the carrion that had tempted him from the heavens. With a flex of the wings, the hunter of the dead skimmed the temple's stone headdress and rose on another thermal. She watched from inside the dark confines of the crypt, dank earth and bare stone all around, a squat doorway ahead, her only way out.

She stepped under the limestone lintel and blinked at the intensity of the light. Above, the bird still climbed; below, the Great Plaza was devoid of human life. Beyond the pair of stelae, guarding the foot of the steps, a dozen raccoon-like coatimundis scampered and rolled in the dust, chasing and freezing, their long tails accentuating their fitful movements. Something caught their attention. They froze, heads raised, bodies alert and the next instance fled up the steps and through the ruins. They had vanished before the woman appeared.

Arriving from the eastern side of the temple, she appeared at a run and only paused when she reached the stone sentries. Sucking in air, she glanced back in the direction she had come, before turning her attention to the Plaza. Caught between the fear of what lay behind her and the need to find something ahead, her eyes flicked up to the temple vault above. Only then did she see the woman's face. It was Hera and she was starting to climb towards her, using both hands and feet to aid her ascent.

Gasping for air she reached the top and stumbled through the doorway, into the shadows, just as a group of men emerged at a run from the direction she had arrived. They stopped in the middle of the Great Plaza and divided, heading off in pairs to all points of the compass; the pyramid temples ignored as senseless dead ends.

The Plaza was quiet again and Hera had managed to regain enough breath to stand and peer out through the entrance. Realising the men had gone, her sister started to examine the chamber. Could Hera sense her presence? She wanted to say something, but there was no sign she was aware of her.

In the dim light, she saw that Hera had a camera grasped in one hand. She had removed the memory card and was frantically surveying the rough-hewn walls. Something caught her attention and she moved deeper inside the tomb and knelt low in one corner. Near the floor, where the walls met, one stone was deeply pitted. She took an empty chewing gum wrapper from her walking shorts and wrapped it around the memory card before carefully pushing the small, metallic package into a narrow crevice running half the length of the cornerstone. She pressed it in as far as possible, grazing her index finger and drawing blood. Only then did her sister look up in her direction, hand still resting on the fissure hiding the SD card. The pose was held for an instant as if for a photograph and then she was back at the doorway searching for movement below.

The Plaza was silent and empty and before she could move towards her sister, try to speak to her or attempt to let her know she was there, her twin was gone. She watched from the raised threshold, a helpless spectator, as Hera reached the lowest step still clutching the camera and immediately dashed north towards the trees between Temple One and The North Acropolis.

A shout from the highest ledge of the pyramid opposite drew her attention to a man who had been working his way around the tomb on lookout. He had spotted Hera just before she made the trees. His cries soon drew others back to the Plaza. Some of the men she recognised from the original photograph, including both Tom and Leonard Fosse. The group divided again with the six men she had seen in her vision, disappearing directly into the forest after Hera, whilst the others fanned out to either side.

Alone in the tomb, the darkness intensified and the slot of light from the drama below shrank into the distance. She felt waves of sadness wash over her, a sense of unutterable loss. Sobs wracked her body, warm tears dripped into the dust and then she was awake, alone in her dark hotel room, curled up and sobbing. Her pillow was soaked with tears and the despair from the dream still crushed her.

She climbed out from beneath the mosquito net and walked back and forward across the room. The emotions subsided and she began to think more clearly. Was it all about photographs? After all, that is what had started this quest. Hera had hidden a camera memory card from the men who were hunting her. Why had she bothered to take the empty camera with her? Of course, it was obvious. If her pursuers found the camera in the tomb they would find the card was missing and search for it nearby. What could possibly be on the card that made it so important? Surely her sister would not have taken a picture of anything so significant it warranted such a pursuit? The ongoing search for Hera was not a hunt for her but for the digital record of some incriminating activity and as yet they had found neither the card nor her sister.

Her thoughts turned again to Tom. Did this latest dream condemn or exonerate him? Neither, she supposed. She knew he had been at Tikal with her sister and that Hera had made a break for it, he had said as much himself. What she did not know was in what capacity he had been there. She might be able to forgive him his unsavoury past and all his lies to her if he really wanted to find Hera for her own sake and not just for what she had taken. She needed his strength, his composure and his love. She could not deal with this on her own. She felt so lost without him.

The tears started to flow again and a determined effort was needed to stifle the sobs. At the open window, she sat and sightlessly stared out into the cloud-smothered night. What had Hera seen and captured that was so incriminating? Despite her fears, she knew that she had to return alone to Tikal. Her sister's final pose, hand over concealed fissure where the card rested, had been unnatural, a waste of valuable time unless Hera knew she was there and wanted her to find it.

FORTY-ONE

At seven the next morning, she was once again outside the Tikal hotel where the first tour group had stopped for lunch. Her plans had almost fallen at the first hurdle. She knew that tomorrow, November 1st, was a national holiday for Día de Muertos but had not realised that October 31st, All Saint's Day, was also part of the two-day celebration for the dead. She had paid over-the-odds to obtain a taxi and might have to fork out even more to return to Flores, but with only two days left and Tom returning later that day, she had to act immediately. She had eventually found a taxi outside the *Parroquia Nuestra Señora de Los Remedios*, the church in Flores, not at the hotel. The fewer people knew of her actions the harder it would be to trace her movements.

By the time the taxi pulled in outside the hotel at Tikal, a buffet breakfast was in the process of being set out inside the dining room. She waited until the driver pulled away before turning from the hotel and heading towards the monuments. The chain across the site entrance announcing it was closed for the next two days was neither unexpected nor a deterrent and soon she was standing alone in the Great Plaza. She had cursed the national holiday when trying to procure a taxi but now, with nobody to observe or comment on her presence, it might prove a blessing. She had the place to herself

A haze was rising from the forest as the sun started to climb and it felt as if she had walked into the past. She would not have been surprised to see an ancient Maya priest in full sacrificial garb, step out from the temple ruins.

Standing in front of the Temple of the Jaguar she gazed around the site that had come to dominate her life ever since discovering the picture of Hera. In a way it was ironic. She had been looking to reconstruct a man's life from photographic evidence and in so doing was reconstituting her own. A year ago, her sister had been photographed on this very spot before escaping into the jungle.

She turned towards the steps and started to climb. She was in no rush, even if the card was still there she was not sure she wanted it. Each step was an effort. The last week had been a maelstrom. She felt exhausted, physically and emotionally drained, but the only alternative was to return home immediately and forget about her sister and Tom. She knew it was not an option. The past had caught up with the present.

Halfway up she paused as a noise below drew her attention. A small animal with a long snout and stripped bushy tail scurried across the plaza. It was one of the coatis she had seen in her dream. She glanced up at a sheet of translucent, white cloud still thin enough to reveal a hazy sun. There was no sign of a vulture or any other birds come to that. The air felt heavy, not from the excessive humidity, it was still too early for that. Maybe another storm was brewing. On the top step, she turned again, paused and helped herself to a drink from her water bottle.

Without people, the Plaza had changed. It felt like an ancient stage setting: the monuments were the scenery, the silence an expectant hush before the drama unfolds. Behind her the gaping black entrance awaited. She turned and stepped over the stone sill into the cool interior. Her eyes struggled to adjust to the contrast from the light outside. She dropped her daysack and retrieved her torch. Casting the beam round the small cell she illuminated ellipses of rough wall and uneven floor. The empty chamber was surprisingly small, more like a corridor than a room. Various would-be graffiti artists had scrawled their tags on the stones or scratched primitive images.

At first glance, the large stone in the corner seemed flush with its neighbour. She brushed the wall where she had seen Hera hide the wrapper and the superficial dirt flaked off exposing a deep crevice. Running her fingers along the crack she could feel nothing. Lying on her side she managed to lower her line of sight to look directly into the fissure. Right up in the corner, the reflective green and silver of a discarded wrapper shone in the dark. Shoved deep inside the gap it required the nail file from her bag to tease it out.

She did not open it immediately but went and sat outside on the top step. The morning sun warmed her after the chill of the tomb. The compound was still silent, even the birds seemed to be off duty. She unfolded the packet, which was dirty but dry and allowed the tiny, plastic card to slide into the palm of her other hand. The yellow label stated it was a SanDisk Extreme with 32GB of memory. How could something so apparently innocuous be so much of a threat?

Carefully rewrapping it in a tissue she slid it into her pocket. What secrets did it hold? She had to know. She needed access to either a card reader or a computer with an SD card slot. Her phone's microSD slot was unsuitable. Her laptop would do, but she was unwilling to return to the hotel just yet and no longer trusted the privacy of her machine. No one must see the images before she knew exactly what was on them. An Internet café or hotel business centre was what was needed. The *Hotel Posada de la Selva*, where she had been dropped off, advertised such facilities.

She walked back through the ruins, oblivious to her surroundings. Her daypack pressed against her back, hot and cumbersome, and yet the piece of folded tissue paper in her pocket with the tiny memory card felt far heavier, its minuscule dimensions capable of shaping or fragmenting her world. Was this fragile item the sole reason for Tom's quest?

Thoughts about him stirred such conflicting emotions. She had left a message for him at the hotel desk just to say she was sightseeing and that she would catch up with him later. How on earth could she pretend to him that nothing had changed? She felt certain her face would be an open book, whatever she chose to say. From their very first meeting, the intensity of his stare had been able to peel back her protective veil.

Growing up she had prided herself on the ability to keep her thoughts and dreams to herself. Today was going to prove the ultimate test.

FORTY-TWO

Back at the hotel, the restaurant was busy with the late risers. Fortunately, the compact business centre, little more than a glass-framed booth, was empty. Three computer terminals, a printer that doubled as a photocopier and a solitary landline phone seemed to be the extent of their facilities. One solitary shelf, with directories, a couple of business reference books, a tub of pens and a stack of unused A4 paper completed the room's contents. The woman, who had shown her in and logged her on, had left and a single fan was the only sound to distract her from the task in hand. She took a seat at the screen hidden from the windows and inserted the SD card into the appropriate slot.

The screen projected the name of the memory card as 'L.F. 2018'. Of course, it was not Hera's camera. It belonged to Fosse. Both Anthony's email about Fosse's involvement with the Mexican cartel and Tom's account of him taking pictures of the gang suggested that Leonard Fosse had been employed by a crime syndicate – no wonder the Intelligence Services had him under surveillance. Why any organisation involved in large-scale, illegal activities would want a visual record was beyond her. The question now was how did the camera come to be in Hera's possession? Had Fosse's given it to her or had she taken it?

Hundreds of stamp-sized images appeared on the screen. She scrolled down row after row and randomly clicked on one, a picture of a smartly dressed man filled the screen. It appeared innocuous enough. He was a

248

short, stout man in an open-collared, white shirt and dark grey trousers, sporting a bushy moustache and neatly trimmed black hair. The only thing demanding extra attention was his gaze. His eyes were cold and hard and the direct stare at the camera was uncompromisingly hostile.

She right-clicked the mouse and was provided with the option of properties. This in turn produced a wide range of facts about the image: its resolution, pixel count, ISO speed, f-stop and length of exposure. It was the next set of data that grabbed her attention, the exact date and time the picture was taken and a geotag giving detailed coordinates of where the picture was taken. No wonder the pictures were so important. It was a precise record of who, when and where.

She opened the following image and the same individual appeared in the same setting, flanked by two smartly dressed men. Not one of them was self-consciously posing and some transaction was taking place. The photo had captured a document being passed between one of the new pair and the man with the icy stare from the previous image. The picture's properties showed that it had been taken the same day as the previous image but an hour later. The much higher ISO number suggested the use of a zoom lens and sure enough, the focal length was twenty times greater - a telephoto lens had been employed. The photographer had not been in the immediate presence of his subjects. He had been far enough away not to be obtrusive, maybe even far enough away not to be observed at all.

The next few pictures were very similar, taken of the same men at a distance, apparently involved in some sort of business transaction. Was Fosse being employed to record potentially incriminating, blackmail material, or to provide detailed evidence for insurance purposes?

She skipped to a picture several rows further down and felt the bile rise in her throat. The quartered body of a man lay in a pool of blood, straddled by a heavily tattooed individual, brandishing a chain saw. The next picture if anything was worse, a naked woman spitted like a pig, from mouth to anus, on a long metal spike and held aloft by two similarly decorated, shorn-headed men. The third, cruelly surreal, was a human face sewn into a football.

Over the next half hour, she felt emotionally violated as if she had travelled through hell: hangings, beatings, rapes, decapitations, mutilations and beheadings polluted the exposures. A range of fiends, some tattooed, some masked, posed with brandished weapons, during or after the appalling acts of barbarity. These nightmarish images were sickeningly interspersed with shots of moneyed normality: men in suits, smart cars and palatial settings.

One series of shots reminded her of some Ancient Roman spectacle: public buses held up at gunpoint, women being raped, men armed with knives, hammers and machetes butchering each other, while gang members looked on approvingly. The sequence ended with an apparent survivor embraced and the dead piled into a mass grave. The bloody games and sacrifices of the Maya carved into stelae over a thousand years ago reinvented by the drug cartels and recorded digitally in high definition. What made men want to record their most barbaric, bestial acts? Carnage and unmarked, mass graves seemed to be the emblems of this pitiful country.

Fosse had methodically and in gruesome detail chronicled the gang's activities, all their activities. How could someone have gazed on these scenes without going mad, capture them for posterity and not be fundamentally and eternally corrupted? What could possibly have persuaded Fosse to accept this contract, it had to be more than just money.

She minimised the screen while she had a drink. The feeling of nausea would not leave her. She was not sure she could face any more? Resignedly lowering the water bottle she knew she had to see it through. The final images might unlock the secrets to all those questions that had haunted her. If it held anything of her sister's fate or Tom's involvement, it would be there, just before Hera obtained the camera and hid the memory card. She scrolled down to the final rows and sure enough, they were of Tikal a year ago, or to be precise a year come tomorrow, November 1st. Fosse must have had more than one camera. The picture that she had found in his attic obviously came from a second camera.

Three rows from the end, she found a range of beautiful atmospheric shots of Tikal's monuments that could have graced any Guatemalan publicity material, but for the presence of cruel-looking, armed men. Posturing on the steps, leaning against stelae, triumphal atop pyramids, their crude, attitude-ridden poses dominated and corrupted the scenes. Their harsh tattoos and hard faces as severe as the monuments they populated. It was Fosse's typical style, a commentary on the modern by reference to a landscape, a study of modern tyrannical power set against the monuments of former, cruel despots. It also collaborated Tom's account of the gang members posing for photographs.

The next three pictures were more distressing - a man was being beaten and kicked. In the first frame, he was on his knees, his hands raised in supplication. She remembered the face from her dream as belonging to the man who had stumbled in front of Hera. The second picture was of two men kicking him, one to the groin the other to the face. The shot was in the Great Plaza and the body was by the steps of the acropolis, level with the central clump of trees. The two men inflicting the kicking were Scar Face and Tattoo Arms. Why would anyone want to record such hate, such violence? Was it pure sadism or was it a sign of power, a warning to others?

The last of the triptych was Tattoo Arms dragging the beaten body by his hair, along the lower step of the Acropolis. The beaten man's face was a bloody mess, his clothes drenched in gore and he appeared to be unconscious, if not dead. The body was being dragged along the step where she had made out streaks of blood in the picture. If Tom could be trusted with some details, this must have been Andrew, the member of the team who tried to escape. The frozen moment that had started this life-changing quest for her sister was only a matter of seconds away.

The final shot on the memory card was of Tom being handed or handing over a machete to a man in military fatigues. It was impossible to tell which way the weapon was being passed. Hera was also in the shot, kneeling, head down. Hirsute Man stood over her, pistol loosely held by his side. If pictures told a story this was one of a potential execution. Tom was either being forced or actively participating in the preparation for her sister's death. She felt on the point of screaming and only by reminding herself that Hera had escaped with the camera, an event that must postdate this picture, kept her emotions in check although her hands were badly shaking.

Fosse must have swapped to one of his other cameras at this point. Hera's immediate fate would have been recorded, she was sure of it. Maybe if she had been prepared to go on looking through the attic that Friday she would have found the pictures that followed. The pictures that not only connected this terrifying image with the one she had saved but those that recorded the events after her photograph. How would that have changed things? Would she have gone to the police with more incriminating photographic evidence? If the mystery had been taken out of her hands would she ever have made this trip? Her twin sister would have remained a secret, nothing more than a noteworthy coincidence, a conversational reference to someone in another world who looked just like her.

She removed the camera card. She had seen more than she could stomach. She placed it in her purse, went and found the woman who had logged her on and paid for the time she had been there and then left the hotel. The haze above the trees had thickened and like some massive greenhouse, the heat and humidity were building. She needed to walk, to think, to get away from the overwhelming degradation of those images. Strangers approached and to avoid them she swung off along path away from the hotel, indifferent to where it led, just desperate to clear her head.

She halted in a clearing by a fallen tree, its smooth white trunk, bone-like. The bird and insect noise throbbed in the groggy, pre-storm atmosphere. She needed to rally her thoughts and try to remain calm. Hera could not have been executed or Tom would not still be looking for her. Somehow she had managed to get away and to take one of Fosse's cameras. What was Tom's role? Did his account of making a break for it with Hera still make sense? It did not explain how she got hold of Fosse's camera. How did that last image connect with the one she had found? What narrative could tie them together? Neither image decisively condemned or condoned his involvement. If he was being forced to decapitate Hera no wonder he could not tell her the truth. It was no clearer as to whether he was acting under duress or a willing participant. What was patently clear was the incriminating nature of those horrific images and the reason Hera was being hunted.

Her distressing train of thoughts was disturbed by the screech of an owl. She listened and the harsh sound was repeated from the branches nearby. Surely owls were nocturnal creatures, what was disturbing this one? She stood up and cautiously moved towards the screeching. Above was a large nest. She stood still and waited. The shrill cry came again from within a mass of twigs and moss. What on earth was happening? Was it an owl's nest or was an owl attacking some other bird's fledglings? The screeching stopped and a green-headed parrot, yellow flecks of plumage above a black beak, appeared. It looked around and as if for luck screeched one last warning call before disappearing to a cacophony of juvenile chirps and squawks.

She had read about parrots' abilities to imitate other sounds. This one was probably guarding young and had adopted the call of a more menacing owl to scare off potential predators. She returned to her fallen tree and wondered how parrots had first learnt to mimic other birds. She had read about cases like the South African Drongo capable of imitating up to twenty different bird alarm calls but never experienced it first-hand.

Slowly an idea started to shape. Robert the Bruce had allegedly been taught a propitious lesson by a spider, why couldn't she learn from a yellow-naped parrot?

FORTY-THREE

She was being played by Tom for some purpose and needed to force his hand but was in no position to do that directly. Any accusations would probably be refuted with further lies and might place her in greater danger without getting any closer to her sister. She could not do it, but Hera might.

If Hera was to reappear, Tom might reveal his true intentions. If a parrot could make other birds think it was an owl what would it take to persuade Tom that she was Hera? She needed to build an identity that could stand up to the kind of checks that might be done at short notice. She could start with registering at Hotel Posada de la Selva under her sister's name. This would create an account that could be checked and reports of her appearance should stand up to any inquiries.

She removed her make-up, mussed her hair and changed into spare shorts and t-shirt she carried in a watertight bag as a last resort. Some dust rubbed into her clothes and skin made her look less like a tourist. Dressed in this fashion she would stand out from the majority of the hotel clientele and make her more memorable. It also concealed any clothes Tom might recognise.

Returning to the hotel desk, she booked for that night in her sister's name, employing a story about having changed her mind over the hotel she was staying at in Flores. She excused her lack of luggage and passport by claiming it was still at her previous hotel. Fortunately, the receptionist did not need to see any identification until she returned later and checked in properly. She then asked if she could send an email to her hotel, as they were not answering the phone, to give them prior notice that she would be checking out later that day. It was not *Hotel Posada de la Selva's* policy to allow guests to use their email account, but the young man serving wanted to be helpful and with a quick look round the foyer to check his boss was not prowling, swivelled the screen round and pushed the keyboard across, asking her to be brief. Her luck held as the receptionist was immediately summoned away to attend another guest.

Swiftly, while he was distracted, she emailed herself at the *Casa Maya Donna*, pretending to be Hera. The message, really for Tom's attention, had to be suitably cryptic to conceal the holes in her fabrication yet persuasive enough for him to believe she would visit Tikal alone. It could not give any hint that his cover was blown. The brief message stated that Hera knew she was looking for her and that she had things of vital importance to share, but it was not safe to meet in town. The suggestion was that they meet at Tikal, the following day, at noon. It would be deserted and give them the time they needed. She was to come alone otherwise Hera would not show.

The site would be closed for the Day of the Dead which would not only mean that if Tom decided to follow her he should prove easy to spot but also that his responses to the person he thought was her sister would not be inhibited by onlookers. The setting for the rendezvous should stir his memories of Hera and thereby aid her deception. She signed it, "Your sister, Hera." Hopefully, the message was plausible and would warrant her actions in Tom's eyes. She sent the message just as the hotel receptionist returned to check her progress. She thanked him and said she would return later that evening.

Outside, an irate taxi driver who had been waiting over an hour to transport hotel guests to Flores was quite happy to take her in place of his tardy passengers. She asked him to drop her at a camping equipment shop she had noticed on the outskirts of town. The store appealed largely to tourists and hopefully would not be closed during a public holiday. Her next task was to try to look as much like Hera as possible. If she could recreate Hera's appearance from the photo and reappear in the same location, Tom might be convinced. It was a ploy of smoke and mirrors. As far as she knew the last time Tom had seen Hera she was wearing the beige t-shirt, matching walking shorts, olive socks and the walking boots from the photograph and that would probably be his overriding memory.

Fortunately, the well-provisioned camping outlet was open, at least until lunchtime. With most historical sites closed the town's tourist-based retailers were doing a roaring trade. While the shop assistant was busy kitting out a couple for what looked like some extreme, jungle adventure, she scoured the shelves and racks for suitable attire.

Gradually she managed to find items that approximated fairly closely to what Hera had worn in Fosse's picture. Refusing a bag she deliberately crushed her purchases into her daypack before leaving the store. If she was to play the role convincingly, Hera's clothes needed to look creased and worn, not pristine. To her mind, a woman in hiding was not going to be the epitome of fashion and was going to travel light.

She did not want to return to The *Casa Maya Donna* and the possibility of facing Tom. The less time she spent with him before tomorrow the less likely she was to betray herself.

The town was in a festive mood with many stalls selling items for *Madre de Dios*, ideal for just wandering and filling time. The forged email from Hera would be sitting in her hotel pigeonhole alongside her key, easily accessible to anyone anxious to know its contents. Her imagination was already fabricating images of Tom using some slight diversion to check the nature of her message.

The next job was to check on Tom's claim about being called away to view another cadaver. She had tracked down the contact number of the morgue at Melchor de Mencos the night before but had failed to get a response from them. This time when she phoned, she was surprised to find it answered by a man with passable English. He explained that he was not in a position to tell her anything, as he was only a security guard and the mortuary was closed. It seemed the national holiday even extended to the dead.

Taking on the role of a distressed female tourist she fed the man a line about checking on a friend who was supposed to have been staying in Melchor de Mencos but had disappeared. She claimed the police knew nothing, nor did the hospitals and she did not know where else to look. She just wanted to know if a Caucasian woman in her twenties, with black hair, had been brought in over the last few days. The man excused himself and the line went silent. She was almost on the point of cancelling the call, believing he had forgotten her when he returned. As far as he could see it had been a quiet week and no one matching that description had been brought in. Tom had lied to her again. What had demanded his attention so urgently in Melchor de Mencos and forced him to stay overnight?

FORTY-FOUR

The phone call had been made in a quiet corner of a square otherwise buzzing with life. Once concluded, she moved back to join the melee and approached a stall selling hand-made jewellery. Bending over to examine an intricate pair of earrings and with her mind half on Tom's latest deception, she was only partially aware that her daysack had been jostled. She turned in time to spot a young boy slipping away from her through the crowd. The pocket on her daysack that held her purse was wide open and the purse was gone. The boy was already halfway across the square and still moving with a sense of urgency. The full impact of the loss hit her like a head-on collision. It was not just a few notes and credit cards that had been taken; they were of no importance compared to the main item stashed there - the memory card.

She desperately tried to push her way back through the crowd in the direction the boy had fled. It had to be him. No one else was in a rush to get away from the stall. She struggled clear of the press of bodies and to her relief, the boy was still in the centre of the square, being restrained by a man. The man was Michael.

Michael's explanation was quite simple. He had seen her in the crowd looking at jewellery and had pushed his way through to greet her. Before he could make her aware of his presence he had noticed the boy close behind her loosening one of the zips and removing the purse. He had managed to catch the child before he had a chance to escape from the square. The culprit, probably only six or seven, had given up shouting and looked miserable and on the point of tears. Michael handed back her purse before cross-questioning the little thief. A stream of distressed Spanish spilled from the boy's mouth.

"He says he needed the money. He knows it's wrong, but he was sent out to buy some items for *el Día de los Difuntos*, what we call *el Día de los Muertos*, and he lost the money his mother gave him." The boy now looked truly wretched and she was starting to take pity on him.

"What did he need to buy?" she asked.

The boy's words were quieter and more subdued as if he realised how much trouble he was in. Again Michael translated, "It was a few things for his father's grave." The boy's admission brought her up short. She had been on the point of scolding him and sending him away with a flea in his ear or at least she was going to ask Michael to give him a serious tongue-lashing.

"What things?"

Michael responded without involving the child who was wiping his nose on a grubby sleeve. "It is customary for families to go to the cemeteries where their family are buried and place tokens on their graves, you know food and drink that will encourage them to visit."

"I thought it was like our Halloween, a big fright fest."

"No, no, not at all. For us, it is a time to invite our dead back to earth. We clean up the cemeteries and often make *ofendas*, private altars, where we place things to welcome them back. If you go to the cemetery you will see most of the graves have offerings: candles, flowers and photos of loved ones."

"I noticed all the marigolds on sale."

"Their bright colours and pungent scent are supposed to attract the dead. They only come back to us for 24 hours, so everything is done to encourage and assist their journey."

She looked at the little boy still downcast and sniffling, opened her purse and pulled out a few notes. She knelt down until she was at his eye-line and offered the money. At first, he did not seem to understand the gesture as if it was some sort of trick. Michael explained it was a present and suddenly as if a cloud had lifted, the boy's face lit up and with a stream of *"gracias"* and *"muchas gracias"*, he was off again, back towards the stalls, money clasped tightly in his hand.

"That was very kind of you," Michael said.

"It was nothing. I just hope he has enough to get what he needs."

"You gave him plenty. Anyway, what are you doing here? I thought you would be on the way home by now and staying out of trouble."

"The day after tomorrow. I was just doing a bit of shopping, picking up a few souvenirs."

"There is something you should see before you leave. Have you got time?"

She was only too glad of Michael's invitation. He had not only saved the memory card but was also providing her with something to fill up the time before she returned to the hotel and faced Tom. They walked across town with Michael commenting on the celebrations that were going on everywhere. It was not only the cemetery that was being prepared; it also seemed that many of the houses were open to the street and a thorough clean in progress. At regular intervals, pine incense reached her nose. Michael explained that originally the ceremony was based on an Aztec goddess, Mictecacihuatl, the goddess of the dead. The dead were encouraged back to their graves and then welcomed home, so it was important for their return visit that the houses were spotless. After a night's entertainment, the dead would be escorted back to their graves for another year.

They arrived at a cemetery she had passed in the taxi just a few nights earlier. It was now heaving with life. Everywhere people were busy tidying up the multi-coloured graves, laying out offerings and making giant kites from bamboo poles and tissue paper before attaching messages to them. The atmosphere was not the hushed, reverential tone adopted in English churchyards but a vibrant, joyous and noisy celebration with people drinking and partying while working together.

"I read about them, but why kites?" she asked, astonished by the atmosphere.

"It is a way of guiding the dead back to their family. Soon the first ones will be finished and you can see them being launched. It is quite an achievement. Some can be up to ten metres in height."

They wandered amongst the families working on their bright creations, sticking and colouring patterns onto their homemade kites. Harnessed to secure anchors, the first massive kites were soon being hauled upright by excited groups of young men and released to the heavens. Michael offered her some snacks he had brought with him as more and more bright shapes danced into the air. Soon after, he made his excuses. His father was expecting him. They had their own preparations to make. She thanked him and it was only after he had left that she remembered that he had probably meant they had to get ready to invite his mother home. If this was the first year without her, she realised how important this day must be for both Michael and Pedro and yet he had given up the last few hours to her, a woman he hardly knew. She hoped that one day she would be able to show the same level of kindness to someone passing through her life.

She wandered on her own amongst the town's families. Back home she would have felt an intruder straying on other's grief, here, she was welcomed with offers of food and drink as picnics were enjoyed at the gravesides, songs sung and more kites launched.

By late afternoon people were starting to head off, to wait at home for the return of the dead. As the cemetery cleared she spotted Felipe and his mother. They were just blowing out the candles on a church-shaped tomb painted in blue and white. Both of them seemed pleased to see her but could not stay as one of Felipe's brothers was expected. Felipe leaned forward to blow out the last candle explaining that some people thought the dead returned in the form of moths and if a moth was burnt by one of the candles, the deceased would not be able to return the following year.

The cemetery soon held only a handful of people tidying up. She could not put off her return to the hotel any longer. She checked her phone to find two messages from Tom asking where she was. She replied excusing the delayed response as poor reception and informing him that she was on her way back.

It was as she crossed towards the exit that she suddenly heard a shout, "*Señorita*". She turned and there was the little boy who had tried to rob her. He ran across to her carrying a small kite, very much homemade, very much a child's creation. He pushed it in her direction saying, "*El obsequio, el obsequio*," until she took it, nodding her head in thanks. She suspected he had made it as a present for her. She smiled, said "*gracias*" and then he was gone, scurrying between the gravestones to an exit on the far side of the cemetery. She attached the kite to her bag and continued towards the nearest exit allowing the kite to flutter free in the slight breeze that stirred amongst the gravestones..

FORTY-FIVE

She was tired and the walk back to the hotel was long but not long enough, and before she was fully prepared she had re-crossed the causeway and arrived back at the *Casa Maya Donna*. Her room key and email message were waiting for her, but then she had expected nothing else.

Instead of going to her own room, she went straight to Tom's. He would be expecting her and it was better that she initiate action rather than have him unexpectedly turn up. He seemed truly glad to see her and concerned that she had been out so long. The embrace and the kiss felt so contrived she felt that he must guess something was wrong. It was one thing to deceive someone on the phone but quite another to simulate warmth and desire in the flesh. Her body felt unyielding even to herself and the smile forced. She excused her distracted state as the result of a long day of sightseeing and the shock of the email she had found on her return to the hotel.

He seemed to accept her excuse and quickly turned his attention to the message from *Hotel Posada de la Selva*. Even though he had almost certainly read the message earlier she wanted to gauge his reaction, but she did not dare look at him while he read, scared that at any moment she would reveal her deep distrust and fear. Fortunately, Tom seemed oblivious to her state or accepted it as a natural response to the message. He also accepted her need to meet Hera but was averse to her going alone. He argued that she might need his help, promising that he would wait at the entrance, but she refused to be swayed. Hera had insisted she came alone and reluctantly Tom agreed. She made him promise. If she was to get to the truth it was essential the subterfuge worked and Tom felt he had a free hand to follow her or remain in Flores, as he saw fit.

She excused herself soon after, claiming the need for a shower and a change of clothes. Only as she was leaving did she remember to ask about his trip to the morgue. With difficulty, she held his gaze as he told her it had been a mistake and the body was nothing like Hera. The girl had been older and was not even dark-haired. He lied so well, so fluently, no twitch or break of eye contact, it was as if he truly believed the things he was telling her. Was there any possibility he was telling the truth? After all, she had not asked the man at the morgue about other corpses. He had said only that there were no young bodies fitting the description she had given him. Would he have bothered to tell her of any others that did not fit her criteria?

Before leaving, she explained that she felt a bit under the weather and would probably have a nap before they went out that evening. His face registered concern, but he was too preoccupied to delay her departure.

Alone back in her room all her doubts and fears flooded back. What would Tom be doing right now? Whether he was acting on his own or as part of a group, she was certain he would be using his phone, either to relay the new information or to check the hotel at Tikal to see if her sister had checked in yet? She could not do much about the first possibility, but the second was a different story.

She phoned the hotel giving her sister's name and then informed them that she had a booking for that night but was delayed and was not certain what time she would arrive. The hotel was extremely helpful, reassuring her that even if she arrived after hours, there would be a night porter on who could check her in and that the room would be held.

Alone in the quiet of her room, she considered her options. The visual record of the cartel and its activities should go straight to the authorities and yet without it, she had no way of applying pressure to find out what had happened to her sister. It was also her safety net. With it she had a bargaining chip, without it, chillingly, she might be excess to requirements. Hera must have shared the same thoughts. Why else would she have bothered with the camera? Once she had found out where Hera was and felt they were both safe, she would pass on the pictures to those agencies that dealt with international crime. It could be done anonymously and hopefully, that would ensure no connection was ever made back to her or her sister. For now, the memory card was her lifeline.

It would be stupid to take it with her and naive to leave the card unattended in her room. It had to be concealed somewhere, but where? Hera's idea of using a chewing gum packet sprang to mind and sifting through her possessions she found a second small tin of mints she had bought on the first day in Flores. It had been less than a week ago but it felt like another age so much had happened and so much had changed. She carefully removed the mints and wrapped the memory card in some tissue paper before placing it inside and recovering it with mints. The tin was so non-descript that the best hiding place for it would probably be in plain view, on the table beside her bed. She had learnt this the hard way when searching deserted properties for *the Gazette*. The house clearance firm had found newsworthy items she had overlooked as too trivial or mundane to warrant examination.

Having disposed of the card she moved on to trying out her disguise. In the mirror, her slightly oversized t-shirt and baggy shorts already appeared to be reshaping her identity. Her legs looked thinner and her upper body had lost some of its definition. Both items were deliberately chosen slightly too large to make herself seem thinner, more like the photograph. The socks were fine. She turned them over at the top in the same manner as Hera had worn them. The boots were far too new and bright, so she spent ten minutes scuffing them on the wall of her bathroom. The rough plaster soon removed both shine and colour and by the time she had finished the boots gave the impression of having tramped the length and breadth of Guatemala. Next and most important was the face. She tried to do her hair and makeup in a style reminiscent of Hera's, brushing the hair forward to create a long fringe and removing all signs of makeup except for a natural tone blusher and pearl highlighter to accentuate her cheekbones. When she felt she had achieved a slightly gaunter look she studied herself in the mirror.

At a distance not even her closest friends would now be able to tell them apart, the outfit, hair and even the recent tan were spot on. If her dreams could be trusted, her mannerisms would also be similar to Hera's. The only aspect that was distinctly different was the accent and she was sure she could do something about that. She changed back to her old look and made sure that everything she needed for the transformation was crumpled back inside her pack.

She lay down on the bed and watched the fan's fins blur at full speed. Only now did the immensity of what she was planning to do strike her. Just how safe was it? Would Tom ever hurt her? She could not believe that someone who had made love to her as he had could ever harm her. She wanted to believe that if he cared about her, he would try to sort something out. If not and it was all an act for the sake of the pictures, they would prove her security. What if things did go wrong? She needed a fallback, an escape plan. The pictures might buy her time, but what could she do to stop the kind of pursuit Hera had faced?

FORTY-SIX

Her thoughts trailed back to her Renaissance studies and Machiavelli's pragmatic approach to power. His line from *The Prince*, "Never attempt to win by force what can be won by deception," had stayed with her. She was in no position to use or threaten force so maybe deception could be taken further than merely imitating Hera.

If Tom was as ruthless and manipulative as his files indicated, she needed a weapon, figuratively speaking. Maybe *Los Zetas's* savage reputation could be her defence. What if they believed Tom was a threat? Whether he was working for or against them, such a scenario would have critical implications for him. As a last port of call, to save both her and her sister, this might be the most effective weapon she could wield and one she was sure Tom would fear. Was she prepared for the consequences of such action? She opened her laptop and brought up a new word document and then recovered her notebook. She congratulated herself on recording information this way, it meant she now had access to all the research she had done on the drug cartels.

The essence of her plan was to suggest that Tom already had the pictorial record of *MS-13* and *Los Zetas's* activities and might be looking to make capital from it. If she could imply that Tom's chequered past and changing allegiances included dealings with rival cartels, she could sow the seeds of doubt. Recent arrests of major figures within *Los Zetas* had led to predictions of the organisation fracturing, with the ensuing internecine struggles ripping the cartel apart. If this were true they would be more sensitive than ever to rumours of betrayal. The threat of *Los Zetas's* retribution would be more effective than anything she could physically achieve.

What would be the outcome of such a deception? She had seen the barbaric pictures of *Los Zetas's* acts of vengeance. Was it signing Tom's death warrant? Was she prepared for that? Surely Tom would be able to look after himself; after all, he was highly trained in survival skills. He would be forced into hiding and would no longer be a threat to either her sister or herself. Any such scheme would have to be her final act of desperation. It would be her and Hera's lifeline if Tom left her with no alternatives.

Her notes stated that the American government believed *Los Zetas* to be "the most technologically advanced, sophisticated, and dangerous cartel operating in Mexico" but their area of influence and involvement was far greater than that. Her research had shown they were a global phenomenon and not restricted to Mexican borders. They were heavily involved in North America and Europe, especially Italy, working with the *Ndranghta*, a mafia-type organisation with international operations. Her new employer, *the Guardian*, had a considerable readership in those countries. Any article she wrote for them, involving the cartels and implicating Tom, would surely be picked up by *Los Zetas* if they were as technologically sophisticated as claimed. If not, one of their associated crime syndicates would spot it and ensure it was passed on.

If the worse should come to pass, she needed the equivalent of a loaded gun. If she was right, *Los Zetas* were desperate for Fosse's film or would be if they knew it existed. It was a mystery to her why they would ever have sanctioned such an incriminating piece of evidence in the first place. Maybe power and hubris were natural concomitants. She realised misinformation needed to have veins of truth running through it to be believable. Her article had to connect with what could be checked of Tom's history, the things she had discovered about him in the police records. His undercover work, sometimes as an agent provocateur, provided ample material for implicating him in gang activities, betrayals and counter-activities. It was the equivalent of what she had been doing for *the Gazette*, rewriting the history of individuals from snippets of evidence, but the consequences here would be far graver. Her choice of adjective seemed morbidly appropriate.

Gradually her article expanded like a web, weaving in elements of Tom's life with international, criminal activities. Just as she had intended to use Tom as the epitome of fire fighting, now he became the living embodiment of the drug cartels. There was already an ideal example in existence. A blond-haired American known as *La Barbie* had run *Los Negros*, an armed wing of the *Sinaloa* Cartel employed to counteract *Los Zetas*. She implied that Tom was *Los Zetas'* own ruthless blond *Dirección*, the man responsible for a particular region's policy and activity. The implication was that this was or had been Tom's role. Nothing that could be checked could be definitive, just inferred. She then introduced the photographic record sponsored by the gang, its explosive content and its disappearance a year ago. Tom's ruthless pursuit of these pictures she connected to Fosse's unexpected death. The English location was clearly detailed to give it a greater relevance to a largely English readership. Only then did she suggest he had already acquired the memory card but as yet had not disposed of it.

The article then attempted to give a character profile of this elusive criminal. The accusations were hedged by terms such as, "allegedly" and "purportedly." His time spent at Liverpool University fortuitously coincided with a large increase in drugs entering the UK and Liverpool becoming the hub of a national distribution network, largely supplied by the Columbian *Cali Cartel*. This implicated Tom in their activities. She progressed to his time in North Carolina, when the US government purportedly had a tacit agreement with *Sinaloa*, to refrain from prosecuting members of the gang in return for information on rival gangs, including *Los Zetas*. That period coincided with the arrest and sentencing of twenty-six members of *MS-13* in Charlotte including their leader, *The Wizard*.

By highlighting Tom's history alongside gang activity the implications were there for readers to grasp. By placing Tom in North Carolina at this time it inferred he was somehow involved in this mass arrest and conviction. She suddenly remembered that his relationship with her sister had started when he had been based up near her in Virginia, the home of the CIA. This fortuitously coincided with the start of the CIA's alleged non-intervention policy with *Sinaloa*. The more straws she wove into the fabric of her text the more solid the construction appeared to be.

She continued to highlight his undercover training and skills acquired as a police officer in Guatemala City, including some of his citations and then his ruthless and vicious training for the *Kaibiles*, a former recruitment centre for *Los Zetas*. These were the facts that would hold up to scrutiny and act as ballast for the insinuations.

How close, she wondered, did her fabrication approximate to the truth? In writing the piece she had almost convinced herself of his guilt. On the other hand, if he was working undercover, this might endanger his life. But if he was innocent, she would not have to use it. The words in front of her were now a primed weapon that she was not sure how to aim or fire. Was it even loaded if she could not get it published? Could it be accurately aimed or was it a blunderbuss approach, scattering shot amongst the guilty and the innocent alike?

She added an extended covering letter to Anthony. She owed him the truth and only this would persuade him of the importance of publication. The letter detailed her predicament: the recovery of the picture, the discovery that her look-alike was a twin sister, Hera's kidnapping a year ago, escape with the incriminating film and unknown whereabouts since and Tom's ambiguous involvement. She asked him to pass the article on through his contacts to *the Guardian* if she had not contacted him within 24 hours. Once she pressed the send button the consequences might be out of her control. She set the email up to be automatically sent in 48 hours, that would give her a chance to cancel it later or use it as a lever if things did not work out as she hoped.

The laptop and therefore the message could not be safely left in her room. She would have to find somewhere to conceal it. Was it fair to ask Felipe to look after it until her return and did she have an alternative? Maybe she could book some kind of storage space, such as a locker, somewhere around town. At last, it was done. The gun was loaded and ready to be aimed. Outside she realised the night had arrived and still there were fifteen, interminable hours to wait.

Dressed immaculately, Tom called for her at seven. As planned she made her excuses, feigning a migraine and after expressing his sympathies and checking if she needed anything, he quickly took his leave, promising to look in on her later. Spying on him through a crack in her shutters, she observed that he did not return to his room but continued downstairs. From her bathroom window, she caught sight of him walking briskly away from the hotel. Now was the time to act before he returned. She hurried down to the restaurant and ordered some food to be delivered to her room.

Unobserved, she slipped out of the hotel through a service door. Acutely aware that she did not want to be seen skulking through the backstreets of Flores with her laptop, she targeted the nearest large hotel. They refused to place anything in their left-luggage room unless she had stayed with them and it was only after some discussion and a bribe that the young man on the desk agreed to store the laptop for 48 hours. She watched the man unlock the door behind the counter and place the case on a rack. Paying both the deposit money and the far larger bribe, she received a form acknowledging the storage and then left, relieved that she would not have to ask Felipe. She had been away from her hotel for no more than twenty minutes.

She slipped back into the hotel. The courtyard tables were filling for the evening sitting. As she entered her room, the pungent aroma of her evening meal struck her. It had been delivered and set on her bedside table while she was out. She had not expected it to be ready so quickly. Turning to the bed, she could have kicked herself. There on the pillow lay her open notebook. In her rush to utilise the time while Tom was away, she had forgotten to hide the notes, the rough draft for her article betraying Tom to *Los Zetas*. How stupid could she be? She checked the time. The room had been empty for less than twenty minutes. Tom could not have seen it and it appeared not to have been moved. Even if the waitress who had delivered her meal had spotted it, surely her scrawlings and schematics would mean nothing to any of them. What was happening to her? She was becoming suspicious of her own shadow.

She ate hungrily and felt more composed by the time she had finished. Her mind kept returning to her delayed email. It was like one of those letters left with attorneys to be opened in case of death. The reality of tomorrow was starting to sink in. Was it too late to just call it off, pretend she was too ill to go to the meeting or go and claim her sister never showed? How would she ever find her sister if she could not elicit the truth from Tom? With such turbulent thoughts, sleep was impossible, but she needed to create the impression of it for his benefit.

By the time he looked in on her, she had eaten, disposed of the tray and was lying in the dark with a bottle of aspirin and glass of water beside her bed to bolster the impression of an invalid. After knocking gently, Tom quietly entered. She could sense him standing next to the bed, staring at her. Forcing her breathing into a regular, shallow pattern she hoped that this and the dimmed light would be sufficient to mislead him. She smelt his aftershave and felt the tears welling beneath her closed eyelids.

He left as silently as he had entered and only when she was sure he had gone did she open her watery eyes. The night stretched dauntingly ahead, filled with thoughts and doubts of how tomorrow would play out.

FORTY-SEVEN

As expected, the night was interminable; each long minute dragged out and weighed down with fear. Again and again, she found reasons not to go through with her plan and then persuaded herself to the contrary. Again and again, she went over her actions for the following day. Once at the site she would adopt Hera's appearance and then, well before midday, hide somewhere near the Great Plaza and wait for Tom. If he did not show up it meant he trusted her to deal with her sister alone and did not intend anything bad. If he showed she would confront him as Hera and then...Her mind twisted through numerous possible scenarios.

The wind outside was increasing in strength and forced her to go over and close her shutters to stop them banging. Across the courtyard, a light was on in Tom's room. He too was up late. Was he also finding it difficult to sleep?

When morning did arrive she joined Tom for breakfast but ate little and wore dark glasses to create a sense that she was suffering from the after-effects of a migraine. It was not difficult to create the impression of exhaustion; the night had left her feeling drained and fearful. Neither said much and breakfast turned out to be quite a desultory affair, taken inside because of the gusting wind.

Tom again pleaded that he be allowed to escort her but finally seemed to accept that she needed to see her sister alone. He also voiced a few concerns about how her sister could possibly have known she was staying at The *Casa Maya Donna*. Her fabrication was already starting to creak and she was glad of the tight time frame. She deflected his concerns as best she could and promised to find him as soon as she returned.

Despite initial problems finding anyone prepared to do the run, Felipe managed to book her a taxi after she explained that she had promised to meet up at the Tikal hotel with someone she had met while visiting the site. The taxi arrived promptly and would get her there well before noon, but Tom accepted her excuse that she was too anxious to sit around at the *Casa Maya Donna* and that she would prefer to wait at one of the lodges or hotels near the site. This served the dual purpose of further limiting the time she had to dissemble in front of him and would allow him to arrive at the ruins before her, or so he would think. She left him with a kiss. Hadn't Judas done the same? Was she betraying him? Surely not, he had forced her into this course of action.

The driver seemed set on getting to Tikal as quickly as possible and by ten-thirty he had dropped her at the hotel where her sister was supposedly registered. She waited for him to leave before moving away from the entrance. The sky was a tumultuous pallet of dark blue, black, white and grey, as dangerous looking thunderclouds, crowded in over the forest.

The entrance gate was closed and unmanned, as it had been the day before. She slipped past unobserved and as soon as she was out of sight of the entrance changed into her crumpled outfit. Putting the last touches to her face and hair, she considered again what she was getting herself into. Just how reckless was her plan to shock Tom into revealing his true identity? Despite all her efforts, her greatest hope was that the trip would be an uneventful one. That she would spend a few hours on her own and then return to the hotel and a man she could learn to trust again and continue her search for her sister some other way.

If that was not to be the case and Tom did follow her, she needed to stay in control. Where should the meeting occur? It would help to be able to see him coming first and if possible stop him approaching too closely.

The longer she could keep him at a distance, the more chance her disguise had of working.

She had made a point that morning of wearing a bright red and yellow, knee-length, floral dress, white sandals and striking makeup as well as blow-drying her hair to give it extra body. If Tom remembered her like that, there was less chance of him recognising her in neutral, beige working clothes, with flattened straight hair, a fringe and devoid of obvious makeup. Her flamboyant, feminine appearance on departure had suggested she was heading on a date rather than a reunion. As for the voice, she was not sure. Tom obviously knew Hera's voice, but it had been a year since he last heard it. She had only heard Hera whisper. That's what she'd do, stick to a whisper and pretend she had a sore throat. Any slip in accent might then be ignored. Hopefully she would not have to say much before she knew the truth.

The wind had picked up another notch and was scattering leaves and twigs across the causeway. This could be a problem, it would make it difficult communicating with Tom over any distance. She needed to find a way to communicate with him without being too close. She surveyed the ruins around her. The same buildings she had gazed on with awe, just days before, now took on a different appearance. They had become places of potential refuge and concealment. Recalling the layout of the central complex she settled on the Temple of the Masks, where she had strayed on her first visit.

She arrived at The Great Plaza. It was bathed in a strange light, a golden glow from refracted rays passing through a shrinking window in the clouds. Abandoned over a thousand years ago, devoid of tourists, the atmosphere had a profoundly solemn air, like a deserted cathedral. The spirits of the dead could be sensed in every stone and every carving. What events had these temples borne witness to? In how many ceremonies and sacrifices had they played a key role and what part would they perform in today's events? As she crossed the Plaza she felt the ruins sensed her presence. The eerie light only added to the haunting effect.

The rope around Temple 2 was still in place. She slipped under at the same point she had done on the first day and began to climb. Breathless she arrived at the tomb and turned to survey the empire that lay all around. Had Lady Kalajuun Une' Mo' stood here some 1300 years ago and gazed out from her future burial place with the same sense of awe and trepidation? The sun's oblique rays exposed fractures in the approaching storm clouds and glowed preternaturally off the bottle green forest below. Those pyramids poking above the trees were illuminated by the same peculiar glow, radiant against the liquorice black skies. It was as if the city was recharging, coming back to life.

She took a brief drink and stepped into the tomb. Her vantage point allowed her a view over the acropolises on either side and down the length of the Plaza in the direction anyone would arrive. Shrouded in darkness, she would be all but invisible from below. If Tom was coming, he would know by now that Hera had still not checked into the hotel and probably assume she had stayed somewhere else where she could not be traced. He would arrive early and like her, probably try to find an unobserved vantage point. If he only wanted the best for Hera there was little reason why he should not reveal himself as soon as she appeared. If on the other hand he just wanted the camera memory card, he would probably remain concealed until he was certain Hera was alone and unable to escape.

She rehearsed her lines and Tom's potential responses. She experimented with the accent she had chosen, a southern states' lilt, rough grated by an infection of the throat. Her voice in the darkness of the tomb sounded distant, disembodied and not of her own making. She forced her thoughts back to Tom. If she could keep him outside, on the lower steps, she might just be able to persuade him that Hera had returned and force him to reveal his true intentions before she owned up to her deception. She needed him to glimpse her at a distance, to set up the right expectations. From here she could see if he came alone and make a decision in advance on how and whether to confront him. She checked the time and realised it was only fifteen minutes shy of midday. The wind gusted even stronger up here above the protection of the trees and she withdrew deeper into the tomb to escape its hot breath carrying the vanguard of the approaching storm.

FORTY-EIGHT

A figure entered the plaza from the north side of Templo del Gran Jaguar. It was Tom. Instinctively she had known he would come although she had clung to the vain hope that he would not. Was he here for Hera or for her? He hesitated near the acropolis, checking the area ahead for signs of life. It was not too late, she could step back into the dark, hide and wait for him to leave, return to Flores and pretend her sister had failed to turn up. He was unlikely to choose her hiding place as a suitable site for his own concealment as the precarious steps would stop any hasty descent in pursuit of Hera.

She stepped forward scanning the dark skies, pretending not to have seen him and then moved back into the dark. He had spotted her and had started to cross the plaza. His actions did not appear secretive or menacing but open, unrushed and direct. She watched him pass the clump of trees near the centre and arrive at the foot of the Temple of Masks. Without hesitating, he began to climb and too late she realised her mistake. She was trapped, nowhere to turn and nowhere to run. The stairs, tumbling away below her tomb, were the only way in and the only way out.

The eerie light that had guided her here had dwindled to a grey half-light. When she first saw the temples, they had appeared impressive structures, dwarfing the hordes of tourists, but in comparison with the louring cloud formations above, they were mere baubles. A strange twilight had immersed the world and the forest now appeared flat and lifeless as the storm closed in on Tikal.

From inside the chamber, she watched him climb. His progress had a sense of inevitability, each step systematic and unfaltering. It felt like the cogs of a timepiece moving towards the point where they enable midnight to strike. He did not look up to where he was heading or back to what lay below, just kept on coming.

Finally, with just a dozen steps between them, she made her move. Partially emerging from the shelter, he immediately registered her presence. Buffeted by storm gusts raking over the sepulchre, she ordered Tom to stop. The wind ripped the words from her mouth and shredded them, yet he seemed to sense their meaning and his upward progress stalled. His stare was indecipherable. She wanted him to speak, but he just looked at her and then started to climb the last twelve steps at the same determined pace.

Like some lachrymose fanfare, the heavens opened with a vengeance. The precursory spits of rain were overhauled by a torrent bursting across the plaza from east to west, blasting into the face of their pyramid. With only five steps between them, she shouted out her instruction again, adding that she had the film, but the words were mere droplets in the deluge that now engulfed the site.

The storm drove in through the entrance of the tomb and tried to crush Tom against the face of the pyramid. He had stopped but seemed unperturbed, motionless and alert. His mouth opened, but the rain-drenched winds swept the nascent sound away. He started up the final steps and arrived at the ledge embracing the tomb, hesitated momentarily and then stepped towards her. Framed in the doorway she had nowhere to go.

It was then that one of those indelible moments occurred, an instant drawn out over eternity and revisited for as long as the memory persisted. He smiled but not the twinkling eyed, closed mouth smile she knew. This was an open-mouthed, hard smile while his eyes remained as cold and implacable as a glacier. He stood there, the rain lashing him from behind, his blond hair matted to his skull. Water streamed down his face and his light blue clothes had turned midnight blue with the torrents of rain now spilling from the heavens. His right arm reached forward, his hand open in a gesture or demand for her hand or for the film, she would never know.

At that instant, a jagged shaft of the most intense light cut through the rolling, black mass above and slashed towards the temple, flinging her back into the tomb. The accompanying boom of thunder was ear-splitting, echoing round the chamber and through the floor where the lightning had thrown her. She felt as if she had been hit by a wrecking ball. Outside, she could see Tom lying on the top tier, his face bleeding from fragments of rock that had exploded away from the crown of the temple where the lightning had struck.

Dazed and bruised, she staggered back to her feet. Her insides felt scrambled. Only the entrance of the tomb had protected her from the exploding fragments of stone. She forced herself out through the doorway into the mouth of the storm that tore at the ancient temple. Tom did not move. She bent over him and with difficulty dragged him back against the wall of the tomb. He opened his eyes and stared at her with a look of confusion and then another crack jerked his body sideways.

At first, she thought it was another clap of thunder, but no burst of lightning had forewarned them and a dark, bloody flower was blooming on Tom's shirt. His face, distorted and raked with cuts from the stone chips, revealed the agony he was in and yet he managed to speak and through clenched teeth spat out his only word to her, "Run!" With what strength he had left he pushed her away. Her back struck the entrance wall to the tomb and knocked the air out of her body. Gasping for breath she regained her balance and without turning to him again, took off down the steps.

The howling wind that should have hindered her, held her upright during her breakneck descent. Another shaft of lightning sliced through the heavens and vanished into the trees, illuminating three, armed figures climbing down from Maler's Palace where they had been concealed. The ensuing explosion of thunder, as if the world had been ripped apart, shook the ground beneath the city. She had no time to think, the armed men were only fifty yards away. Somehow they had found her and Tom.

She turned south and fled towards the reservoir before cutting back behind the temple and heading towards the north acropolis. Her actions were instinctive. She needed to confuse them, to buy time. Whoever Tom was, she could not leave him alone with these killers. Scrambling up to a new vantage point she watched as two of the men clambered up the steps towards where Tom had been lying. The other man had disappeared in pursuit of her. The two men climbed quickly despite the raging elements. She thought she recognised one of them, but the rain and wind blurred everything.

Despite her elevated place of concealment, she could not see Tom. He must have dragged himself back inside the tomb. The two men reached the top step and stood either side of the entrance, braced against the walls. Simultaneously they disappeared inside and then a bizarre lull in the wind allowed Tom's voice to be heard from deep within the tomb, calling out for help. The box-like space amplified his despairing cries that echoed around the unresponsive, stone monuments and then the momentary calm was gone. The wind tore back through the plaza with renewed determination, drowning out his pitiful cries.

His desperate appeal recalled her nightmares, then as now she was incapable of action. How had these men found them? From the recesses of the tomb, an agonising scream pierced the storm and was then abruptly stifled. The horrendous cry reverberated in her ears long after the sound was snuffed out.

The two men re-emerged, dragging Tom's body. Another streak of lightning lit the scene like some Hieronymus Bosch painting of hell. They hauled his body to the edge of the platform. She could now identify the two figures, they were the same two she had seen replacing drums at Uaxactun. The younger man masked in tattoos grabbed Tom's hair and wrenched his head off the floor. The blood still streamed from the many cuts and scratches. Dragged to his knees, she noticed his arms move in a vain attempt to break free. He was still alive. If she broke from cover now would they stop? Could she save him?

The older man drew a machete from a scabbard tied to his back. The hand holding the blade was raised to the heavens. Lightning spiked the sky splintering the darkness. With petrified horror she watched as the arm swung in a great arc, severing Tom's head in one swift, single strike. The headless body toppled forward onto the top step. In slow motion, it tottered on the edge and then rolled down to the next step, bounced on the soaked stones and continued to plunge. Picking up speed, the carcass tumbled, smashed and twisted on its descent. As Tom's battered head was held aloft, a modern sacrifice to the ancient god Huracan, an involuntary scream was ripped from her lungs. She clamped her hands over her mouth, but the men were already staring in her direction. As if synchronised, both immediately started to descend after Tom's lifeless, battered corpse.

She could not move. The shock and absolute horror of what she had just witnessed had immobilised her. Another flash of lightning revealed the third man reappearing from behind the temple. The booming thunderclap that followed shook the ancient stones around her feet and liberated her limbs. She turned and fled, scrambling, slipping and sliding over the drenched ruins. Blind panic surged through her, muting the pain from the scrapes and scratches. Behind she could sense the hunters gaining on her.

Once down from her hiding place and in the lee of the acropolis she quickly made the trees behind the West Plaza. Running as hard as she could, she fled along the winding trail that disappeared into the forest. The savagery of the wind, mercilessly whipping at the trees, drowned out any chance of her progress being heard. Her clothes stuck to her drenched body and water coursed down her face, arms and legs. Grazes, scratches and cuts bled freely.

The fingers of the storm had now closed to a fist and smashed into Tikal with unrelenting anger. The ancient Maya gods were set on crushing the city, roaring out their anger. Jagged forks of lightning chased each other through the sky in search of new sacrifices for the blood-soaked site. Further narrow tracks carried her away from Tom's butchered corpse. She was disorientated, agonized and traumatised but kept on running, unaware of where she was or where she was heading.

Time meant nothing as she crashed through the undergrowth. Minutes perhaps hours passed before she broke into a clearing. Night had descended on the world and only the searing bolts of lightning illuminated her way. A ruined structure lay ahead of her. Somehow her path had led her towards Complex P. The altar of dream-like visions was briefly silhouetted. She was being hunted along the same trail Hera had been pursued exactly a year ago. Pausing by the altar sheltered between the twin pyramids, she glanced back, sucking in great gasps of air into her tortured chest. The men emerged from the forest and quickly covered the ground towards her. They knew where she was and would not let her escape a second time.

Branches lashed her legs and arms, her lungs screamed for air as her heart agonised to pump the blood faster. She ran, stumbled, fell, dragged herself up and ran again. The muscles in her legs were stretched to breaking point and still she imagined the killers gaining on her. Tom's end had been horrific, but at least it had been quick. She had read about and seen some of the atrocities they inflicted on women. Agonising, drawn-out torture awaited her capture. Those loathsome creatures would not hesitate in physically and sexually violating her at their leisure, before killing her.

She forced her battered, pain-racked body onwards. Another clearing and she realised that the trail she was following would only channel the men towards her. Yet again, she changed direction, selecting another track illuminated only for an instant. The undergrowth grew denser and ripped at her skin and hair. She cut back on herself along an animal track in an attempt to confuse her pursuers. Suddenly she was out in the open, stumbling over a bare rock outcrop stripped of trees. It was one of those bald spots she had seen from the air, a limestone mound of giant boulders, devoid of vegetation. Torrents of rain bounced off the glass-smooth rocks and swept down them in cascades. Gripping at any handhold or foothold available, she scrambled up and over the giant rocks and across the deeply creviced and eroded surfaces.

She reached the highest point and another blinding flash illuminated the jungle, spreading endlessly in every direction. The lightning had also highlighted her, exposed and vulnerable, caught in the open. She rushed to clamber down the other side, back to the concealment of the forest. The slick surface beneath her boots offered no grip and suddenly she was slipping, her feet sliding from beneath her. Prone and helpless, she started to slide, picking up speed, incapable of slowing her progress or altering her path. Ahead, a slash in the rock, cut across her way. For an instant she was air bound and then her body crashed against the far wall of the rock fracture. She tumbled into the opening below, landing on her back, unable to move. Desperately she tried to suck air into her crushed lungs. Above her, framed by the fissure she had fallen through, the storm raged and the torrents gushed down the rocks into her cell. She could do no more. If this was to be her end so let it be, but please let it be quick.

FORTY-NINE

She lay in that confined space for what seemed an eternity, too frightened and hurt to move, straining for sounds above and expecting any moment to be discovered.

Why had they killed Tom? How had they tracked them both? Was it looking at the photos at *Hotel Posada de la Selva*, the fake registration or the notes for her article left open on the bed? Could they have been after Tom anyway? Her body hurt so much it made her cry out each time she tried to ease her weight. The ghastly memory of Tom's final moments kept on replaying in vivid detail. The thunder still echoed above her and the rainwater cascaded down the rock face, filling the space where she lay. Soon she was half submerged. If she did not move soon she would drown. Maybe that was the way to go. Just let the water wash her away and try not to fight it.

She dragged herself into a sitting position to raise her head above the swelling torrent and bit on her hand to stifle the scream of pain. She might have let herself go if it had only been about her, but now it was about much more than Juno Argent. Hera was depending on her. No one had ever depended on her before and rather than it being the burden she had always assumed, it was a strength beyond anything she could have imagined. With another muffled cry of pain, she dragged herself up onto a narrow ledge, inches above the river that now coursed through her refuge.

Huracan continued to pound the forest for hour after hour whilst she clung to her precarious shelf. The fissure she had tumbled into was probably part of the network of caves and watercourses lying below Tikal. Michael had told her it was the third level of that ancient world and the home of the gods of the underworld who waited to bring death and disease to the surface. The water below her plunged in torrents deeper into the cave and If her strength gave out she would slip into the deluge and be swept down with it, yet another sacrifice to unappeasable, savage deities. At times she could feel her grip relaxing, her hold on life loosening, thoughts of a quick escape from the pain, the fear and the enduring nightmare only a fleeting decision away. Everything could be over and finished in an instant.

Fuck them. She would not roll over and die for them. She was not going to be another one of their victims. The anger rose in her chest, gripped her mind and clenched her spirit. Those men were unspeakable monsters, their actions beyond comprehension. She had eluded them and was not going to give them the satisfaction of dying. She would survive and somehow she would make them pay.

The hours passed and gradually the storm abated. She was left bruised, battered and bleeding, as the waters below dispersed. She dared not risk trying to climb out yet, even if her body was capable of it. They had chased Hera for the last year; they were hardly likely to give up on her after a few hours, even in the face of such a thunderstorm. She lowered herself back to the floor of the cave and lay back in the dark, wet recess trying to ease her agonised body. Despite the pain and the fear, exhaustion overtook her and she dozed.

Yet again dreams awaited, but this time it was different: no nightmarish jump-cuts between fears, no sense of ineffectuality, no snakes or armed men, just a vision of Hera untroubled and unhurried. She emerged from a light reminiscent of dawn's first radiance and floated towards her. They were both dressed identically. Hera smiled at her and held out her hands. They touched and she heard her whisper, "Thank you." The vision started to disappear. She clung on to Hera's hands, but they also began to fade and soon she was gone. Unable to hold on to her sister, she awoke with the same sense of utter loss she had experienced before, tears streamed down her face, but it was no longer agonising. In this dream her sister had not been scared and hunted, ripped from her without acknowledgement. She had been at peace, able to take her leave.

She dug out the torch from her daypack, which had remained on her back and probably protected her from the worst of the fall. Shielding the now feeble glow with one hand she cautiously scanned the fissure. Leaves, twigs and bones were heaped on another shallow ledge, above where the water had coursed through the cave. It appeared to be some kind of animal's lair. The thought of coming face-to-face with a Jaguar or Puma no longer scared her. Exhaustion and pain permeated every bone in her body, but her dream had left her sorrowful yet serene, like some all-consuming sedative. Her end was not going to be here, she knew that now.

Playing the torch over the bones, something glinted amongst the leaves. Reaching across, her body complaining at each new demand, she discovered the shiny item was attached to a chain. She rubbed the small shape on her t-shirt, already knowing what she had found. In the palm of her quivering hand lay a teardrop moonstone, enclasped in silver. Emily Argent, their mother, had left both twins with identical charm necklaces - a silver teardrop of the moon. Maybe someday soon she would be able to take Hera's necklace back to their mother and tell her of her lost daughters.

Somehow, in a blind panic, she had taken the same path as her sister had taken a year ago. Whether it was fate or her sister had guided her here she did not know, but she had fallen into the same cave as Hera. Her sister's last hours had been spent, down here, alone. Had she been too badly hurt to escape? Had an animal found her hiding in its den? Had she just given up? No, she knew that was not true. Illogical guilt, that she had not been there for her sister, twisted her insides and was only gradually soothed by the realisation that Hera could finally rest in peace.

She kissed the necklace and pocketed it before unsteadily clambering to her feet. Despite the pain, her legs took her weight. She squeezed her body into the gap and slowly levered herself up. Fraction by fraction she inched her way up towards the night sky and the starlight that now shone above. Although the unyielding rock walls cut into her knees and arms, the despair and self-pity that so nearly crushed her earlier were forced into abeyance. Her sister had been hunted and left to die by those bastards. She would show them that they were not prepared to be victims. She would survive and keep Hera alive in her head and her heart and in every gene and chromosome.

Her arms hooked over the rim of the crevice and somehow she managed to drag herself out. She lay there panting, unable to move, her body burning with the effort, the night breeze cooling her agony. Above the scattered stars celebrated her escape and the forest chorus proclaimed her survival.

Had her sister known she would come for her? She lay motionless on the rock staring up at a thin moon and millions of stars. She recalled the private look Pedro and Michael had shared and Pedro's enigmatic words, "Our forests hold many secrets!" Had he guessed Hera's fate? She sat up, oblivious to her agonised bones and torn skin. *El Día de los Difuntos* had lived up to its name, reuniting family with their loved ones. Back home, materialistic lives had fractured the connection with the mystical. The dead were buried or cremated and lost to the living. In Guatemala, where suffering seemed endemic, death was not the end. It was a world closely enmeshed with the numinous. She sat there for the rest of the night, undisturbed by any animals.

Just before dawn she opened her daypack and retrieved her dress from inside. It was not the dress she wanted but what she had wrapped it in. To ensure its bright colour had not been spotted in her pack she had used the tissue paper that made up the boy's kite as wrapping paper. Although creased and bent it still resembled a kite. The string was still attached and as if in sympathy a breeze over the forest tried to pull it from her grip. The vigil over her sister was almost concluded. She waited until the sun emerged on the horizon and then let the kite go. It fluttered for a second or two above the cave entrance and then climbed into the sky, showing Hera the way. She watched until it grew so small and distant it only existed in her memory. Her sister, so distant in life yet so close in death, would not be lost again.

The howler monkeys' barks heralded the new sun and the forest awoke around her. A distant throaty cough alerted her to a jaguar slinking towards its daylight retreat. As soon as there was enough light in the sky, she said a final farewell to her sister and carefully worked her way back south to where she calculated Tikal lay.

After a time, she heard and then spotted, a tour group clambering over some of the ruins. She slipped back to the nearest small clearing and changed into her crushed, damp floral dress and sandals. With her blood-stained, soaked and torn t-shirt, she dabbed at the worst of the blood and mud, brushed her hair and retrieved her sunhat and cracked sunglasses to shade her battered face. The make-up she had brought to play the role of her sister concealed the worst of the cuts and grazes.

She emerged tentatively, close to Complex P, as an early tour group explored its recesses. Emerging from the trees she was spared only the briefest of glances. Slowly and painfully she made her way past the entrance gate, trying to appear relaxed and unscathed. If any of the men who had chased her had remained behind to keep check she must not give them pause for thought. No one seemed to pay her any attention and there was no indication that anyone had discovered last night's murder. The killers must have removed Tom's body, and the rain cleansed the bloodstains. Fortunately, neither Michael nor Pedro was on duty. It was hard enough appearing to move freely let alone having to explain to them why she was there.

She avoided the hotel in case the person who had booked her in as Hera was on duty. Nobody seemed to pay her any undue attention as she waited for a taxi. She soon managed to pick up a lift as a group of four tourists from Flores were dropped off by the same driver who had driven her to Pedro's house. For some reason, he seemed pleased to see her and quickly transferred her back to The *Casa Maya Donna* at a discounted rate.

Re-entering her room she could not tell if any of her possessions had been disturbed. The bed was freshly made and the towels replaced, but nothing was missing, the little plastic memory card was still there concealed in the tin of mints. She cleaned herself up before recovering her laptop from the hotel where she had left it.

The email to Anthony was now unnecessary and would remain unsent. After a moment she deleted it. She did not want to remember Tom as she had painted him but as he had been with her. Staring across the courtyard at his room, her feelings were so confused. The door was open and a cleaner was stripping the bed. She walked round and peeked in. There was no sign of him ever having been there. Any luggage he had, was gone. Had he taken it with him? Had he been planning on leaving immediately after confronting Hera? Or had someone else removed his things? She felt her eyes welling up and quickly moved on so as not to attract attention.

Her flight was that evening from Guatemala City. Her connecting flight from Mundo Maya Airport was at four. As the taxi pulled away from *Casa Maya Donna* the tears coursed down her face. She was leaving her sister and for all his faults, the man she had loved, neither had existed for her two weeks earlier and both would stay with her for the rest of her life.

She had taken her leave of Felipe surprising him with a big kiss. In turn, he had given her a beautiful Maya scarf embroidered with the Maya zodiac and symbols. "*Adios Senorita*. This is so you don't forget your time with us," he had needlessly added with that big, beautiful, gleaming smile. She had left a farewell message on Michael's phone but could not face doing the same for Pedro. She needed time to work out what to tell him about Hera.

She felt unconcerned for her own safety. The men who chased her last night were hunting Hera Lane, not her, not Juno Smith, as it stated on her passport. Her sister was now resting peacefully where no one would ever trouble her again, alongside the remains of Tikal that had been such an important part of her life. She glanced at the small tin of mints in the bag on her lap. There would be a time to consider how to share Hera's legacy – the photos. When and with whom, she would decide.

Printed in Great Britain
by Amazon

53427402R00167